Praise for *The Lady's Slipper*

"A fight to save a rare orchid turns deadly. Charles Cutter and Burr Lafayette are at their best."
—Steven J. Pruett, executive chairman, Cox Media Group

"Fair warning: Be ready to keep reading once you start this page-turner about the brilliant but troubled, and always surprising, Burr Lafayette. Even readers of the series won't see the twist coming at the end."
—Leland K. Bassett, president, Bassett Entertainment Group

"*The Lady's Slipper* is a great read! Cutter paints a picture of an orchid that turns deadly and mixes it with a brutal murder and a devastating trial."
—Kieran Fleming, executive director, Little Traverse Conservancy

"Burr Lafayette returns in *The Lady's Slipper*, a courtroom drama with an unlikable client, an unlikely solution, and his own demons. Cutter's dialogue, descriptions, and the twists and turns of the story make this another gripping mystery in the Burr Lafayette series."
—Ben Beversluis, editor, retired, The Grand Rapids Press

"Myth and murder go hand in hand in *The Lady's Slipper*. Cutter's sense of place, his characters, his story, and most of all Burr Lafayette, make this a real page-turner. Well worth the read."
—Glen Young, Bear River Literary

"A Charles Cutter mystery is pure Michigan."
—Peter Anthony Holder, The Stuph File

THE LADY'S SLIPPER

MURDER IN HARBOR SPRINGS

THE LADY'S SLIPPER

Murder in Harbor Springs

Charles Cutter

M·P·P
www.MissionPointPress.com

Copyright © 2026 by Charles Cutter
All world rights reserved

This is a work of fiction. Names, places, and incidents are the products of the author's imagination or are used fictitiously. Any resemblance to actual events or locales or persons, living or dead, is entirely coincidental.

No part of this book may be reproduced, stored in a retrieval system, or transmitted in any form or by any means electronic, mechanical, photocopy, recording or otherwise, without the prior consent of the publisher.

Mission Point Press

Published by Mission Point Press
MissionPointPress.com

Cover Design: John Wickham
Interior Design: Sarah Meiers

Hardcover ISBN: 978-1-965278-93-2
Softcover ISBN: 978-1-965278-94-9
Library of Congress Control Number: 2025914167

Printed in the United States of America

For Christi, Charlie, Tom, and Kathryn

*"The average dog is a nicer person
than the average person."*

—Andy Rooney

Prologue

The Legend of the Lady's Slipper

Many years ago, an Ojibwe girl lived with her family in a village in the north woods. Her name was Manoomin, which means "wild rice." The people lived in a great forest on the shore of a deep blue lake. The forest sheltered the people and gave them rabbits, deer, and bear to feed and clothe them. The lake was full of walleye, pike, and perch. When the lake froze, the people fished through the ice.

Summers were short. Winters were long and dark.

Manoomin's brother, Nejik, was the fastest boy in the village. Nejik, which means "otter," was the village runner and delivered news and messages to the other villages.

One year, winter came early. It snowed and snowed. The wind blew the snow into big drifts. The lake froze quickly, and the ice was thick.

During the deepest part of winter, a terrible disease struck. One by one, the people became ill with fever and could not leave their shelters. But a village across the lake had medicine that could cure them. Nejik was to run to the village and get the medicine, but then he became sick. Manoomin was the only one who was not sick, so she would be sent to the village to get the medicine. She dressed in a heavy deerskin robe and moccasins lined with rabbit fur and started across the lake. Manoomin walked toward the fires of the village, but she sank in the snow that covered the ice, and the ice creaked underneath her. At last, she made it to the village. She told her story to the village elders. They fed her and gave her the medicine. An old woman took her into her lodge and told her it was too dark and cold for her to go back that night. She covered Manoomin with a robe, but the girl knew she had to leave right away.

Manoomin started back across the lake through the snow. She saw the blue and green lights of the northern lights in the sky, the spirits of the dead.

She worried that the people of her village would join them if she didn't hurry. All at once, the snow gave way, and she sunk up to her arms. She tried to climb out, but the more she struggled, the further she sank. She knew she had to be clever to find a way to escape from the snow. She lay back and shut her eyes. She shivered in the cold. As she lay there, the snow loosened its grip. She turned on her stomach and paddled with her arms. Slowly, she swam her way out of the snow. She was free, but she had lost her moccasins when she dug her way out. She searched and searched but they were buried in the snow. She started out again, barefoot. Her feet ached from walking in the snow, and the ice and snow cut into them. Her feet began to bleed. There was blood in every footprint, but Manoomin knew she had to keep going.

It was dawn when she reached her village. She cried out and fell into the snow. Her family ran to her. They took her to their lodge, bandaged her bloody feet, and laid her on a robe in front of the fire. The medicine healed the people, but Manoomin was feverish until the snow melted.

When spring came, Manoomin and Nejik searched for her lost moccasins. They couldn't find her moccasins, but they did find a beautiful flower no one had ever seen before. It was pink and white and shaped like a moccasin and grew wherever she had stepped with her bleeding feet.

The flower grows in wet, boggy soil in the north woods and can live for a hundred years, but if any part of the plant is picked, the entire plant dies.

The Ojibwe named it the Moccasin Flower. Today, it is called the lady's slipper. It is the story of the bravery, courage, and will of a young girl.

CHAPTER ONE

Collin Murphy lay on his belly on the only patch of dry ground he could find. Next to a mucky pond, cedars all around him, breaking up the sunlight. The swamp smelled like mud, rotting plants, and the sweet, spicy smell of the cedars. The wind whispered in the trees. Waves washed up on the beach. It was sunny and seventy, a perfect summer day.

He propped himself up on his elbows, his Detroit Tigers baseball hat, the one with the Old English *D*, on backwards. He focused his camera on a turtle the size of a dinner plate sunning itself on a fallen log in the pond. The shutter clicked. He turned the camera on a lady's slipper at the edge of the pond. The flower was soft pink and bright white. It was shaped like a moccasin and hung from a single stalk. Insects buzzed around the flower. He took a picture of the single flower, then a picture of a colony of the flowers. He turned the camera on a water bug skimming across the pond.

Collin put the camera down and sat up, cross-legged. He watched a couple in their twenties stroll down a woodchip path on the other side of the pond. They held hands and walked past a massive beech tree with silver bark. The tree was easily a hundred years old.

He looked back at the pond. A frog peered at him with black eyes. A water bug darted across the pond, too close to the frog. The frog swallowed it.

He looked at the beech tree again and saw another couple walking down the path, their backs to him. They stopped next to the tree. The man was well dressed and looked like he was in his sixties. The woman looked younger. Collin picked up his camera. The man turned toward Collin, then back to the woman. They looked like they were arguing.

The man pointed at the tree. Collin zoomed in. The tree was covered with carvings cut into the bark. The man and the woman started back the way they had come. Collin took another picture, then looked back at the frog, sunning itself.

A dozen teenagers led by a fortyish woman came down the path from the other direction. She pointed at the trees, the plants, and the pond, talking the whole time. A man in his late thirties at the back of the group held the hand of one of the girls. They stopped under the beech tree. Collin zoomed in again. The carvings were initials, many of them encircled by hearts. The woman ran her hand across the bark.

The well-dressed man and the younger woman stopped and looked back at the teenagers. He pointed at them and then at the tree. The woman pushed his arm down.

The fortyish woman started down the path. The teenagers and the man followed her. The well-dressed man and the younger woman started off again. Collin got back on his belly and crawled up to the flowers.

"They're beautiful. And mysterious. I can see why there's an Ojibwe legend."

He took out his knife and scraped mud off the side of his camera. He didn't hear the footsteps behind him. A man kicked him in the side, then clubbed him on the head. He ripped the camera from Collin's hands.

A splash. The turtle lunged at the frog, tearing it apart. Blood spread across the pond.

* * *

"Sit down, Mr. Lafayette."

"Your Honor, I'm not—"

"I said, 'sit down.'" The judge banged her gavel.

"Your Honor—"

"If you say one more thing, you will be arguing with yourself out in the hall." She pointed at Burr's chair. "The last time you were here, I told you to polish your shoes, which you haven't. If I ever have the misfortune to see you again, do not come back into my courtroom until you have polished your shoes."

Burr Lafayette, late forties and still standing, looked down at his cordovan, tasseled loafers. Italian leather. Five hundred dollars a pair.

They could use a little polish.

He pulled down the cuffs of his button-down, baby blue pinpoint oxford shirt, which didn't need pulling down. He straightened his red silk foulard tie with the black diamonds, which didn't need straightening, then ran his left hand along the crease of the slacks of his thousand-dollar tropical wool charcoal suit with the gray pinstripes, now slightly threadbare.

He looked up at the judge.

"Not another word," she said. "And no more of that silly primping."

Burr sat, slowly, like a dog who knows what it's supposed to do but doesn't want to do it.

Collin Murphy, the picture of fashion in a summer-weight khaki suit, a white shirt, and an orange and blue pastel tie, sat next to him.

He doesn't dress like a professor.

But he did look like a professor. Late thirties, about 5'9", on the thin side of slim. Shaggy brown hair hung over his collar. Green eyes, pointed nose, thin lips, and a scholarly look about him. Except for the bandage on his forehead.

Claire Fisher, from the Friends of the Conservancy, sat to Collin's right.

Burr's Aunt Kitty sat at the end of the table. She was the reason Burr was here.

How do I get myself roped into these things?

"Mr. Dahlberg, you were saying?" the judge said.

"Thank you, Your Honor. I do understand that you had discretion to grant the plaintiff a temporary restraining order. Respectfully, however, I don't think the fact situation warranted a TRO. And if it did, Mr. Lafayette should have notified me."

Burr stood. "Your Honor, I did notify Mr. Dahlberg."

"You called my office when you were almost to Grand Rapids. There was no way I could have possibly gotten here in time."

That was the plan.

The judge shook her head, then looked at Dahlberg. "I note that you're here now, Mr. Dahlberg. Is there anything you'd like to say regarding the TRO?"

"I ask that you dismiss the temporary restraining order issued against my client Dewey Ballantine and permit him to proceed with the sale of Thorne Swift."

"Nonsense," Burr said, under his breath.

The judge glared at Burr, then looked back at Dahlberg.

"Your Honor, we need not get to the merits of the TRO. My client, Dewey

Ballantine, is a resident of the state of Michigan and the Little Traverse Conservancy is a Michigan corporation. Because they are both legally considered residents of Michigan, there is no diversity, and, as much as I respect your jurisprudence, the federal district court for the Western District of Michigan does not have jurisdiction. This case must be dismissed."

"Nonsense," Burr said again, not so much under his breath.

"If the plaintiff wants to pursue its cause of action, it must do so in a state court." Dahlberg cleared his throat. "It is my understanding that there is a very fine circuit judge in Emmet County."

That will be the end of me.

Dahlberg smiled at Burr and sat.

Roy Dahlberg of Dahlberg and Langley lived on Lake St. Clair in Grosse Pointe Shores. He represented the Fords and Detroit's silk-stocking families. The patrician's patrician. Dahlberg was mid-sixties, slim, tan, silver hair. Black suit with a white chalk stripe, starched shirt with French cuffs, gold cuff links, and a gray silk tie. You got what you paid for when you hired him.

Burr had sparred with Dahlberg in his previous life. Many times. Burr had represented parts suppliers that Ford didn't want to pay. He'd won most of the time, but he'd met his match with Roy Dahlberg.

Burr stood. He pulled down his cuffs and reached for his tie.

"Stop primping and get on with it."

If Burr had met his match with Roy Dahlberg, he was afraid he might be in over his head with Judge Elizabeth Abbott. She was about thirty-five and a recently appointed federal district judge. A former U.S. prosecutor, she got straight to the point and did not suffer fools gladly. And she was easy on the eyes. Tall, blonde hair in a bun, and pink lipstick.

Her lipstick is the same color as the lady's slipper.

Burr sat at the plaintiff's table in the courtroom on the second floor of the federal building in downtown Grand Rapids. It was government-issue white with a government-issue linoleum floor, two shades darker than the walls—largely because the litigants walked on the floor and not on the walls. But the pews in the gallery were red oak with a champagne finish, and polished until you could see your reflection. Burr's own table, also red oak, showed the wear and tear of a lawyer fighting the lawyer at the table across the aisle.

The courtroom was largely empty except for a sixtyish man with salt and pepper hair, a pencil mustache, and a sincere blue suit.

Does he have something to do with this?

"Your Honor, the diversity of the parties need not be an issue," Burr said.

"It most certainly is."

Burr made a face at Dahlberg. "It's not your turn." He turned back to the judge. "Your Honor, this case involves a federal question."

Judge Abbott bit her lip.

"The showy lady's slipper is an endangered species. It has been so classified by the federal government. As a result, it is a protected species, and it cannot be destroyed. This is clearly a federal question."

Dahlberg jumped to his feet. "That is patently untrue, Your Honor, that flower is a weed that grows everywhere, including in one of the most inhospitable swamps in Michigan, commonly known as Thorne Swift, and the subject of this misguided litigation. Furthermore, it is not protected from development on private property. And Thorne Swift is private property. The lady's slipper may be protected somewhere, but it's not protected in Michigan."

I was hoping Dahlberg didn't know that.

Burr ran his hands through his hair, front to back, which he did when he was flummoxed. Which was now.

Maybe the judge doesn't know.

Burr was in his late forties. At one time he'd been six feet tall. Still lean. He had a hawk nose, sky blue eyes, a strong jaw, and straight white teeth. He had acorn-colored hair, longer than was fashionable, and a few gray hairs, which he pulled out as soon as he found them. His eyebrows arched when he spoke.

"Your Honor, the lady's slipper is an endangered species. At the very minimum, the defendant is required to file an environmental impact statement." Burr looked over at Dahlberg, who was still standing. "Would you please sit down?"

The blonde judge banged her gavel. "Mr. Lafayette, while this may come as a surprise to you, I am in charge here." She cleared her throat. "Mr. Dahlberg?"

"Thank you, Your Honor." Dahlberg straightened his tie.

Why does he get to do that?

"Your Honor, this is all very simple. First, an environmental impact statement is not required on private property. Second, this is just a straightforward real estate transaction. My client, Dewey Ballantine, is merely selling his property.

"That's all there is to it," Dahlberg said. "Thorne Swift is a swamp. The buyer, who is here in the courtroom, is going to develop it into single family homes. Which will add to the tax base of Emmet County. And Emmet County can certainly use the revenue."

Dahlberg looked at the man sitting in the back of the courtroom.

That's why he's here.

"Everybody wins. The county, the buyer, and my client." Dahlberg put his hand on his client's shoulder.

Dewey Ballantine, age fifty, sat to the right of Dahlberg. He was short, dumpy, two chinned, and balding. Front to back and back to front.

I wonder if ever the twain shall meet.

Burr, also still standing, said, "Your Honor, my client has a lease on the property. The defendant can't sell it."

"Mr. Ballantine terminated the lease."

"He can't do that."

"He most certainly can. And he did." Dahlberg opened a folder and took out a legal-sized document.

That's at least thirty pages.

Dahlberg flipped through the document. "Your Honor, this is the lease between Mr. Ballantine and the Little Traverse Conservancy for the property, commonly known as the Thorne Swift Nature Preserve. The language regarding termination is on page fifteen."

Dahlberg looked up at Judge Abbott. "May I read it to you?" he said sweetly.

"No, you may not," Burr said. "That lease or whatever it is has not been admitted into evidence."

"So moved," Dahlberg said, more sweetly.

"Stop it, both of you." The judge slammed her gavel again.

I don't think she's too happy.

"Mr. Lafayette, just what would you have me do?"

"Your Honor, I ask that you retain jurisdiction of this case, enjoin the termination or the lease, and prohibit the sale of Thorne Swift."

"If wishes were horses," Dahlberg said, quietly.

"I heard that."

"You were supposed to."

The judge looked at Dahlberg. "What is it that you want?"

"I ask that you dismiss this case for lack of jurisdiction."

Burr walked around his table and took a step toward the judge. "Your Honor, because of the endangered status of the lady's slipper under federal law, this case clearly involves a federal question."

Dahlberg stood. "There is nothing endangered about the lady's slipper. This is about terminating a lease and the sale of real property. That is a matter of state law."

Burr took another step toward Judge Abbott.

"Stop right there. Not one step closer."

Burr put his left foot forward.

"Go back to your table and sit down."

"Your Honor—"

She pointed at his table.

How can I possibly win if I can't even figure out where I stand?

Burr backed up. "Your Honor, this is clearly a federal question. You must retain jurisdiction."

The judge sighed. "Mr. Lafayette, what do you want?"

Dahlberg walked around his table toward the judge. "Your Honor—"

"You stay at your table, too."

Dahlberg backed up. "Your Honor—"

"Please be quiet, Mr. Dahlberg," Judge Abbott said. "Mr. Lafayette, what do you want from me?"

"I ask that you enjoin the sale of the property that my client leases from Mr. Ballantine while an environmental impact statement is prepared."

"Your Honor, that is the equivalent of taking jurisdiction, and there is no jurisdiction."

The judge opened her file again. She thumbed through it, stopped, and studied a piece of one of the pages. She sighed again, then looked at Burr.

"Mr. Lafayette, on May 15th, I granted you a temporary restraining order that gave you two weeks to document the lady's slipper on Mr. Ballantine's property. I note that you haven't done that. That was a month ago. Why should I give you any more time to do anything?"

Burr rocked back and forth, heel to toe.

"Your Honor, you graciously agreed to this emergency hearing. Please let me tell you why this is so important."

The judge looked up at the ceiling, then back at Burr.

"As long as you're here, you may as well."

"First, as to the question of jurisdiction, I would like to add the Friends of Thorne Swift as additional plaintiff. The Friends of Thorne Swift is a Delaware nonprofit corporation formed specifically to preserve and protect Thorne Swift from development. My client is represented by Claire Fisher who is sitting to the right of Dr. Murphy."

Collin put his hand on Claire's. She took it off.

Claire Fisher was mid-thirties, slim, mousey shoulder-length hair pulled behind her ears, a few freckles, a turned-up nose, and no makeup. She wore a white blouse, black slacks, and a matching black jacket. Burr thought she'd done her best to make herself look unattractive, and had failed.

Dahlberg launched himself to his feet. "Your Honor, this is the height of judicial fraud. Defense counsel has concocted a scheme to keep this case in your courtroom when it clearly belongs in state court. Mr. Lafayette is perpetrating a fraud on the court."

"Respectfully, Your Honor, Delaware companies are commonly used as 501(c)(3)s, particularly for fundraising purposes, which this is."

She shook her head, then looked at Burr. "At this point, I'm not sure it matters who the plaintiffs are. The court accepts the addition of Friends of Thorne Swift as an additional plaintiff." She turned to Dahlberg. "You need not say anything, Mr. Dahlberg. I take judicial notice of your objection."

"Your Honor—"

"Your objection is noted." To Burr, "Please continue."

"Thank you, Your Honor. While we are grateful that you gave my client a week to finish its research on the lady's slipper, we were unable to do so."

"A week is a week," Dahlberg said.

Judge Abbott glared at Dahlberg. "I didn't ask for your opinion." She turned to Burr and sighed.

"I object," Dahlberg said.

"So noted." The judge turned back to Burr. "Please enlighten us, Mr. Lafayette."

"Your Honor, my client was unable to complete its research. The caretaker ejected Professor Murphy the first time he was at Thorne Swift. That was one of the reasons I requested the TRO, which you so graciously granted. The next time Professor Murphy tried to do his research, he was attacked. He was clubbed and seriously injured."

Judge Abbott sat up straight. "Who attacked him?"

"Unfortunately, Your Honor, Professor Murphy didn't see who attacked him."

"I'd like to see what's under that bandage," Dahlberg said.

I'm sure you would.

Burr looked at Collin. The white bandage on his forehead was mostly unnecessary, but Burr, ever the showman, had insisted.

"We would be happy to show you, Your Honor, but Professor Murphy's doctors warned him about the risk of infection."

"A likely story," Dahlberg said.

Collin pushed his chair back. "You have no idea what happened."

"Sit down," Burr said.

Collin started for Dahlberg. Burr pulled him back.

The judge slammed her gavel. "Mr. Murphy, sit down this instant."

"I was—"

"I said 'sit down.'"

Burr pushed Collin back in his chair.

"One more outburst like that and I will hold you in contempt. Do I make myself clear?"

"Yes, Your Honor," Burr said.

How can a professor of botany be such a hothead?

"Continue, Mr. Lafayette," the judge said. "Without the drama."

Burr smiled at Dahlberg, then looked back at Judge Abbott. "As I was saying, Your Honor, Professor Murphy was beaten and was unable to complete his research."

"Who beat him?" Dahlberg said.

The judge rapped her gavel. "Mr. Dahlberg, the last time I checked, I was in charge here." Then, to Burr, "Who beat him?"

It was Dahlberg's turn to smile.

Burr looked down at his shoes, still in need of polish, then back to the judge. "Unfortunately, Your Honor, Professor Murphy didn't see his attacker."

"You could at least show us what you have," Dahlberg said. "Like the pictures he took before."

"Stop it, Mr. Dahlberg." Judge Abbott rapped her gavel again, this time a little harder. "Mr. Lafayette, please show Professor Murphy's work and the pictures you do have.

I didn't know we were playing Simon Says.

"Unfortunately, Your Honor, Professor Murphy's attacker stole his camera."

"Show what you do have," Dahlberg said.

Burr took a step toward Dahlberg. "Should I address you 'Judge Dahlberg?'"

Judge Abbott banged her gavel this time. "Stop it. Both of you." Then, "Mr. Lafayette, show us what you do have."

"Your Honor, Professor Murphy had a digital camera. All of the pictures were inside the camera."

"So, you don't have anything to show the court?" Judge Abbott said.

"No, Your Honor. That's why we need more time."

"How much more time do you need?" the judge said.

"Respectfully, Your Honor, Professor Murphy needs time to recover from his injuries before he can do any more research. He also needs a new camera."

"How much more time do you need?" the judge said again.

Burr rocked back and forth on his feet again. He looked up at the ceiling, then over at Dahlberg, then at the judge. "Your Honor, I think it will be at least a month before Professor Murphy will be able to resume his research."

"A month?" Dahlberg said.

"A month?" the judge said.

"Yes, Your Honor." Burr smiled at Dahlberg again.

"I object, Your Honor," Dahlberg said, not smiling. "The lady's slipper won't be blooming in a month. If you give them another month, it won't bloom again for an entire year."

Exactly.

"And we'll have to wait a year to sell the property," Dahlberg said.

You are so right.

"Which will not only delay the sale of my client's property but could well cause the sale to collapse."

That's the plan.

"Your Honor, it's not my client's fault that Professor Murphy was beaten and his camera was stolen. For all we know, Mr. Dahlberg and his client were behind it."

Dahlberg jumped to his feet.

"Who else would care enough to do it?" Burr said.

"How about one of your tree hugger friends. Just to make it look good. Or perhaps Professor Murphy, and I take great liberty in even using 'professor' to describe him, is faking it."

"That is uncalled for," Burr said.

Dahlberg wasn't through. "Your Honor, Mr. Lafayette's client has had over a month to complete the research. And then they were granted even more time. This is a swamp next to Lake Michigan. My client is merely trying to enjoy the benefits of private property. If you grant Mr. Lafayette's request, this will be the equivalent of taking private property, which is prohibited by the fifth amendment."

"Nonsense," Burr said. "The property will still be there in a year. If it's so valuable, a year is nothing. But if this sale proceeds, the lady's slipper will be gone forever."

"Those weeds are everywhere."

"They are endangered."

Judge Abbott slammed her gavel. "Stop it, both of you."

The judge pursed her pink lips and looked down at Burr. "Mr. Lafayette, what exactly would you have me do?"

"Your Honor, we ask that you give us enough time for Professor Murphy to recover from his beating, which may well have been at the hands of Mr. Dahlberg's client."

Dahlberg jumped up again. "Stop right there, Lafayette. This is an outrage. There is absolutely no foundation for this slanderous accusation."

"Mr. Lafayette, you are out of line," the judge said. "Way out of line."

"I'm sorry, Your Honor. We need a year to finish. Because of Professor Murphy's injury and the blooming cycle of the flower."

Judge Abbott drummed her fingers on her desk. Finally, "I find for the defendant. Mr. Dahlberg, your client may proceed with the sale. I will retain jurisdiction. Case dismissed." She stood and walked out.

She may as well have flown out on her broomstick.

CHAPTER TWO

"Jacob is right," Aunt Kitty said.

Burr looked out the window. Clear blue skies above a cornfield, the corn on its way to knee high by the fourth of July.

"Jacob is right," Aunt Kitty said again. She picked a dog hair off her black skirt.

I know where this is headed.

They had just crossed the Thornapple River on I-96, just east of Grand Rapids.

Burr looked at the oil pressure gauge. He didn't love many things, but he did love his sailboat, his shotgun, and his Jeep—a black Grand Wagoneer, the kind they didn't make anymore, the one with the fake wood panels on the sides. Even if he had to add a quart of oil every time he got gas, which was every two hundred miles. The rear window wiper had never worked right, so he broke it off once and for all. The tan leather seat was every bit as comfortable as a La-Z-Boy, and it didn't show dog hair, not that he cared if it did. He'd liked his blue Jeep better, but it had ended up in a tree just off M-119 in the Tunnel of Trees. But that was another story.

She shouldn't wear black in my Jeep.

"Are you listening to me?" she said.

"Yes."

"Then why don't you answer?"

Burr looked over at her. "I didn't know you were asking me a question." He knew perfectly well what was coming next. He just didn't want to be a part of it.

"That dog of yours sheds everywhere."

"Zeke isn't here."

"It doesn't matter. He was here."

"Zeke rides in the backseat."

Aunt Kitty slapped Burr's knee. "That's not true and you know it. That dog rides shotgun every chance he gets."

She's way too smart for me.

Zeke-the-Dog, Burr's aging yellow Lab, was Burr's constant companion and best friend. But he did shed, and he did ride shotgun.

"I'm sorry, Aunt Kitty. I'll wipe off the seat next time."

"No, you won't."

You're right. I won't.

They had left Judge Abbott's courtroom half an hour ago, defeat in hand, and were on their way back to Burr's office in East Lansing.

"You can't carry on like this. Dog hair everywhere. A broken down law practice, and a fire trap of an office building that's falling down around your ears."

Burr took his hands off the steering wheel and ran his hands through his hair, front to back.

"Keep your hands on the wheel."

"I'm steering with my knees."

"I know why you do that." She slapped him on the knee again.

Burr jumped and his knees came off the steering wheel. The Jeep swerved.

Aunt Kitty grabbed the wheel. "You're going to kill us."

Except for Zeke-the-Boy, Kathryn Lafayette—Aunt Kitty—was Burr's only living relative. She was his grandfather's sister. Tall and thin, with a pointed nose, a white ponytail, and clear blue eyes—like Burr's, but fiercer. An aging beauty, she had gone to law school when it was almost impossible for a woman to become a lawyer. She spent most of her time trying to preserve what made Northern Michigan a special place. Which was why Burr had been in court this morning.

"You're lucky the judge didn't throw you out. She doesn't like you."

"I'd have been luckier if she had thrown me out."

"No, you wouldn't. She's a fine judge." Aunt Kitty looked out her window, then said, "She was appointed by Reagan not too long ago. She's from an old East Grand Rapids family. She went to Kalamazoo College, then Michigan law school.

"Great pedigree."

"If it's in dog terms, you can understand it. The rumor is she wants to run for the U.S. Senate. You need to stay on her good side."

"If I hadn't been in court, I could have been working for a client who might actually pay me."

"Do you have any of those?"

"Many," Burr said, who didn't.

"If you had stayed at Fisher and Allen, you could have done this pro bono while you made money practicing law. All you did today was escape without getting thrown out."

"I am painfully aware of that."

"Although the judge did retain jurisdiction."

"Jurisdiction doesn't matter. We lost."

"It matters for the appeal."

Burr looked over at Aunt Kitty.

"Keep your eyes on the road."

"There's nothing to appeal and no reason to do it."

"Nonsense."

"The most we can hope to do is slow them down."

"Did you know the lady's slipper wasn't endangered?"

"Yes."

"Then why did you bring it up?"

"It was all I had, and I was hoping Dahlberg didn't know. Or the judge."

"Did Collin know?"

"He's the one who told me."

"It didn't work."

"It was the only way to get the first TRO."

"You went to all the trouble to have Collin do a study and get beat up for a flower that isn't endangered."

"I didn't know he was going to get beat up."

"I surely hope you didn't." She looked out the window, then back at Burr. "Judge Abbott didn't rule that the lady's slipper wasn't endangered."

"If she thought the lady's slipper was endangered, she wouldn't have ruled that Ballantine could proceed with the sale." Burr looked out his window, then "she effectively ruled that it wasn't endangered."

"Collin is a brilliant botanist."

What does that have to do with anything?

"He may be, but he's a hothead."

"He's passionate about his work, and he's a damn good botanist."

"It wouldn't matter if he was Charles Darwin. If the lady's slipper isn't endangered, Ballantine can sell Thorne Swift to whomever he wants, and the buyer will be able to do whatever he wants."

"That awful Johnson Smart was there today. He's the one who wants to buy it. He was the one in the back of the courtroom. With the salt and pepper hair."

"And the sincere blue suit."

"Don't be smart with me."

They crossed the Grand River at Portland.

We'll be back in half an hour. If I can last that long.

"Thorne Swift is private property, and it's zoned single family residential."

"The Conservancy has a lease."

"Which Ballantine terminated."

"He can't do that."

Burr cleared his throat. "Respectfully, for such a brilliant and learned lawyer, you have a painful disregard for the law and the facts."

"It doesn't matter what the law and the facts are. You can't let Johnson Smart buy Thorne Swift."

"Judge Abbott just ruled that he could."

"That seventeen acres on Lower Shore Drive is the last big piece of property on Lake Michigan close to Harbor Springs."

"Which is why Smart wants to build million-dollar cottages on it."

"You've got to stop him."

She's not listening.

"Aunt Kitty, the way to stop Johnson Smart is to raise the money and buy the land from Ballantine."

"It's too expensive."

"My point exactly."

Aunt Kitty picked another dog hair off her skirt. "Damn that dog."

Now she sounds like Jacob.

"You should never have named your son after your dog."

Here we go again.

"My dear Aunt Kitty, there is no greater honor than to be named after Zeke."

"It will be terrible to go through life as Zeke-the-Boy." She shook her head. "Named after a dog."

It had always surprised Burr that Grace, Zeke's mother and Burr's former wife, had allowed their son to be named Zeke.

Aunt Kitty looked out the window.

"Zeke-the-Dog and Zeke-the-Boy. It's too much."

* * *

"I can't hear a word you're saying," Eve said.

"I said I'm not going to do it," Burr said.

"Come out of the closet so I can hear you."

"I like it in here."

"There are some things you've got to do."

Burr quite liked his closet. It was the only part of his building that had turned out. It was a walk-in closet the size of a bedroom, paneled in cedar. Burr loved the spicy, musty smell. It reminded him of the cedar closets at Cottage 59 on Harbor Point where his aunt lived. It also reminded him of the cedar swamps in Northern Michigan, like the one where the lady's slipper grew. Which he'd just as soon forget. If anyone would let him.

"Come out of that closet."

All of Burr's favorite things were in his closet. His duck decoys, his waders, his shotgun, and his Barbour jacket. He tripped over his seasonal affective disorder light.

"I wondered where that was."

There was almost eighteen hours of daylight now, and Burr was nearly manic. He didn't need the light now, but he would this winter.

He turned off the light and stood in the dark.

"Burr, please."

Eve opened the door to the closet. "For God's sake, you're standing in the dark."

"It's dark when the lights are off."

Eve took Burr by the hand and led him to his desk. She sat in one of the two matching blue leather wingback chairs across from him. Zeke-the-Dog napped on the matching leather couch against the wall. Burr opened his desk drawer and took out a No. 2 yellow pencil.

"Don't tap that pencil."

Burr tapped his pencil on his walnut desk, just slightly smaller than a Buick 225. His office was paneled in cherry. The floors were hardwood with Oriental throws. Behind him, a window the size of a movie screen looked out on downtown East Lansing. Burr liked his office, but he liked his closet more.

Eve reached across Burr's desk and took his pencil. She dropped a pile of pink phone messages in front of him.

He shuffled through the pile but didn't look at any of them. "There's a lot of them."

"Enough for double-handed canasta," Eve said.

"I'm popular."

"You're going to be a lot less popular if you spend all your time in the closet."

Eve McGinty had been Burr's longtime, long-suffering legal assistant at Fisher and Allen. He'd begged her not to follow him to East Lansing when he resigned.

Eve had divorced well and quit anyway. She said she wanted a perennial garden with full sun and moved to East Lansing. Burr thought there must have been a perennial garden with full sun somewhere in Detroit.

Eve was five-four, petite, with chin-length brown hair, a turned-up nose, and a mouthful of white teeth. She was a year older than Burr, which she didn't like and which he never let her forget. She had the beginnings of crow's feet around her eyes which makeup couldn't quite cover up, which she also didn't like. She had bright brown eyes that could start a fire and a wit to match.

Burr knew she was smarter than he was and could never figure out why she worked for him.

She favored gold hoop earrings which she tugged on when she was anxious, which was now.

This can't be good.

"You have got to return those calls," Eve said, still tugging.

"I don't know who they're from."

"That's because you haven't looked at them."

Burr swiveled in his swivel chair and looked out his window.

It's a fine summer's day, and I'm stuck in here.

"It doesn't matter that it's a fine summer's day. You've got work to do."

How does she know what I'm thinking?

"Half of those messages are from your aunt. Half are from Claire. The rest are from your creditors."

"Three halves are more than all of them."

"Turn around and look at me."

Burr did as he was told. For a change.

"This is the last day you can appeal Judge Abbott's dismissal."

"I know."

"Is it ready for me to type?"

"No."

"When will it be ready?"

"Never."

"What do you mean?"

"I'm not going to file an appeal."

"Why not?"

"Because I'm not getting paid."

"There's nothing new about that."

"Very funny."

Eve leaned toward Burr. "This is pro bono."

"It was pro bono. Now I need to get paid."

"You can do a little work for charity."

"Are you working for charity?"

"What do you mean?"

"Do you expect me to pay you to type the appeal?"

"Of course I do."

"Not only do I work for free, I pay you while I'm working for free."

Eve picked up the phone messages and sorted them into piles. She pushed them at Burr. Burr pushed them back. She pushed them back at Burr.

Jacob walked in. "Is this phone message tug-of-war?" He dropped an accordion folder full of a hundred pieces of paper on the pink slips, then sat next to Eve in the matching wingback chair. He pulled about five sheets of paper from the file, neatly stapled, and slid it across Burr's desk. "I finished the motion and typed it myself. All you have to do is sign it."

Burr slid it back to Jacob, who slid it back to Burr.

"I'm not going to play this silly game." Jacob twirled a curl in his steel wool hair, which he did when he was anxious, which was now. "I've done all the work. All you have to do it sign it."

"As soon as I sign it, I'm working for free again."

"We're all working for free on this," Jacob said. "We must save the lady's slipper."

Burr slid the folder to the side of his desk, then shuffled through the messages. "That's what all these are about."

"Except the ones from your creditors," Eve said.

"I expect to get paid before them."

Jacob Wertheim, the Wertheim in Lafayette and Wertheim, had hair like steel wool. He was short and wiry, like his hair. Olive skin, prominent nose. Not big—prominent. A bit younger than Burr.

He ran a thumb and forefinger along the knife-like crease in his linen pants that went nicely with his midnight blue blazer, starched ivory shirt, and peach-and-coral pastel tie.

Jacob is natty.

When Burr resigned from Fisher and Allen, Jacob had insisted on coming with him. Also, despite Burr's protests. They started an appellate practice—only appeals, state and federal, mostly state. Mostly court of appeals, some supreme court. Complicated, esoteric appeals. Jacob did the research and the writing. Burr did the oral arguments and dealt with the clients. Jacob was a brilliant researcher, but he was deathly afraid of courtrooms, clients, and public speaking. He didn't drink, but he did smoke marijuana. He said it helped his anxiety. Burr thought Jacob must be anxious most of the time because he almost always smelled like marijuana. Like now.

He pushed the motion toward Burr. "Sign it, Burr. Please."

Burr pushed it back.

Jacob handed it to Eve. "You sign it."

"I can't do that."

"You've signed Burr's name for years."

"Burr, please," Jacob said. "We don't even know if the appeal will be granted."

"The appeal will be granted."

"How do you know?"

"Because you wrote it."

"This will take care of two-thirds of your messages," Eve said.

"And make the other third worse," Burr said. "Because we won't get paid."

The door to the hallway opened and slammed shut. Claire Fisher ran into Burr's office. Zeke barked from the couch.

A third of the messages just showed up.

"Why haven't you called me?" she said, out of breath. She brushed a hair off her face. "I had to take the stairs."

That's a story for another day.

"You must help."

"I'm sorry, Claire, but …" Burr said.

Jacob picked up the motion. "We were just about to file the appeal."

Claire grabbed it from him and ripped it up.

"Forget the appeal," she said. "Collin's been arrested."

CHAPTER THREE

Burr brought Claire a side chair. "I had to take the stairs," she said again, still out of breath.

The damn thing is broken again.

"I'm so sorry," Eve said. "There's a repairman on the way."

Fat chance.

"The accursed thing never works," Jacob said.

Buying the Masonic Temple building seemed like a good idea at the time. Red brick, six stories, and narrow. Very narrow. Burr would rent out the first five floors, retail and office, and put his office and living quarters on the top floor. The realtor had told him the building had good bones, but the renovations and the new elevator had nearly broken him, and no one wanted to rent it. He only had one tenant, Michelangelo's, a quite nice Northern Italian restaurant on the first floor, but Scooter, the owner, was chronically late on the rent.

Burr didn't like elevators. He didn't trust them. He always took the stairs, but everyone else quite liked elevators.

Eve brought Claire a glass of water. "Catch your breath."

"Things can always get worse," Burr said, mostly to himself.

"I beg your pardon," Claire said.

"Nothing."

Claire took a sip, then a deep breath.

"How can we help?" Jacob said.

We can't possibly help.

"It's Collin. He's been arrested."

"What happened?" Jacob said.

"It's that awful caretaker. Frank. Frank Slaughter."

What a name.

"He's the caretaker at the preserve in the summer." She stood, walked to the door, turned, then walked back. "He's the one who threw Collin out of the preserve. Collin thought Frank was the one who beat him and took his camera." She walked around Burr's desk, then sat down. "He didn't know for sure. He never saw who hit him." She shook her head. "This is so terrible."

"So, he and Collin had a fight?" Eve said.

The last thing I need is to get involved in an assault and battery.

"I don't know."

Claire sat back down. Zeke came over and licked her hand. "Thank you."

Zeke wagged his tail. It thumped on Jacob's leg.

"This wretched cur will be the end of me." He picked a dog hair off his slacks.

We're not getting anywhere. Which is fine with me.

Jacob slid his chair away from Zeke. "Please, Claire, tell us what happened and how we can help."

Claire crossed her legs, uncrossed them, then crossed them again. She looked at the painting of Walpole Marsh in November, mallards landing on a pond surrounded by sand-colored cattails, their brown heads blowing in the wind, the white seeds blowing off.

I wish I was there.

"What happened?" Jacob said.

"Frank Slaughter is dead," she said.

"Dead?" Jacob said.

"Dead?" Eve said.

"He was murdered, and the police arrested Collin."

"Murdered?" Jacob said.

"Murdered?" Eve said.

"He was stabbed."

Claire scratched Zeke's right ear, the one that always hurt.

Zeke yelped.

"He likes his left ear scratched," Burr said.

"I'm so sorry, Zeke." Claire scratched Zeke's left ear. The aging Lab groaned.

If dogs could purr.

"Why was Collin arrested?"

She looked back at the painting of the marsh, then she scratched Zeke's right ear. He yelped again, "I'm so sorry." Zeke limped back to the couch.

"Claire," Burr said.

"The police think it was his knife," she said.

"His knife?"

"The police said Frank was stabbed to death."

"Why do they think it was Collin?"

"They said he was stabbed with Collin's knife. So they arrested him."

She looked at Burr. "That's why I've been trying to reach you. I finally had to drive down here." She paused. "You really should have returned my calls."

"I'm sorry, Claire, but I'm not a criminal lawyer."

"But you've done murder trials. And won."

Even a blind squirrel can find an acorn.

Truth be told, Burr had done criminal work—but not by choice. He'd been head of the litigation department at Fisher and Allen. A hundred lawyers strong, and one of Detroit's premier law firms. But he did commercial litigation, nothing criminal, never criminal law. He'd been the best commercial litigator in Detroit until his disastrous affair with a client. He'd been almost old enough to be her father. It was a terrible mistake that had cost him his practice and his marriage. He moved to East Lansing and started an appellate practice. His esoteric practice couldn't be any further from criminal law, but somehow he'd been roped into murder cases. Not quite unmitigated disasters, but close, and he was damned if he was going to get dragged into another one.

"I'm very sorry about Collin. I'm not a criminal lawyer, but I can get you a good one."

"You know Collin, and you know what's going on."

"I'm sorry, Claire."

She reached across the desk and put her hand on his. "Please, Burr."

Burr pulled his hand back.

"Burr's right," Jacob said. "He's not really competent to do criminal law."

Thank you. I think.

"What happened?" Eve said.

Traitor.

Claire turned her chair toward Eve. "Collin got a call from the Harbor Springs police. Four days ago, I think. They asked him to come in for an interview. That's what they called it." She took a deep breath. "He asked what it was about, but they wouldn't say. So, he didn't go in. They called again. He said 'no' again. Then they came over. They pretty much barged in. Collin got mad and threw them out before they could even get in. He's got a temper." She looked away, then back at Burr. "They came back with a warrant and took him to the police station."

"When was this?" Burr said.

Eve looked at Burr. "I thought you weren't interested."

"I'm not, really," Burr said, who was getting interested.

"The police said they'd found a body and wanted to know where Collin was on Saturday."

"That's almost a week ago," Jacob said.

"Collin said he couldn't remember. The police told him not to go anywhere. On Thursday they told him to come to the station. He didn't. Then they arrested him. He's been in jail ever since."

"Has he been charged?" Burr said.

Claire looked at Burr. "Do you care?"

I'm starting to.

Claire turned her chair to Burr. "That's why I called. Collin's in trouble and he needs help."

"Has he been charged?" Jacob said.

"I don't know."

"The police can't hold him without charging him," Jacob said.

Eve looked at Burr. "If you'd returned Aunt Kitty's calls, you'd probably know."

Thank you for that.

Claire put her hands on Burr's desk and leaned toward him. "Collin's in jail and he needs your help."

"Burr's not a criminal lawyer," Jacob said.

* * *

"I object, Your Honor," Aunt Kitty said.

"Please sit down, Miss Lafayette. You are out of order."

"Your Honor," Aunt Kitty said, "respectfully, it is the prosecutor who is out of order."

"Please sit down or I will have you removed from the courtroom."

"Your Honor—"

Judge Bailey pointed a manicured finger at Aunt Kitty's chair. "Sit."

Aunt Kitty stayed on her feet.

"Now," he said.

The Honorable Paul Bailey, District Court Judge for Emmet County, was used to having his way. He was the grandson of George Bailey, the founder of Bailey Motors, the biggest car dealership in Northern Michigan. It was on US-31 in Petoskey, overlooked Little Traverse Bay, and built at a time when no one thought much about the view. The dealership sold millions of dollars of cars year in and year out, and the used car lot had a multi-million dollar view of the bay. Judge Bailey was used to having his way, and he intended to have his way now, even if he was wrong.

He pointed to Aunt Kitty's chair with a manicured index finger.

Judge Bailey wasn't particularly smart. All the lawyers dreaded facing him, but he had been elected and re-elected time and again because of his name. Bailey Motors did so much advertising that its name rubbed off on the judge's campaigns. Not that anyone ran against him anymore.

He was in his fifties, solidly built, and fussy about his appearance. He had a razor cut and a manicure every week, bleached teeth and dark brown eyes with contact lenses. A strong jaw and a straight nose. He wore a tailored three-piece suit, expensive and fashionable but wasted under his robe. He didn't look like a movie star, but he didn't look like a judge either.

"I said sit."

"Your Honor, I must ask that you dismiss the charges against my client." She put her hand on Collin's shoulder. "His habeas corpus rights have been violated."

The prosecutor stood. "That's not true, Your Honor—"

"It most certainly is," Aunt Kitty said.

"That is ridiculous," the prosecutor said.

Calvin Truax was a tall, gangly man approaching sixty. His eyes bulged in their sockets, and his nose looked like a crow's beak. His Adam's apple looked like a golf ball, and it bobbed when he spoke. His hair was thinning, but he did have clear blue eyes.

"Your Honor—"

"Miss Lafayette, sit down."

Aunt Kitty was nothing if not stubborn, and no one would ever accuse her of bowing to authority. She started to say something, but a hand pushed down on her shoulder. She sat.

"I beg your pardon."

"Burr Lafayette for the defense, Your Honor."

Burr, with Jacob, Eve, and Claire in tow, had just rushed into Judge Bailey's courtroom, unannounced and uninvited.

The courtroom was on the first floor of the Emmet County Courthouse, a red-brick Victorian building left over from the logging days of Northern Michigan. It was trimmed in post-Victorian shabby. The linoleum floor was peeling, the walls and ceiling looked like they'd come down with the flu, and the pews were flaking, like they'd been in the sun too long, which they hadn't, because there were no windows in the courtroom.

"What in God's name are you doing here?" Truax said.

Burr sat between his aunt and Collin, dressed in a stylish orange jumpsuit. He looked at the prosecutor and smiled.

He looks like Ichabod Crane.

"I object to this interloper barging in," Truax said.

Interloper?

Judge Bailey looked down at Burr. "Who did you say you were?"

"My name is Burr Lafayette. I represent Mr. Murphy."

"I represent Mr. Murphy," Aunt Kitty said, who looked every bit the part. She wore a black suit with a knee-length skirt, a white blouse, and no jewelry.

"Your Honor, this is totally unacceptable," Truax said.

"Your Adam's apple is bobbing," Burr said.

Truax turned red and covered his neck with his hands.

Burr had crossed swords with Truax before. He'd beaten him in a murder trial, but Truax was a good lawyer, and Burr wasn't excited about fighting with him again.

Truax dropped his hands. "Your Honor, we extended Mr. Murphy the courtesy of turning himself in, which he refused. Police found him. He resisted arrest. They had to bring him in forcibly. It was Friday. You were not available over the weekend. And today is Tuesday."

"What about yesterday?" Aunt Kitty said.

Truax turned a deeper shade of red.

"Your Honor, the statute requires a person accused of a crime to be charged within forty-eight hours. My client cannot be charged."

Burr looked at Judge Bailey. "May we have a minute?"

The judge shut his eyes, then nodded.

Burr sat. Aunt Kitty didn't. She looked down at him. "Truax didn't charge Collin in time. This cannot stand."

Burr looked up at his aunt. "We plowed this ground before."

"And you won."

"That wasn't the reason."

"It certainly was."

Burr's neck was starting to hurt. He touched Aunt Kitty's sleeve. "Would you please sit down?"

"I will not."

"As long as we're here, we might as well find out what this is about."

"We can find out when Truax starts playing by the rules and when Bailey isn't too lazy to come to work."

The judge looked at him sideways. "I beg your pardon?"

Burr stood. "Your Honor, we'd like to proceed with the arraignment."

Truax looked at Burr. "That's the first sensible thing I've ever heard you say."

Collin jumped to his feet. "You had no reason to arrest me." He took a step toward Truax. "Let me go."

Burr grabbed Collin by the arm. "Sit down. You're making things worse."

Collin shook off Burr's hand and started for Truax.

"Bailiff, restrain the defendant," Judge Bailey said. A sleepy-eyed, slack-jawed bailiff looked up from what might have been a nap. "Bailiff," he said again.

The bailiff, a well-fed man in his forties, pushed himself to his feet, lumbered over to Collin, and put his hand on Collin's shoulder.

"Let go of me."

"Cuff him," Truax said.

The bailiff looked at Judge Bailey, who nodded. He spun Collin around and cuffed his hands behind his back. Then he pushed him down into his chair.

"One more outburst and you'll find yourself back in your cell," the judge said.

"Which is where you belong." This from Truax.

Burr leaned over to Collin. "This is not helping."

"I didn't do anything."

"Let's hear what they have to say."

Aunt Kitty poked Burr. "Collin has been mistreated."

"You're not helping either," Burr said.

Judge Bailey banged his gavel. "What is going on down there? You're all going to find yourself in jail if you don't behave."

Burr stood again. "I'm sorry, Your Honor. Emotions are running a little high."

"I should say so," the judge said. "Control your client or you won't like what happens next."

"Yes, Your Honor." Burr sat.

Judge Bailey studied his fingernails. Then he took out a handkerchief and polished them one by one. "Where were we?" He looked down at the court stenographer, a skinny, thirtyish woman with the reddest fingernails Burr had ever seen.

She and Bailey make quite a pair.

Truax stood before she could say anything. "You were just about to read the charges against the defendant."

"I was?" The judge shuffled through his papers. Then he looked down at Truax. "Mr. Truax, why don't we start with you telling us what happened."

Burr stood. "Your Honor, the prosecutor has no firsthand knowledge of what did or did not happen. This is hearsay."

Judge Bailey scowled. "While it may come as a surprise to you, Mr. Lafayette, I am familiar with the rules of evidence. And this is not an evidentiary matter. This is an arraignment."

"Yes, Your Honor, but in an arraignment, it is customary for the presiding judge to read the charges and for the defendant to enter a plea."

The judge thrust his hand out to Burr, palm first. "Stop right there. Your reputation precedes you." He wagged his finger at Burr. "This is my courtroom, and I'll do as I damn well please. Is that clear?"

Burr sat but didn't say anything.

"Is that clear, Mr. Lafayette?"

Burr nodded.

"Mr. Lafayette, the court reporter cannot record a nod. Please answer the question."

"Respectfully, Your Honor, if you would like a narrative, I think it would be better if the investigating officer testified as to what he found."

The judge scowled. "At this rate, I'll be up for reelection before we get through this." He looked at Truax. "Proceed." Then at Burr. "Not one peep out of you. Do I make myself clear?"

Burr nodded.

"Speak when you're spoken to."

I thought I wasn't supposed to peep.

"Yes, Your Honor," Burr said.

The judge nodded at Truax.

"Thank you, Your Honor," Truax said, standing. He opened a file and flipped through it. "On Sunday, July 22nd, Jill Slaughter, the wife of the deceased, reported her husband missing. She said she hadn't seen him since Saturday. The police started looking for him. They got a list of friends from his wife and started calling. No luck. They checked with his employer, the Little Traverse Conservancy." Truax looked at Claire, then back at the judge. "He was the caretaker at the Thorne Swift Nature Preserve in the summer. He didn't show up for work, and they hadn't seen him either." Truax put his hands in his pockets.

Nice touch.

"On Monday, the police found his truck, a white Ford F-150."

"Where was it?" the judge said.

"It was just off Bull Moose Road, Your Honor."

"Where is that?"

I wish he wasn't paying such close attention.

"Bull Moose Road is at the end of Fourth Street on the edge of Harbor Springs. Fourth Street runs along the base of the bluff, just west of the post office. The Conservancy has a nature preserve on both sides of the road after the houses end. There's a turnaround at the end of Fourth Street. Mr. Slaughter's truck was just off the turnaround. The police searched the area; there was no sign of Mr. Slaughter, and they didn't find anything." Truax paused. "At first."

The judge leaned toward Truax.

Now I'm getting interested.

"They expanded the search further into the preserve. The area is heavily wooded and parts of it are swampy. There is a boardwalk that runs through the wettest part of the preserve. It ends up at Second Street. They searched and searched but didn't find any sign of Mr. Slaughter."

The judge leaned further toward Truax.

If he leans any further, he's going to tip over.

"Then they called the state police post in Petoskey. They sent a tracking dog and a handler."

"What kind of dog?"

"I'm not sure," Truax said. "A Lab, I think."

Another traitor.

"They went back to the preserve and gave the dog something of Mr. Slaughter's so he could get Mr. Slaughter's scent. Then they took the dog into the preserve. The dog ranged all over the preserve. Nothing. Nothing for over two hours."

Truax knows how to tell a story. I'll give him that.

"They were on the boardwalk again and just about to give up when the dog ran off into the swamp. It's thick in there. Trees, brush, and marsh grass. Wet and swampy. They lost track of the dog. They called and called. She wouldn't come back. Nothing. The dog was gone and they were getting worried."

Truax put his hands in his pockets again.

More drama.

"They didn't know what to do. They waited and waited. And waited. Then they heard the dog bark. Out in the swamp."

"What did they do?" the judge said.

I think we're about to be euchred.

Truax cleared his throat. "They took off through the swamp toward the barking. It was a tough go. The swamp was almost impassable. They slogged through the ooze. Finally, they saw the dog. She looked at them and kept barking. They were exhausted by the time they got there. The dog was in mud almost up to its chest.

"They didn't see anything at first—just the dog barking. They bent down and felt around in the water and the muck. They found Mr. Slaughter's body." Truax paused.

He's letting it sink in. Nice touch.

The judge studied his fingernails again.

What's so special about his fingernails?

"Then what?"

"Mr. Slaughter was dead. He had been dead for some time. One of the officers went to get the medical examiner. He came, examined Mr. Slaughter, then his body was removed."

"What did he find?"

"They found that Mr. Slaughter had been stabbed in the back. Multiple times. And in his right eye. Once."

The judge shuddered. Burr looked over at Collin, staring at Truax.

"How does this implicate Mr. Murphy?" the judge said.

Truax smiled, a nasty, know-it-all smile. He bent down and picked up a brown eight-by-eleven envelope off his table, then made a show of opening it.

I don't think I'm going to like what's inside.

Truax took something out of the envelope. He closed his hand around it before Burr could see what it was. The prosecutor walked up to the judge and opened his hand, his back to Burr.

He's doing that on purpose.

"What is it?" Judge Bailey said.

"This, Your Honor, is the murder weapon." Truax opened his hand.

The judge shuddered. "It looks like a Swiss Army knife."

Truax nodded. He turned to Collin and showed the knife. "It belongs to the defendant, Collin Murphy."

Burr jumped to his feet. "Objection, Your Honor. There is no proof of that whatsoever."

"Your Honor, Mr. Murphy is known to have a Swiss Army knife," Truax said.

"I have one," Burr said. "So do five million other people."

"Be quiet, Mr. Lafayette," the judge said. "Mr. Truax?"

"We are confident it's Mr. Murphy's knife," Truax said.

Burr looked down at Collin. "Where's your knife?"

"I don't know."

Burr shook his head, then looked down at Collin again. "You're going to need to know."

The judge sat back in his chair. He folded his hands together. "Mr. Truax, let's go back a step. How do you know this knife is the murder weapon?"

The prosecutor smiled again.

Truax has Bailey right where he wants him.

"The medical examiner identified it as the murder weapon."

"I object, Your Honor."

"What is it this time?" The judge gave Burr a peeved look.

"Your Honor, this is a probable cause hearing. It's not a preliminary exam."

"You are quite right, Mr. Lafayette."

Maybe I'm getting somewhere.

"Overruled." To Truax, "Is that all you have, Mr. Truax?"

"No, Your Honor."

Burr still standing, "I object."

"So, noted. Sit down." The judge waved Burr off. "Continue, Mr. Truax."

Burr stayed on his feet.

"I said sit down."

"Your Honor—"

"Mr. Lafayette, you have two choices. You can sit down and be quiet, if that's possible. Or you can stay on your feet and walk out of here. You choose." The judge smiled at him.

Burr sat.

Truax looked at Burr. He swallowed, and his Adam's apple bobbed.

"You should have that looked at," Burr said.

"I beg your pardon."

Burr put his hand around his Adam's apple. "You look like you've got a golf ball stuck in your throat."

"Stop it, Mr. Lafayette," the judge said. "Mr. Truax, let me see the knife," Bailey said. "No, never mind. Do you have anything further?"

"Your Honor, Mr. Murphy and Mr. Slaughter were seen arguing at Bar Harbor on the night that Mr. Slaughter went missing. Mr. Murphy was overheard telling Mr. Slaughter that he would kill him if he didn't give him his camera back."

"That doesn't prove anything," Burr said.

Judge Bailey looked down at Burr. "You're quite right, Mr. Lafayette, but it's enough." The judge looked at Collin. "Mr. Murphy, stand up."

Collin stood. Burr stood next to him. "Your Honor—"

"Don't say a word. Mr. Murphy, I find that there is sufficient evidence to charge you with murdering Frank Slaughter. The charge is open murder. How do you plead?"

Collin tried to get his hands in front of him, but the handcuffs kept his hands behind his back. He didn't say anything.

"How do you plead, Mr. Murphy?"

"This is crazy."

"I'll give you one more chance, Mr. Murphy."

Collin started around the table toward Judge Bailey. Burr grabbed him by the shoulder and pulled him back. "Your Honor, Mr. Murphy pleads not guilty."

"Enter a plea of not guilty. Bailiff, return Mr. Murphy to the county jail."

"Your Honor, we request that Mr. Murphy be released on bail."

Judge Bailey sat back in his chair. "Are you kidding me? I had to have him cuffed."

"Your Honor, Mr. Murphy may be high spirited, but he is not dangerous, and he is not a flight risk."

"He tried to come after me."

"Mr. Murphy was stretching his legs."

"Nonsense," the judge said.

"The preliminary examination will be three weeks from today. Bailiff, take Mr. Murphy to the jail." He tapped his gavel and left.

CHAPTER FOUR

Burr dipped his spoon into his navy bean soup and steered a floating chunk of ham around the bowl, guiding it safely to shore.

"Stop playing with your food," Aunt Kitty said.

He steered the ham around a menacing reef of navy beans.

"Stop it."

Burr kept steering.

Aunt Kitty reached over and sank Burr's ham with her spoon.

Burr's not-so-merry little band—Aunt Kitty, Jacob, Eve, and Claire—sat at a window table at the Petoskey Big Boy, where US-31 and US-131 came together. The Big Boy hadn't been Burr's first choice. He'd wanted to go to the Mitchell Street Pub in downtown Petoskey because they had Labatt on draft. Aunt Kitty chose the Big Boy because they didn't have Labatt on draft and didn't serve any alcohol whatsoever. They also didn't have a whitefish sandwich, so Burr ordered their year-round navy bean soup, which was good for yachting with ham and beans and the hot chocolate. He and Zeke-the-Boy frequented the Big Boy in Grosse Pointe, largely because of the sugar-inducing coma of their hot chocolate, which was as much whipped cream as it was hot chocolate. That, and the cherry with the stem. He always asked for two cherries.

The rest of them, except Burr and Jacob, went to the salad bar. It was a fine salad bar, but Burr refused to have anything to do with salad bars.

I'll be damned if I'll go to a restaurant and make my own salad.

Jacob had the grilled cheese sandwich on white with the crusts cut off, as always.

Burr studied his soup.

"Look at me when I'm talking to you."

She must think I'm still twelve.

"And stop acting like you're twelve. You've got to figure out what to do."

Burr sank the rest of his ham navy. He looked at his aunt. "At the moment, there's nothing to do."

"Nonsense. At the very least, you can get bail for Collin."

"If he hadn't gone after Truax, I probably could have."

"Collin's got a short fuse, and it gets him into trouble," Claire said. She picked at the chicken Caesar salad she'd made for herself at the salad bar.

Just like Eve.

"Wait till Bailey cools off. Then try again," Aunt Kitty said.

"There's also the appeal," Claire said.

"I filed it," Jacob said.

"What do we do about that?" Claire said.

"We wait." Burr ate one of the cherries.

This would be a lot better if it was in a Manhattan.

"We can't just wait," Claire said. "We have to do something."

"Waiting is Burr's favorite strategy," Eve said. She picked at her salad bar chicken Caesar.

Burr studied his remaining cherry, then, "It doesn't seem like a professor of botany would have such a short fuse."

"It makes perfect sense to me," Jacob cut his grilled cheese sandwich into one-inch squares.

That is playing with your food.

"Collin is a brilliant botanist. He's passionate about his work, and his students love him," Claire said. "You have to get him out of jail."

"My dear, Claire," Burr said, "I probably could have gotten bail if he hadn't gone after the judge. As it is, there's no chance."

"You are so positive," Aunt Kitty said.

Claire stood. "I'm going to find a lawyer who can get this done. You're fired." She walked out.

* * *

Burr sat on *Spindrift* and stewed in his juices. That and what was left of his third very dry, very dirty, Bombay Sapphire gin martini on the rocks with four olives.

After he'd been fired, Burr and Zeke drove around Little Traverse Bay to the Harbor Springs city marina. While Burr launched his dinghy, Zeke stood in chest-deep water and drank from the bay. Burr wasn't a big fan of wet dog smell, but he'd given up trying to keep Zeke out of the water a long time ago. But as much as Zeke loved the water, he was no fan of Burr's tippy dinghy and refused to come out of the water. Burr had seen this movie before. He found a stick and threw it on the beach. Zeke, true to his genes and his training, fetched the stick and brought it back to Burr.

"You just couldn't help yourself."

Burr loaded Zeke into the dinghy and pushed off from the beach. Zeke sulked in the stern with the stick in his mouth He smelled like the beach and the wet dog he was.

"You don't much look like a commodore being rowed to your man-of-war."

The wind blew from the southwest. A light chop on the bay, a cloudless late July day, and the temperature in the mid-seventies—a perfect summer day in Harbor Springs, better known for ten months of winter and two months of bad skating.

Burr rowed them out to *Spindrift*, his aging thirty-four-foot, cutter-rigged sloop, moored on a buoy in the harbor. Burr pulled alongside and hoisted Zeke's front legs onto *Spindrift*'s deck, then lifted his dog by the hips and pushed him on board.

"There was a time when you could do this by yourself."

Burr tied the dinghy to the stern and climbed aboard.

He went down below and pulled up one of the floorboards. The bilge was about half full of water. He turned on the batteries at the instrument panel, then turned on the bilge pump. Zeke looked down at him from the cockpit but made no effort to come down below.

"Zeke, old friend, I've seen worse."

Spindrift had been built in 1940. She was in good shape but looked her age. She had oak planking, varnished mahogany cabin sides, gunwales, trim, and a forty-seven-foot spindly pine mast with more rigging than Burr had names for.

Burr loved *Spindrift*—not as much as he'd loved *Kismet*, but *Kismet* was about five miles west, sitting on the bottom of Lake Michigan in two hundred feet of water.

He climbed up to the cockpit, turned the key in the ignition, and pushed the starter button. The engine turned over but wouldn't start. He pulled out the choke and tried again. The starter whirred, but the engine wouldn't kick in. He stopped when he smelled gas.

"Flooded," he said. "Damn it all."

He waited ten minutes, then tried again. The starter groaned. Nothing. Burr tried again. Still nothing.

"Zeke, the battery is just about run down. Like me."

He waited another five minutes, then tried again. The engine caught.

"Will wonders never cease."

He let the engine idle for another five minutes, then put it into gear. It stalled.

"Damn it all."

He pushed the starter again. The engine started. He put it in gear. This time it kept running. He shifted back into neutral. He went to the bow, got the boat hook and cast off the mooring line. Back in the cockpit, he put the engine in gear and made for the city docks. He'd seen an empty slip and wanted to tie up before anyone else did or the harbormaster could tell him no. He believed that asking for forgiveness was better than asking for permission. That, and a twenty-dollar bill.

Burr single-handed *Spindrift* into the Slip 61 and tied her up by himself. Burr went back down below, found a six-pack of Labatt in the bilge, and put it on ice. Then he mixed himself a martini.

"Just like me. On ice."

He climbed back into the cockpit.

"Zeke, I've been fired before, but I've never been fired from a pro bono job. I wasn't even getting paid."

He took a swallow of his drink.

"It's not the worst thing that ever happened." Another swallow. "But it didn't do much for my oversized ego. As Eve calls it."

Sometime later, Burr made his way down below, scrambling out of the question. He lit the alcohol stove, opened a can of Bush's Vegetarian Baked Beans, and ruined its healthiness by dumping in half a can of Koegel's sliced Vienna franks. Zeke's favorite. He mixed the rest of the Koegel's with Zeke's dog food and ate the beans and franks out of the pot.

"Being fired has its advantages."

* * *

A rap on the cabin top. Zeke barked.

"Quiet." Burr untangled himself from his sleeping bag and rolled on his other side. Another rap. Another bark.

"Burr. Burr. Come up here this minute."

"Damn it all."

"I know you're down there. Come up here this instant."

Aunt Kitty.

"It's almost noon."

Burr sat up. His head wasn't pounding, but it was fuzzy.

"Come up here this instant or I'll come down there."

No rest for the weary. Or the wicked.

He managed to get out of his sleeping bag and into yesterday's clothes, wrinkled but not too worse for wear. He'd look for his shoes later. He pushed back the hatch cover. Aunt Kitty glared at him. He squinted in the sun, also glaring at him.

"Take Zeke ashore and come right back."

Since he'd lost his own mother, Aunt Kitty was the closest thing to a mother he had, and he knew enough not to argue with her. Ten minutes later, Burr and Zeke sat across from her in the cockpit, the sun in Burr's eyes, which wasn't helping.

"Where are your shoes?" she said.

Burr looked at his bare feet.

"Never mind," she said. "You simply cannot carry on this way."

"What way?"

"You know what I mean. You can't drink alone."

"I was with Zeke," Burr said, who knew he shouldn't have said it as soon as he said it.

"I thought you quit."

Burr looked away. "I'm on vacation."

"Vacation? You most certainly are not on vacation."

Aunt Kitty flipped her ponytail over her shoulder. She smoothed out her Pappagallo skirt that went nicely with her orange top and espadrilles.

Burr looked at her. "I was fired. You were there."

He reached across the cockpit and put his hand on Aunt Kitty's arm. "Claire fired me, and I couldn't be happier." He smiled at her.

She pushed his hand away. "You were not fired."

"I know what being fired sounds like."

"Well, then, you're unfired." She scowled. "You're rehired."

She doesn't like it when her grammar is incorrect.

Burr smiled.

"What are you smiling about? There's nothing remotely humorous going on here."

Much better grammar.

Burr's head was clearing, and he was ready to match wits with his aunt. As best he could.

"You're saying either she didn't fire me. Or, if she did fire me, she's rehiring me." Burr smiled again.

"There's nothing funny about that."

"The funny part is that either way, I'm not getting paid. Whether I'm fired or hired. I'd much rather be fired and not get paid than be hired and not get paid."

Aunt Kitty turned red underneath her Harbor Springs tan.

She looks like a resorter, but she's tough.

His aunt sighed. "Please, Burr. We need you. We really do."

Not so tough now.

"You're the only one who can save the lady's slipper."

"The lady's slipper doesn't need saving. It's not endangered. According to Judge Abbott."

"You're the only one who can save Thorne Swift."

"I'm the only one who will do it for free."

"What about Collin?"

"First things first."

Tough again.

"Judge Abbott denied your petition for reconsideration."

Burr sat up straight. "She what?"

"She denied your petition so the sale can go through."

Burr leaned back against the gunwale.

"If you ever called your office, you'd know. Heaven forbid, you would actually be there."

"It's only been a day."

"Most people work during the week."

Aunt Kitty put her hand on Burr's arm. "Burr, you simply must stop that awful Johnson Smart. You can't let him destroy Thorne Swift and the lady's slipper." She leaned back and looked out at the bay. "And all it stands for."

That's a bit dramatic.

"Burr, please."

* * *

"I object, Your Honor," Dahlberg said, out of breath.

"Your Honor," Burr said, standing. "There is nothing for Mr. Dahlberg to object to. He's lucky I invited him."

Judge Abbott pulled down the left sleeve of her robe, then the right. "Must we start out like this?"

"Your Honor, I was not notified of this emergency hearing," Dahlberg said, still huffing and puffing.

"Then why are you here?" Burr said.

"Your Honor, the defendant requests a thirty-day postponement so we can properly prepare."

Burr scowled at Dahlberg, then looked up at Judge Abbott. "Your Honor, this is an ex parte request for a temporary restraining order. The defendant need not be here. I only notified him as a matter of courtesy."

"Courtesy," Dahlberg said. "Courtesy," he said again. "I had to break all the speed limits to get here in time."

I may have given him too much notice.

"Furthermore, not only did you dismiss the Little Traverse Conservancy's case, you denied its motion for reconsideration. We shouldn't even be here." Dahlberg took a deep breath.

Dahlberg is getting his breath back.

"And there's the matter of jurisdiction."

"You retained jurisdiction, Your Honor," Burr said.

Burr looked down at his entourage, just Jacob and Aunt Kitty. There was the small problem of Collin having been charged with murder, which he didn't want Judge Abbott to know about. There was a good chance that she didn't know. Two different courts, federal and state, a hundred fifty miles apart, and not much communication between the two.

Hopefully, Dahlberg doesn't know either.

Burr had given in to Aunt Kitty, but he had no idea what to do. Judge Abbott had denied his motion for reconsideration and dismissed the case. He wished he'd said 'no' to Aunt Kitty. He'd been taken advantage of—his head had been fuzzy, his thinking muddled. And now, his unpaid vacation had ended abruptly. He couldn't figure out how to restart his unpaid case, but it seemed to him that Collin being charged with murder trumped the plight of a flower in a swamp, endangered or not.

The only thing he could think of was to ask for another temporary restraining order, but he needed a reason. He broke the better part of a box of pencils before he came up with something. It was a long shot, but it was all he had.

It looked like Judge Abbott thought so, too. "Mr. Lafayette, we have already been through one TRO and another that I denied. On what possible grounds do you think you should be given a second TRO, especially in light of my past rulings?"

Burr stepped around his table and walked up to the judge. "Your Honor, you did dismiss the litigation and my petition for reconsideration. You did, however, retain jurisdiction, and there is another issue that requires your urgent attention."

"I'm listening."

"Your Honor, the Conservancy has a lease with Mr. Ballantine. He violated the terms of the lease when he terminated it. He had no right to do so. If he is allowed to proceed with the sale of Thorne Swift to Mr. Smart, the Conservancy will be irreparably damaged, and money damages will not be sufficient to compensate for the harm caused. That is why a TRO is called for."

Dahlberg stood. "That's ridiculous. Mr. Ballantine had every right to terminate the lease. There is a termination clause in the lease which Mr. Ballantine complied with to the letter."

"That is patently untrue." Burr picked up a file from his table and opened it. "As you may recall, Mr. Dahlberg admitted the lease into evidence. It does, in fact, have a termination provision, but that provision is inapplicable."

Judge Abbott arched her eyebrows.

"As a bit of history, Mr. Ballantine's father, Justin Ballantine, entered into a ninety-nine-year lease with the Little Traverse Conservancy in 1985. The 'whereas' provision states that the purpose of the lease is to preserve the property in its natural state in perpetuity.

"The rent was to be one dollar per year. The Conservancy accepted the lease and made numerous improvements to the property at its own expense. The improvements were designed to make the property more accessible to the public and to protect its unique features. Thorne Swift is extremely popular and has many, many visitors every year."

"That has nothing to do with the termination provision," Dahlberg said.

"Your Honor, this has everything to do with the termination provision. The purpose of the lease is being carried out. The termination provision applies only in the event that the purpose of the lease is not being carried out."

"That's not true, Your Honor." Dahlberg picked up his copy of the lease. "The termination provision reads in part: 'This lease may be terminated if its intended purpose is no longer being carried out and for other reasons.'"

Burr walked up to Judge Abbott, lease in hand. "By way of background, Your Honor, the defendant, Dewey Ballantine, inherited Thorne Swift two years ago when his father passed away. It is probably common knowledge that the defendant, through a series of poor investments, has fallen on hard times and needs money. That's why he wants to sell Thorne Swift. He's broke."

That's what Jacob found out.

"I object, Your Honor." Dahlberg marched up to the judge and stood beside Burr. "This is irrelevant, Your Honor. Not only is it irrelevant, it is untrue. In any event, Mr. Ballantine had every right to terminate the lease."

"This doesn't qualify as one of the 'other reasons'," Burr said.

"How would you possibly know what 'other reasons' means?"

"Because—"

Judge Abbott rapped her gavel. "Quiet." She bit her lip. "Let me look at the lease." Dahlberg handed her his copy. She studied it, then pointed a long, pink fingernail at Burr. "Mr. Lafayette, I am not going to grant your temporary restraining order."

Damn it all.

"But I am going to stay the sale of Thorne Swift while I review the lease." She tapped her gavel ever so lightly and disappeared through the door behind her.

CHAPTER FIVE

Aunt Kitty stirred the ice in her martini with her finger, then she threw her drink, glass and all, over the railing and onto the lawn.

Burr watched the now empty glass rolling toward the beach.

At least it didn't break.

The glass, cut crystal with a gold rim, had a drake mallard painted on it.

That's my favorite glass.

"I'll get it," Burr said.

Aunt Kitty stood. "I'll get it myself."

The martini making ritual had been going on for years. Burr made Aunt Kitty's martini. Aunt Kitty complained that there was too much vermouth. Burr remade it. She always complained about it, but she'd never thrown her glass off the porch before.

She'd shown him how to make her martini when he was fourteen. A rocks glass full of ice, two jiggers of gin. Only Bombay Sapphire would do. Half a capful of Martini and Rossi dry vermouth. One pimento stuffed olive. She always knew when he made it the wrong way.

Which he had today. He'd put too much vermouth in her glass—three quarters of a capful. It was a mistake, but he didn't think she'd be able to tell.

I should have known better.

Aunt Kitty started for the door. Burr dashed off the porch and rescued her glass. It already had ants crawling in it.

"I wonder what it's like to be a drunk ant? As opposed to a drunk aunt."

His aunt stopped. "I beg your pardon?"

Burr skipped up the porch steps, glass in hand, ants and all. "I'll take care of it."

"I can make my own martini." Burr eased his aunt out of the way. "I'll be right back."

He walked into the foyer, a hardwood floor with an oriental throw, cream walls with a painting of an NM on the wall. "NM" stood for *Northern Mich-igan 32*, a long, narrow daysailer with a mast too tall for the hull. Circa 1930s. There were only two fleets in the world—one in Harbor Springs, the other in Charlevoix. Designed for the deep waters of Little Traverse Bay and Lake Charlevoix, they were fast and uncomfortable. The painting was of *NM 7*, Burr's grandfather's boat. They still raced them in Harbor Springs, but Hull 7 hadn't been in the water since Burr had quit paying the storage bill at Irish. The boatyard had threatened to sell her to cover the past due bills. Burr ignored the dunning letters, one of his specialties. It had worked so far. He patted the picture as he walked by. "I'll get you back in the water."

Burr walked past the living room on his left, the parlor on his right, then through the dining room and into the kitchen, an old-fashioned room with a white tile floor and black Formica countertops. The refrigerator, about the size of a Volkswagen, stood on four legs, a compressor on top. He poured half a capful of vermouth, threw it in the sink. Then dripped what was left into the glass.

Back on the porch, he handed Aunt Kitty her drink.

"Much better," she said, "but still too much vermouth."

Burr sat back down in a forest green Adirondack chair and looked up at the baby blue beadboard ceiling. Cottage 59 was a grand old three-story Victorian with six bedrooms, servants' quarters, and a turret. Burr loved turrets. Cottage 59, the last house on Harbor Point, faced the harbor and backed up to Little Traverse Bay. It had the best view on the Point—a narrow finger jutting into the bay, the deepest and most protected harbor on Lake Michigan.

Harbor Point was one of the first gated communities in Michigan. No cars allowed beyond the entrance, only horse-drawn carriages and bicycles. None of the cottages had names. They were all numbered. Burr thought it the height of snobbery.

Cottage 59 was all that was left of the once considerable Lafayette family fortune. In a reverse primogeniture, Burr's grandfather had passed it to his sister, Kathryn—Burr's Aunt Kitty—but she couldn't sell it. At her death, it was to pass to Burr, unless, of course, something went wrong, which Burr thought was altogether too likely.

Burr looked out at the harbor—a daysailer coming about, a Boston whaler pulling a water-skier. To his right, the tip of Harbor Point, a sand spit with a lighthouse. The water went from sixty feet deep to just two feet at the beach, beached runabouts, swimmers, picnickers, and sunbathers all along the shore.

It's all so resorty.

"Does Judge Abbott know that Collin's been charged with murder?" Aunt Kitty said.

"I don't think so, and I didn't bring it up."

"How about Dahlberg?"

"If he did, I'm sure he'd have told the judge." Burr took a swallow of his martini, dirty with four olives.

"You can't just sit there drinking."

That's what you're doing.

"I know what you're thinking, but I'm not the one with work to do."

He took another swallow.

"Put that down. And look at me when I'm talking to you. You better get cracking."

I haven't heard that one in a long time.

"Put that drink down and hop to."

Or that one.

"How many times have you told me I'm not a criminal lawyer, and here I am again. In another criminal case. Plus, a lawsuit with next to no chance of winning. I'm not getting paid for either one. And you got me into both of them." He looked over at his aunt. She smiled at him. He didn't smile back.

Burr looked longingly at his martini. He knew he liked martinis too much. They had gotten him into trouble, but he had slowed down, sort of. He'd had his first one when he was fourteen, right after he'd made his aunt's.

* * *

Burr ran his fingers across the scratches and dents of his table. Collin sat to his right in his orange jumpsuit and handcuffs. Aunt Kitty sat next to Collin. Truax sat across the aisle.

This is another folly. And not one of my own making. Burr had spent a lifetime waiting for judges.

Judges look at a schedule like it's a suggestion.

At last, the judge made his grand entrance. He sat, then turned the pages on his desktop calendar. He looked down at Burr. "What are you doing here? The preliminary exam isn't for another three weeks."

Burr stood. "Your Honor, we are here to request bail for Professor Murphy."

"I denied bail."

He might have done it. Especially with that temper of his.

"Yes, Your Honor, but I'd like you to reconsider your decision."

"Why would I do that?"

Burr stepped around his table toward the judge. "Your Honor, the court rules allow bail if the defendant is not a flight risk and is not a danger to the community."

Truax stood. "That's right, Your Honor, and while the defendant may not be a flight risk, he certainly is dangerous. That's why he's wearing handcuffs." He pointed at Collin's wrists.

Burr took another step toward the judge. He was close enough to smell the judge's aftershave, a bracing menthol with a bite.

He really is a dandy.

"Your Honor, my client was charged with a murder he didn't commit. He was upset the last time he was in your courtroom. I think you would be too."

"Your Honor, Mr. Murphy has a reputation as a person who cannot control his emotions. He has a violent temper," Truax said. His face turned red.

He looks like a stork with a sunburn.

"Mr. Murphy had a violent outburst in my courtroom. More than one."

"Your Honor, I will be personally responsible for Professor Murphy."

The judge twiddled his thumbs.

This guy and his hands are driving me crazy.

He looked down at Burr. "Mr. Lafayette, I am inclined to grant your request."

"Thank you, Your Honor."

"I haven't finished." He cleared his throat. "Stand up, Mr. Murphy."

Collin stood.

"I am going to grant you bail. You will be under Mr. Lafayette's supervision. One misstep and you will be back in jail. Do I make myself clear?"

"Yes, Your Honor."

"I object, Your Honor," Truax said.

"Of course you do," Judge Bailey said. He turned back to Burr. "Bail is set at two million dollars."

Burr took a step back. "Your Honor, that is much too high."

"That's the number."

Burr walked back to his table. "Collin, that means you need to come up with two hundred thousand dollars cash. Can you do that?"

"Two hundred thousand dollars? Are you kidding? That's ridiculous." He started to pound his hands on the table.

Burr grabbed Collin's hands. "Stop that or you'll be right back where you started." He turned to the judge, "Your Honor, we can't come up with that much money."

"Then Mr. Murphy can continue to enjoy our accommodations."

Aunt Kitty stood. "Your Honor, I'll put up the bail."

"What?" Burr said. "How are you going to do that?"

"Miss Lafayette, the court will take your check."

"Your Honor, I'm a little short of cash, but I can put up the deed to my home."

Cottage 59?

"I am familiar with Harbor Point." He smiled at her. "That will be sufficient."

Cottage 59?

* * *

"I'm not going to do it," Collin said.

"I can't help you if you don't," Burr said.

"Saving Thorne Swift has nothing to do with saving me."

"It has everything to do with saving you." Burr took a forkful of the smoked lake trout appetizer. The crinkled skin was the color of shiny graham crackers. He and Collin sat on the patio at Legs Inn in Cross Village. Burr had taken M-119 from Harbor Springs, twenty miles north, through the Tunnel of Trees, the road so narrow that the trees on either side grew over the road, blocking the sun, and creating a tunnel-like canopy. Its lime, forest, mint, and deep green leaves were beautiful now, but it was spectacular in the fall, yellows, oranges, and reds.

Burr thought it would be a good idea to get Collin out of Harbor Springs and put some distance between them and the disastrous Cottage 59 bail.

So far, it hadn't turned out that way, but the smoked whitefish—flaky, white, and moist—had been worth it. That, and the draft Labatt.

They sat at a table on a bluff a hundred feet above Lake Michigan, the lighthouses at White Shoal, Waugoshance, Gray's Reef, and Skillagalee off to the west.

Burr smelled the smells of the lake below them, the wet sand, and a dead fish or two.

"It's not a coincidence that you're being charged with the murder of Frank Slaughter. He was the caretaker at Thorne Swift and probably the one who beat you up. And took your camera."

Collin picked at the smoked whitefish.

"You were seen arguing with him at Bar Harbor the night he was killed."

"No one knows if he was killed that night."

"That was the last time he was seen alive."

"I told everyone before I ever went to Thorne Swift that the lady's slipper wasn't endangered."

"I was hoping Dahlberg didn't know that. I don't think Ballantine did."

"The Conservancy had a pretty good idea that Ballantine was going to terminate the lease, and they wanted me to document the lady's slipper. Just in case."

Collin took a forkful of the whitefish. He looked at it, put it on his plate, then pushed it around in a circle.

If I did that, Eve would tell me to stop playing with my food.

"What do you want?"

"I want you to tell me what happened when you were beaten up at Thorne Swift."

"There's nothing much to tell."

"What happened?"

"We've been through this." Collin slammed his hands on the table.

"That's why Bailey sent you to jail. Tell me what happened."

"I was lying on my stomach, propped up with my elbows, taking pictures of the flowers. The next thing I remember I had a terrible headache. And my camera was gone."

"Who did it?"

"I have no idea."

"Who do you think it was?"

"I don't know."

"Take a guess."

Collin shook his head.

"Take a guess," Burr said again.

"Frank Slaughter," Collin said.

Burr nodded. "Then what?"

"I went to the doctor."

"What happened to your camera?"

The waitress came to take their lunch order. She was in her early twenties, blonde, and spoke with an Eastern European accent. Stanley Smolak, a Polish immigrant, built Legs Inn seventy-five years ago—a fieldstone building on the edge of nowhere. Cross Village had been a logging village at the edge of a great hemlock forest, the bark used to make tannins for the leather industry. The village had boomed until the timber ran out and the village burned. But Stanley had a vision. He decorated his Polish restaurant with giant pieces of varnished driftwood that looked like monsters. Burr thought they were creepy.

Legs got its name from the white stove legs that had been cemented in a row along the roof of the restaurant. Stanley introduced young Polish workers to Northern Michigan in the summers. He gave them a job, a place to live, and a start in America. And he served the best Polish food within two hundred miles.

"I'll have the golumpki," Burr said.

"And you, sir?"

"Nothing for me."

"He'll have the pierogies," Burr said.

The waitress took their menus and left.

"Your camera," Burr said.

"I haven't seen it since the day I got beat up."

"Do you know who beat you?"

"No."

"You didn't see who it was?"

"No."

This isn't going anywhere.

"Why did you meet Frank at Bar Harbor?"

Collin looked out at the lake.

"Collin …"

He turned back. "He said he could help me get my camera back."

"And?"

"And I met him at Bar Harbor."

This is like pulling teeth.

"And …"

"He said he could help me get it back if I paid him."

"How much?"

"Twenty thousand."

"And that's when you lost your temper."

Collin nodded. "I told him I wasn't going to pay him for what was mine, so he left."

"And then you followed him to the end of Fourth Street."

Collin nodded again. "He parked there and got out of his truck. He waved for me to follow him. I got out and followed him into the woods. On the path. It was dark that night. I lost him. Then I caught up with him."

"What happened?"

"He raised the price to twenty-five thousand."

"What did you do?"

"I went back to my car."

"But you hit him first."

Collin shook his head.

"Did you stab him with your Swiss Army knife?"

"No."

"How did he get stabbed with it?"

"I have no idea."

"It was your knife."

Collin nodded again.

"What happened to it?"

"It was gone when I came to. Whoever took my camera must have taken my knife."

"You said you thought Frank took your camera."

"Yes."

"If you didn't see who hit you, why do you think it was Frank?"

"He was the caretaker, and he was the one who threw me out before."

"And he took your knife at the same time?"

"That's what must have happened."

"And then he stabbed himself in the eye with it."

CHAPTER SIX

Burr killed the mallard with his first shot. He dropped it at the far side of the pond. Zeke stared at the duck floating on its back, then looked at Burr. Burr gave him a line, then, "Zeke, fetch."

The dog quivered but didn't go after the duck.

"Zeke, fetch," Burr said again.

The dog looked at Burr but didn't move. Burr stood and took a step toward Zeke, still sitting. He gave him another line. "Zeke, fetch." The dog stood but still didn't go in. Burr said "fetch" again and gave Zeke a shove. He half jumped, half fell into the pond and swam toward the duck.

"He's too old for this," Victor said.

It was September 25th, opening day of duck season on Walpole Island and Burr's favorite day of the year. He'd started hunting at Walpole with his grandfather when he was twelve, and he'd never missed an opening day.

He and Zeke had taken the ferry across the Detroit River from Algonac to Walpole Island yesterday. They stayed at Burr's cabin, complete with no telephone, on the Johnson River, just downriver from Victor's house. Victor Haymarsh was fifty-five and looked it. Short and thick with a ponytail that hung to his shoulders. Black hair with a few gray hairs that he didn't pull out. He was half Ojibwe, half Potawatomi, and Burr's oldest friend.

Burr took his cigarettes from his parka and offered one to Victor. He lit Victor's, then lit one for himself. He'd given Victor his own pack of Marlboros, tobacco, a traditional gift to a chief, but they were smoking Burr's first. Burr only smoked during duck season, and only when he hunted. This was his first cigarette of the season.

Zeke grabbed the duck and started back. Burr and Victor smoked and watched Zeke swim back with the duck. The dog stopped at the dog ramp. "Zeke, come," Burr said. The dog put his front legs on the ramp but didn't climb up. Burr crushed out his cigarette. He took Zeke by the collar and pulled him up the ramp. "Zeke, give."

The dog let go of the duck, a drake mallard, its head still brown, not yet colored out.

They had set up before dawn in a stake blind on a pond just off the Johnson. There was a fifty-yard channel into the pond, just wide enough for Victor's boat. Burr smelled the gasoline in the bilge on the way in. Victor had built the blind just inside the cattails and camouflaged it with weeds. The pond was about two acres, cattails all around, still green. He'd built a hide for Zeke at one end of the blind—a six-foot deck with two-by-sixes, open on the sides with a roof to hide Zeke, and a ramp so he could get back in it. But today, he couldn't.

"He's too old for this," Victor said again.

"It's his first hunt of the season. He's just getting warmed up."

"You're going to kill him if you keep making him bring back your ducks." Victor lit another cigarette. "Should you even be here today?"

"It's opening day," Burr said.

I know where this is going.

Half a dozen wood ducks drifted in from the river. They flew lazy circles around the pond. Burr raised his call to his lips.

"Don't call. They see the decoys."

Victor put out twenty-three mallard decoys in front of the blind, always an odd number. He said, "The ducks are looking to pair up. An odd number makes them decoy better."

Burr didn't think ducks could count to twenty-three, and he was pretty sure that the wood ducks in the air didn't want to pair up with mallard decoys in the pond, but he let it go. Just like he did every year.

The ducks cupped their wings, dropped their legs, and floated down.

Burr shot two drakes on the right side of the flock, killing one and crippling the other. "Zeke, fetch." The aging Lab launched himself into the pond. He brought back the drake. The crippled duck swam into the cattails. He gave Zeke a line and sent him after it.

Victor shook his head. "You have a trial coming up?"

How does he know?

Zeke disappeared into the cattails.

"Don't you have to work on it?"

"It's opening day," Burr said.

"First things first," Victor said.

"It's a preliminary exam. My job is to listen. I got it postponed until October."

Victor looked across the pond, the cattails rustling where Zeke hunted for the crippled duck.

"There's really not much to prepare for."

Zeke poked his nose out of the cattails, the duck in his mouth. He swam back to the blind, climbed the ramp, and presented the duck to Burr. Burr wrung its neck. Zeke shook himself off and sat back in his place.

Burr and Victor shot five more ducks. Zeke retrieved all of them, but Burr had to lift him into the Jeep.

* * *

Burr tapped his brand-new, freshly sharpened No. 2 yellow pencil, the first of however many he'd go through, depending on how things went. He sat at the defense table, Collin to his right, then Jacob and Aunt Kitty, who'd insisted on being co-counsel. Calvin Truax sat across the aisle. Eve and Claire sat behind them in the first row of the gallery. The rest of the gallery was full, murders not being particularly common to Emmet County.

Burr was perfectly happy in the courtroom. It smelled of Clorox and Spic and Span. It would probably smell like sweat and foul tempers before long.

An eternity of taps later, the bailiff entered—a short man with a full head of blond hair, a crooked smile and a mouthful of crooked teeth. He had on his *de rigeur* uniform: dark brown shirt, tan slacks, and shiny silver badge. His Colt sidearm—not much smaller than a baseball mitt—looked out of place.

"All rise," the bailiff said, lisping.

Judge Paul Bailey made his grand entrance, black robe over a starched white shirt and red tie. He looked over his domain, then sat.

"Be seated," the bailiff said.

"Thank you, Swede." The judge opened a folder, then, "We are here today in the matter of the State of Michigan versus Collin J. Murphy to determine if Mr. Murphy should be bound over for trial for the murder of Frank Slaughter."

Burr started to stand.

"Don't start, Mr. Lafayette. There's nothing I could have possibly said that could cause you to object."

"Your Honor—"

"Quiet. This is a preliminary exam. There is no jury for your theatrics, and I assure you, they will not play well with one." He turned to Truax. "That goes for you, too."

Truax nodded, then looked at Burr, knowingly.

He is impossible to like.

The judge patted the court stenographer's head, the same skinny, thirty-ish woman who had been in the court for the arraignment.

"We are on the record," he said.

She nodded and started typing.

"Mr. Truax, you may begin."

Truax stood. "Thank you, Your Honor. We are here today to ask that you bind Collin Murphy over for trial for the murder of Frank H. Slaughter."

The judge waved at Truax. "Calvin, I know why we're here. Call your first witness."

"Yes, Your Honor. The state calls Lawrence Van Arkel."

A tall, thin man, about sixty, walked up to the witness stand. What had once been his chest had sunk to his waist. He had gray hair, gray skin, gray eyes with bags under them, and a matching gray suit.

Burr had been in court with him once before.

Van Arkel was an MD and the county coroner. He was also a mortician and made his living as an undertaker.

He looks like he could use an embalming himself.

Truax ran through Van Arkel's qualifications. Then, "Dr. Van Arkel, you performed the autopsy on Mr. Slaughter. Is that right?"

Van Arkel nodded.

"Dr. Van Arkel, please answer the question," Judge Bailey said.

The coroner looked up at the judge. "I did, Your Honor."

"You nodded. Miss Spencer can't record a nod."

Van Arkel looked a bit peeved. "Yes," he said.

"Thank you," Truax said. "Were you able to determine a cause of death?"

"I was."

"And?"

"And what?" Van Arkel said.

Judge Bailey rapped his gavel. "Mr. Truax, would you please get on with it. At this rate, I'll be up for reelection before we finish."

Truax turned red.

Red looks good on him.

"I beg your pardon."

"I'll make it easy for you," Judge Bailey said. "Dr. Van Arkel, please tell us how Mr. Slaughter died."

The coroner looked up at the judge. "Mr. Slaughter died of multiple stab wounds."

"And what …" Judge Bailey stopped himself. Then, "… and what caused the stab wounds?"

"A Swiss Army knife," Van Arkel said.

"Thank you, Dr. Van Arkel," the judge said. He looked down at Truax. "We have a cause of death and the instrument that caused his death. That wasn't so hard, was it?"

"No, Your Honor."

"Do you have anything further for Dr. Van Arkel?"

"No, Your Honor."

"I hoped you wouldn't." The judge turned to Burr. "Mr. Lafayette."

Burr knew the coroner was no fool, but he had to try. "Dr. Van Arkel, you are a medical doctor and the county coroner. Is that right?"

"Yes."

"But you don't practice medicine, do you?"

"No."

"What is your occupation?"

"I'm a mortician."

Burr rocked back and forth. "A mortician. That's an undertaker, isn't it?"

"Yes."

"You don't practice medicine. Yet you are the coroner."

It was Van Arkel's turn to turn red.

Judge Bailey slammed his gavel. "Mr. Lafayette, you will stop this line of questioning this very moment."

"Your Honor—"

"Don't 'Your Honor' me. Dr. Van Arkel's credentials are impeccable."

"Your Honor, the qualifications of an expert are always subject to examination."

"Not here they aren't. I take judicial notice that Dr. Van Arkel is qualified. Is that clear?"

Burr nodded.

"Use your words, Mr. Lafayette."

I'm back in second grade.

"Yes, Your Honor."

"Good. Do you have anything you'd like to ask Dr. Van Arkel?"

Burr took a step toward the undertaker. "Mr. … excuse me, Dr. Van Arkel, you testified that Mr. Slaughter died from multiple stab wounds. Is that correct?"

"Yes."

"And the wounds were caused by a Swiss Army knife. Is that right?"

"Yes."

"And how do you know that?"

"The Harbor Springs police provided me the knife, and that knife definitely caused the wounds."

Burr paced back and forth. "But you don't know where they got the knife or whose knife it was."

Truax jumped up. "We will show that next, Your Honor."

Bailey nodded. "You may answer the question, Dr. Van Arkel."

"What was the question?"

"Do you know where the police got the knife or whose knife it was?"

"No, I don't."

"Dr. Van Arkel, just to be clear, you testified that Mr. Slaughter died of multiple stab wounds in his back. Is that right?"

"I did." The coroner squirmed in his seat. "There is one thing I left out."

This could be promising.

"And what is that?"

"Mr. Slaughter was also stabbed in his right eye."

The courtroom gasped. Judge Bailey sat back in his chair. Truax looked like the cat who'd swallowed the canary.

This is terrible.

"I'm sorry," Van Arkel said. "I should have mentioned it sooner."

Burr had made an unforgiveable mistake. He knew better than to ask a question that he didn't know the answer to.

"I have no further questions, Your Honor."

Van Arkel started to stand up.

"Just a minute, Dr. Van Arkel," the judge said. "Did you just say that Mr. Slaughter had been stabbed in the eye?"

Van Arkel sat back down. "Yes. His right eye."

"Wouldn't that have killed him?"

"Your Honor, I'm finished with the witness."

Judge Bailey glared at Burr. "I'm not." He looked down at the coroner. "Would stabbing him in the eye have killed Mr. Slaughter?"

It sure wouldn't tickle.

"It depends on how far in the knife went."

"Do you know how far in it went?"

"It's hard to know, Your Honor. The eye is a bit like jelly."

"Then, what was the cause of death?"

"The multiple stab wounds to the back pierced Mr. Slaughter's heart and lungs. They were more than enough to kill him."

"Then why stab him in the eye?"

The undertaker shuffled his feet. "I don't know, Your Honor. Maybe it was done after Mr. Slaughter was dead."

"In a fit of rage?"

"That would be consistent with the fits of rage we've seen Mr. Murphy exhibit here in court," Truax said.

Burr jumped up. "I object, Your Honor. There is nothing Mr. Truax presented that in any way ties Mr. Murphy to the death of Mr. Slaughter," Burr said, careful not to use "killing" or "murder."

"So far," Truax said.

Judge Bailey wagged a finger at Truax. "Stop it, Mr. Truax." To Burr, "Do you have anything further, Mr. Lafayette?"

"No, Your Honor."

I've already screwed up enough.

"Call your next witness, Mr. Truax."

The prosecutor called Kyle Stone, the Harbor Springs police officer who had found Frank Slaughter's body.

Swede swore in Stone, whose uniform had probably fit pretty well thirty pounds ago. Burr thought he was in his late forties, clean shaven as was his head.

Truax walked up to his witness. "Officer Stone, you were the person who found Mr. Slaughter's body. Is that correct?"

"Yes."

"Would you please tell us how you found it."

"We got a call from Frank's … Mr. Slaughter's wife. She said he didn't come home last night, and she was worried. We didn't think too much about it at first. This stuff happens all the time." Officer Stone and both of his chins smiled at Truax.

"Yes?"

"She kept calling so we started looking for him. We found his truck at the end of Fourth Street tucked back by the old morgue, next to the city well. Anyway, we started looking. Took us two days to find him. We had to get the state police and a tracking dog from Petoskey. She finally found him in the swamp off the boardwalk that runs through the nature preserve." Stone stopped and smiled at Truax.

"Please continue, Officer Stone."

The portly officer puffed himself up. "It was wet in there. Swampy. Belle—that's the dog—is all excited. It's really wet and tangled. We follow her about a hundred feet in. She starts pawing at the weeds. I go over to her. Couldn't see a thing. Too overgrown. Anyway, Belle keeps pawing at the water. I bent over and fished around with my hands. I was soaked up to my shoulders, but it's summer and the water's not too cold. I found him. Pulled him up. Dead as roadkill."

Roadkill?

"Thank you, Officer Stone. And how did you find the murder weapon?"

"I object," Burr said, sitting.

I know where this is going, but it's the best I can do.

Truax looked back at Burr. "I withdraw the question." To Stone, "Did you find anything else?"

Stone shook his head. "Not right away, but we could see he'd been stabbed. From the holes in his shirt and the stab wounds. And his eye." Stone rubbed his eye. "It was something awful."

"What did you do next?"

"We called EMS to get the body out. Then we set out to look for a knife." The pudgy cop sighed. His stomach rolled over his belt. "It was a tough deal. What with the swamp, the water, and the muck." He nodded, agreeing with himself.

Truax tapped his foot.

"Something wrong?" Stone said.

"The knife."

"Oh, yeah. The knife." He nodded again.

"Officer Stone."

"Right," he said. "Well, we couldn't find it anywhere. We got shovels, rakes, buckets, and we looked and looked." He stopped. "But we couldn't find anything."

I can't stand the suspense.

Neither could Truax. "Please, Officer Stone. What happened?"

The cop nodded a third time. "We finally found it. Next to the board-walk. Lucky. Really lucky."

"Thank you, Officer Stone." Truax walked back to his table and came back with something in the closed palm of his hand. He opened his hand, a red Swiss Army knife in his palm. "Is this the knife?"

The cop leaned over the railing of the witness box and studied the knife. He leaned back and looked at Truax. "Sure looks like it."

Truax took a step toward Judge Bailey. "Your Honor, the state would like to introduce this knife into evidence as the murder weapon."

Burr popped up. "Objection, Your Honor. We have no way of knowing if this is the murder weapon."

Truax scowled at Burr, then looked up at Bailey. "Your Honor, we obtained this knife from Dr. Van Arkel who obtained it from the Harbor Springs Police who found it near the victim."

"The evidentiary chain is long," Burr said. "Too long."

"Nonsense," Truax said. "Your Honor, we can call Dr. Van Arkel and have him confirm that this is indeed the murder weapon."

"How would he know?" Burr said. "There's a million of these things out there. I could go to Meyer's Hardware and buy one this afternoon."

"We'll never be done this afternoon," Judge Bailey said, mostly to himself.

"I beg your pardon, Your Honor," Truax said.

The judge ignored him, then, "Bailiff, this knife is accepted into evidence as Exhibit A."

Swede took the knife from Truax and put it on a table next to the stenographer.

"The court, for purposes of this hearing, finds that this knife is the murder weapon."

Truax smiled. His face lost its red.

"I object, Your Honor."

"Of course you do. Overruled." To Truax, "Anything further?"

"I have no further questions," Truax said.

"Mr. Lafayette?"

Burr leaned toward Collin. "Is that your knife?"

"I don't know."

"Good." Burr picked up the knife and turned it over in his hand. It was red and covered with scratches and scrapes.

This thing is pretty beat up.

He walked up to the cop and handed him the knife. "Officer Stone, do you know whose knife this is?"

Stone turned the knife over in his hands. He opened up the can opener, screwdriver, the saw, and finally the corkscrew. "There sure is a lot of stuff on this thing." He put his hand on the corkscrew. "There's even a corkscrew. I don't drink wine, though."

I am in the company of fools and nitwits.

"Officer Stone, do you know whose knife this is?"

"Yes."

"Whose knife is it?"

"There sure is a lot of stuff on this thing," Stone said again.

Burr grabbed the knife.

"Be careful with that," the cop said.

Burr ignored him. "Do you know whose knife this is?

"It's Mr. Murphy's knife."

"How do you know that?"

The portly officer started to sweat. He wiped off his forehead with his county issued handkerchief. "Mr. Truax told me it was Mr. Murphy's."

"But you don't know firsthand?"

"No, I guess I don't."

"You don't even know if Mr. Murphy had a Swiss Army knife, do you?"

Truax stood. "Your Honor, in the transcript of the proceedings in front of Judge Abbott, Mr. Murphy testified that he had a Swiss Army knife."

"He also testified that it was stolen," Burr said.

"We don't know if that's true," Truax said.

Collin stood. "Of course it's true."

"Sit down, Mr. Murphy," the judge said.

"My knife was stolen when I was knocked out," Collin said, shouting.

"Mr. Lafayette, control your client or I will have him handcuffed and removed from the court. Again."

Burr walked to the defense table with the knife in his hand. "Collin, sit down. You're making it worse." He stood with his back to Bailey and Truax, then showed the knife to Collin. Quietly, "Is this your knife?"

Collin reached for it. Burr pulled his hand back.

"The end of the corkscrew on my knife is broken," Collin said.

Burr turned the knife over and found the corkscrew. The tip was broken off.

Damn it all.

"And this." Collin pointed to some faint scratches on the red cover.

"Are those your initials?"

Collin nodded.

How did the police miss this?

"Are you quite through Mr. Lafayette?" Judge Bailey said.

"Your Honor," Truax said. "We can introduce Mr. Murphy's testimony from the proceeding in Judge Abbott's court."

Burr ignored Truax. "Your Honor, this may or may not be the murder weapon, but there is absolutely no evidence to support the fact that this is Mr. Murphy's knife."

Even though it is.

Judge Bailey ignored Burr. "Mr. Lafayette, do you have anything further for Officer Stone?"

I have plenty for Mr. Stone, but I can't risk this knife getting tied to Collin.

Burr put the knife back on the evidence table.

"I have no further questions, Your Honor."

The judge gave them a ten-minute break.

Burr wanted to strangle Collin but thought better of it. Instead, he went outside and stood on the courthouse steps in the October sun, what little there was. A northwest wind blew fluffy cumulus clouds off Lake Michigan. It was sunny one minute, cloudy the next. It felt like the temperature dropped ten degrees when the sun was clouded over. The maples across the street had turned yellow.

Burr took his seat, the last one in. He looked at Collin. "All you have to do is sit here quietly. Don't say a word. Not a word unless I ask you a question."

Swede called them to order.

"You may call your next witness," Judge Bailey said.

"The state calls Paige Turner," Truax said.

What kind of a name is that?

Burr thought her name was funny, but what she was about to say was anything but funny.

Paige Turner was about fifty, still tan, blonde hair, and wrinkles from too much sun. She was skinny to the point of being underfed. Button nose, big white teeth, and a not-too-sincere smile. Pretty, in a Harbor Springs sort of way.

Swede swore her in. Truax started out with her address, somewhere on Pennsylvania Street.

Wequetonsing. I knew it.

Wequetonsing, a hundred or so turn-of-the-century cottages on Bay Street, was the ungated version of Harbor Point. Mostly white cottages with forest green trim, if you could call six-bedroom houses cottages. Summer-only and held together with this year's coat of paint. Most of the cottages had been in the same families since they were built.

"Ms. Turner, you were in Bar Harbor the night of July 21st. Is that right?"

"Yes," she said with a toothy smile.

"And where were you sitting?"

"In a booth. Next to a window. It was dark outside, but you could see the moonlight on the bay. It was beautiful." She smiled again.

Truax didn't smile.

I've never seen him smile.

"Was there anyone sitting in the booth next to you?"

"Yes," she said. "Him. He was sitting in the booth behind me." Paige Turner pointed at Collin. He stared at her defiantly. She kept smiling.

"Your Honor, please let the record show that Ms. Turner is pointing at the defendant, Collin Murphy."

"Let the record show," Judge Bailey said.

That's a fugitive from Perry Mason.

"Was he with anyone?"

"Yes."

"And who would that be?"

"He was with Mr. Slaughter."

"And how do you know that?"

She licked her lips. "I knew who he was from Thorne Swift."

Truax nodded. "Did you hear what they were talking about?"

"I couldn't help but hear. I wasn't trying to eavesdrop, but they were talking so loud, I couldn't help it."

"Of course you weren't," Truax said.

You are so soothing.

Truax looked down at his shoes, which didn't need polishing, then back at Ms. Turner. "What did they say?"

She lost part of her smile. "Mr. Murphy told Mr. Slaughter that he wanted his camera back and he knew he had it."

Truax shook his head. "Who had the camera?"

Ms. Turner lost a little more of her smile, along with some of her patience. "I just told you."

"Please tell us again." Truax tried to smile, but it didn't really work.

Ms. Turner scowled.

That's more like it.

"Mr. Murphy told Mr. Slaughter that he knew that Mr. Slaughter had Mr. Murphy's camera, and he wanted Mr. Slaughter to give it back to him."

Truax nodded. "What did Mr. Slaughter say?"

"He said he didn't have it, but he could get it."

"What did Mr. Murphy say?"

"He said he wanted it now."

"And?"

"How about if I just tell you what I heard?"

It was Truax's turn to scowl. He walked around in a circle, then, "Please do."

"Mr. Murphy demanded that Mr. Slaughter get the camera now. He was mad. I could tell from his voice." She nodded, agreeing with herself. "Mr. Slaughter didn't say anything for a while, then he said he could get it. For a price."

Truax knows right where this is headed.

"How much?" Truax said.

"Twenty thousand dollars."

The gallery jumped in their seats, as if one. They gasped, as if they were all a chorus.

"Then what?" Truax leaned toward his witness.

"Mr. Murphy started shouting. He reached across the booth and grabbed Mr. Slaughter's shirt."

"I thought you had your back to them."

Paige Turner smiled again. "I did, but Mr. Murphy was so loud that I turned around."

"What did you see?"

"I told you. He grabbed Mr. Slaughter by the shirt and started shaking him."

"Then what?"

She lost her smile again. "Mr. Slaughter pulled Mr. Murphy's hands off him. Then he got up. Mr. Murphy said, 'Give me my camera back or I'll kill you.' Mr. Slaughter left, and Mr. Murphy ran out after him."

"Thank you, Ms. Turner." Truax sneered at Burr. "Your witness."

This is just ducky.

Burr walked up to the mostly smiling Paige Turner.

How do I keep from making this worse?

"Ms. Turner, what time was it when you overheard Mr. Murphy and Mr. Slaughter?"

"About midnight, I think."

"Midnight," Burr said. "And when did you get there?"

"I don't know." She paused. "Nine or so."

"Thank you, Ms. Turner. And what were you drinking?"

"Drinking?" She looked up at the ceiling. "I don't remember."

Burr looked up at the ceiling.

It could use a coat of paint.

He looked back at Ms. Turner. "How many drinks did you have? Three, four?"

"I don't remember."

"Five or six?"

"I object." Truax stood. "She said she didn't remember."

Burr looked up at Judge Bailey. "Your Honor, if she doesn't remember what she was drinking or how many drinks she had, maybe she doesn't remember what happened." To the witness, "How many drinks did you have?"

"She said she didn't remember," Truax said again.

"Ms. Turner?" Burr said.

"Asked and answered," Truax said.

Judge Bailey looked at Burr. "Move on, Mr. Lafayette."

Burr paced back and forth in front of the witness, then stopped in front of her. "Ms. Turner, do you know where Mr. Slaughter went after he left Bar Harbor?"

"No," she said.

"Do you know where Mr. Murphy went?"

"No," she said, again.

"Do you know if Mr. Murphy followed Mr. Slaughter?"

"Well, I … no."

Burr took two steps to his left and stood in front of the judge. "Your Honor, I ask that you strike Ms. Turner's testimony. If she doesn't remember what she was drinking or how much she drank, how can she possibly remember what happened that night?"

"Your Honor, I object," Truax said.

"Of course you do." Burr sneered at the prosecutor.

"Stop it, Mr. Lafayette," the judge said. "I am not going to strike Ms. Turner's testimony, but I will consider the circumstances."

"Thank you, Your Honor. I have no further questions." Burr looked at the witness. "This is a real page turner."

Paige Turner didn't smile. Truax certainly didn't smile. Judge Bailey didn't quite smile.

"Call your next witness, Mr. Truax."

"I have no further witnesses, Your Honor."

"That's wonderful news," the judge said. He looked at Burr, "Counselor."

Burr sat in his chair. "We have no witnesses, Your Honor."

"Mr. Truax, you may make your concluding statement, but make it short." He looked at his watch.

Almost lunchtime.

Collin grabbed Burr by the arm. "What do you mean you have no witnesses?"

Burr pushed Collin's hands off his arm. "What part of 'we don't have any witnesses' didn't you understand?"

"My defense. You've got to get this dismissed."

Burr didn't say anything.

"Did you hear me?" Collin grabbed Burr's arm again.

Judge Bailey peered down at Burr. "Is there a problem, Mr. Lafayette?"

Burr pushed Collin's hand away again.

"No, Your Honor."

"Yes, there is," Collin said.

"Young man, you will not speak to me unless I so direct. Is that clear?"

"He's not helping me," Collin said.

"One more outburst and you will find yourself back in an orange jumpsuit. Is that clear?"

Burr looked Collin in the eye. "Not another word. Not one. Do you understand me?" Burr stood. "I'm sorry, Your Honor. My client is understandably upset."

Truax walked up to the judge, his back to Burr. "Your Honor, the state has shown that there is probable cause that Collin Murphy murdered Frank Slaughter. We have shown the three elements necessary to bind the defendant over for trial." Truax emphasized "defendant." "First, there is means. The means is the murder weapon, Mr. Murphy's Swiss Army knife. Second, is the opportunity. We have shown that Mr. Murphy followed the deceased out of Bar Harbor on the night he disappeared. He followed him to the end of Fourth Street, then followed him into the nature preserve where he murdered him. We also showed motive. Mr. Murphy thought Mr. Slaughter had stolen his camera. His camera had the pictures he needed for his study, and he wanted it back. Your Honor, there is more than probable cause to bind the defendant over for trial." Truax looked back at Burr, sneering again.

"You got them out of order," Burr said.

"What?"

"It's means, motive and opportunity. You got the order wrong."

Truax turned red. Again.

"Do you have anything further, Mr. Truax?" the judge said.

Truax looked up at the judge. "No, Your Honor."

"Mr. Lafayette?"

Burr walked up to the judge. "I'll be brief, Your Honor."

"That would be a first," the judge said.

"Your Honor, taking the prosecutor's points in order. While it appears that the knife introduced into evidence may have been the murder weapon, there is absolutely no proof that the knife belonged to Mr. Murphy. None whatsoever."

I hope they don't find the initials.

"As to motive, does it make any sense at all that anyone would kill over a missing camera?" Burr didn't wait for an answer. "It doesn't. Finally, we have no idea if Mr. Murphy had an opportunity to murder Mr. Slaughter. We have no idea if Mr. Murphy followed Mr. Slaughter after he left Bar Harbor. None at all."

Burr looked back at Truax. "And the prosecutor hasn't given us any evidence that Mr. Murphy did."

Burr paced back and forth in front of the judge, stopped, and put his hands in his pockets. He looked up at the judge. "Your Honor, this is nothing but wishful thinking on the part of Mr. Truax. Wishful thinking. Daydreams and chimera."

"Chimera?" the judge said.

"There is no probable cause, Your Honor. I ask that you dismiss this matter." Burr turned on his heel and walked back to the defense table.

Judge Bailey tapped his gavel in the palm of his hand. He rearranged his papers, then he looked at Collin. "Stand up, Mr. Murphy."

Collin didn't move.

"Stand up, I said."

Burr stood and pulled Collin to his feet.

"Collin Murphy, I find that there is probable cause that on the night of July 21st, you murdered Frank Slaughter. You are hereby bound over for trial. Bail is continued."

Judge Bailey tapped his gavel and slipped out before Burr could say a word.

The lady's slipper is a deadly flower.

CHAPTER SEVEN

They adjourned to the City Park Grill after Bailey adjourned them.

Burr made sure he sat next to Eve. She was the only happy one in their unhappy group, and she was happy with him.

Burr suggested they have lunch at the City Park Grill. Eve loved the City Park Grill. It wasn't fancy, and neither was the food. It fronted Lake Street in downtown Petoskey, dark inside, varnished hardwood paneling, almost black with age, furniture to match, and the original tin ceiling from the days when Hemingway ate and drank there. Which was why Eve liked it.

"I like to think of him being here," she said. "Maybe at this table, turning over a Nick Adams story in his mind."

"I'm sure he drank too much and staggered back to Walloon Lake," Jacob said.

Burr ordered a whitefish sandwich with fries and coleslaw.

"How can you order that? After what just happened?" Claire put her hand on Collin's arm.

"Arguing makes me hungry," Burr said.

"Arguing," Collin said, "you didn't even put up a fight."

Burr drank half his beer and waved at the waitress to bring him a second.

"There was virtually no chance the charges were going to be dismissed," Jacob said.

"Not with what Burr did," Collin said.

"What he didn't do," Claire said.

"If you'd called me as a witness, we could have ended it right there," Collin said.

"If I'd called you as a witness, you'd already be convicted."

Collin started to stand. Aunt Kitty, who had the bad fortune to be sitting next to him, tried to pull him back down. He shook her arm off. Aunt Kitty stood.

"Collin Murphy, sit down. This instant. We've all been trying to help you. Especially Burr. You've got to get control of your temper."

I'm going to stop having these lunches.

"I can't see how you did anything for me."

Burr's second beer came. He looked at it lovingly.

"I could have testified," Collin said.

"If I'd called you as a witness, the first thing Truax would have done is ask you if that was your knife."

"So what."

"So, once you said it was your knife, your goose would have been cooked even more than it already is."

"I wouldn't have admitted it."

Burr shook his head. "If you lied, I would have had to tell the judge."

"You're my lawyer."

"I'm also an officer of the court. I don't have to tell Truax or the court anything, but I'm forbidden to allow my client to lie if I know he's lying."

"That's a stupid rule."

Burr ignored him. "Which is why I wouldn't allow you to testify."

"Truax doesn't know it's my knife."

"And I'm not going to tell him," Burr said.

"I still don't see what you did for me."

"Now we know what kind of case Truax has. It would really have helped if someone could testify where you were when Frank went missing."

Collin didn't say anything.

"So, what exactly did you do?" Collin said.

"I listened."

* * *

After the disastrous lunch, Burr rescued Zeke from the Jeep. Burr had let him out after the preliminary exam, but it had been a short walk. He took the aging lab for a longer walk, but he was stiff and Burr had to help him in and out of the Jeep. Zeke didn't hold a grudge, which was one of his many fine qualities.

Burr took M-119 around the bay toward Harbor Springs, Zeke riding shotgun.

The wind had picked up, whitecaps on the bay, leaves blowing off the trees. It was late October, and the afternoon sun had dipped below the trees. The road twisted through the climax forest—maple, oak, beech, ash, and the occasional hemlock. The colors were past peak, but the maples still held onto a few yellow, red, and orange leaves. The oaks held onto most of their leaves—mostly scarlet and brown, with just a few reds.

Burr turned onto Beach Road.

"Zeke, the sun is definitely over the yardarm."

Beach Road opened up onto the bay. Burr drove along the shore in the fading autumn daylight.

"I'm going to need my lights soon. If I can find them."

Burr's seasonal affective disorder was legendary. He would sleep from November to March if he could get away with it.

He pulled into the parking lot of the Harbor Inn, a four-story hotel with white siding and a red tin roof. The Inn rested comfortably on Little Traverse Bay, facing southwest, into the sunset.

He helped Zeke get out of the Jeep and snuck him into the Inn, through the lobby, and into the bar. He found a table facing the bay. Zeke laid under the table at Burr's feet.

The sun had set, twilight now. The bartender lit a fire in the fieldstone fireplace and made a point of not looking under Burr's table. The waiter came over, also careful not to look under the table. Burr ordered his signature martini.

Five minutes later, Stewart Dunleavy sat down across from Burr. "There are no dogs allowed."

Burr nodded.

"Kindly remove him."

Stewart, the innkeeper at the Harbor Inn, was one of Burr's oldest and most difficult friends. Stewart's great-grandfather had built the Harbor Inn at the turn of the century, when two-hundred-foot steamships from Chicago and Detroit brought the resorters, escaping from the heat and the pollen for cool days, clear blue skies, artesian springs, and deep blue water of Little Traverse Bay.

The waiter brought Burr's martini. Stewart scowled at it, then at Burr. "The only difference between that thing and a jar of olives is the jar. I'll have one of those without all the olive paraphernalia." To Burr, "There are simply no dogs allowed. My guests simply won't hear of it."

"Zeke is old, and he's been in the car all day."

"He will ruin my reputation."

Zeke barked once.

Stewart's ears turned red. They matched his nose, which looked like a ripe tomato, but were two sizes too small for the six and a half feet of him, skinny and bent at the neck. "You simply must get him out of here."

He looks like a human walking stick.

"Stay on your leaky boat."

"It's too hard for Zeke."

"The Inn is full."

"And it's getting cold."

"The Inn is full," he said again.

"There's only two cars in the parking lot."

"The tour bus isn't back yet."

The bartender brought Stewart's olive-less martini. Stewart took a big swallow. "The bar is almost full."

"The bar is half full. Maybe."

"I suppose you want to trade for it."

Burr never paid Stewart in cash. It was the genius of the barter economy which Burr usually got the better of.

"Your dog will ruin our image," Stewart said. "We have to protect our four-star rating."

The Harbor Inn had been top drawer in its day, but time had taken it down a couple of stars. The Inn didn't make enough money to pay for the updates it needed, and even though Stewart had married well, his wife didn't want to open her purse for a new boiler.

Stewart put his hands on the table. It rocked back and forth. He took a matchbook from the bowl on the table and wedged it under one of the legs.

"I suppose you'll want to stay here for the trial."

How does he know there's going to be a trial?

"News travels fast. Especially bad news."

"I will need a room."

"We'll be full."

"Starting in November, I could drive a truck through the lobby and not hit anyone."

"You never finished my estate plan."

You don't have much of an estate.

"I'm working on it."

"You've been working on it for years."

"It's complicated."

Stewart eyed his martini, then finished it. He waved to the bartender and held up two fingers. "I assume you want another."

Burr nodded.

The first martini is necessary. The second one is divine.

"I think you're really in the soup this time. Your client has a temper. We had to throw him out."

"What?"

"He barged in here, looked around, and sat down at Dewey's table. He comes here all the time." Stewart pointed to another window table, clearly the best table in the bar. "Dewey was with the guy who's buying Thorne Swift."

"Johnson Smart?"

"Tall, thin guy with a thin mustache. Maybe sixty."

"That's him." Stewart scratched his nose. "It's hard to blame Dewey for selling. Nothing wrong with making a buck."

"What happened?"

"He started yelling, and we had to throw him out. He's got a temper."

Does he ever.

Burr finished his drink and ate the second olive. Their refills came. Burr wouldn't let the waiter take his glass.

There's two olives left.

* * *

The wind blew about twenty-five from the southwest and stirred up the Holiday Pond. Low clouds hurried across the sky. The snow blew sideways and stung his face. There was skim ice in the cattails, brown and bent over in the wind. Their fuzzy white seeds blew like snow.

Burr ducked down in the blind to light a cigarette. It took three matches.

He and Victor had shot three drake mallards with shiny green heads and bright orange legs. Zeke retrieved them all. They'd gone in for lunch and were now back in the stake blind. Zeke shivered at the edge of the dog dock, his eyes fixed on a pair of mallards, a hen and a drake circling the pond. Once, twice, three times, suspicious of the decoys bouncing in the wind. The hen dropped her legs, turned into the wind, and cupped her wings. The drake followed her down.

Burr crushed out his cigarette, stood, and dropped the drake. He let the hen go.

"You could have shot the hen," Victor said.

"I don't shoot hens," Burr said.

"I've seen you do it."

"Only when the hunting's bad."

"I think that's called situational morality."

Burr lit another cigarette—three more matches—and gave Zeke a line on the floating mallard. "Zeke, fetch."

The dog looked at the duck but didn't move.

"Zeke, fetch," Burr said again.

The aging Lab looked at Burr, then at the duck, but he didn't move.

"Zeke, fetch," Burr said for the third time.

Nothing.

"Damn it all. Come on, Zeke."

Zeke walked to the other end of the dog deck. He sat and looked into the marsh, away from the pond.

Victor lit a cigarette on the first try. "He's telling you something, but you're not paying attention."

"He's never done that before." Burr flicked the ash off his cigarette.

"You need to pay attention."

Burr looked out at the dead mallard, drifting across the pond.

"Your dog just quit."

"Quit?"

"Retired," Victor said. "He's all done."

"He's just cold."

"I've seen it before. Dogs get old. They quit. Just like us."

Burr flicked the ash off his cigarette again.

They burn fast in this wind. Probably just as well.

"Zeke lives for this."

"Not anymore. He's all done." Victor picked up his marsh stick.

"You can't go out there," Burr said.

"It's my job."

"You've got a bad hip." Burr took the stick and slogged through the mucky bottom for the duck.

This is why I have a dog.

They shot four more ducks. Burr retrieved them all.

* * *

Burr sat in his Jeep on the ferry. Zeke slept in the backseat. The ferry was part way across the river, waiting for the *Paul R. Tregurtha* to pass. She was a thousand-foot freighter, white bridge in the bow, white cabins in the stern, reddish brown hull. Downbound from Duluth, low in the water, with a full load of taconite pellets from the iron range in Minnesota. The wind had picked up. The snow had turned to rain, and it was all the ferry captain could do to keep the ferry steady in the wind. Burr had the defroster on high. It was all he could do to keep the windows clear.

Twenty minutes later, the freighter was well downstream. The ferry ploughed across to the Michigan side of the river. Burr cleared customs and took I-94 to Grosse Pointe.

He pulled into the driveway at 763 Sunningdale, his former home in Grosse Pointe Woods—where his former wife still lived, where Zeke-the-Boy lived, and where he still made the mortgage payment.

His son ran out and opened the rear passenger door.

"What's wrong with Zeke?" Zeke-the-Boy said.

Burr looked into the backseat. "He's just tired."

I hope that's all it is.

"He's not wagging his tail."

Burr got out of the Jeep and stood by his son. He'd hoped to leave Zeke-the-Dog with Grace while he and Zeke-the-Boy had dinner, but he didn't think he could get him out of the car.

Burr felt Zeke's coat. He was dry and could sleep in the Jeep while they had dinner. Zeke-the-Boy had graduated from Chuck E. Cheese and wanted to have dinner in the grill at the Grosse Pointe Yacht Club.

* * *

Burr tried to get closer to the fire, but Zeke was in the way.

"Aunt Kitty, you simply can't stay here all winter."

"I most certainly can."

She sat in her overstuffed upholstered chair, a Hudson Bay blanket over her legs, a space heater at her feet, and a fur hat pulled down over her ears.

She's not a bit cold.

Burr nudged closer to the space heater. There were another half-dozen space heaters in the foyer along with a half-dozen Hudson Bay blankets piled on a table. Every visitor was to take a heater and a blanket when they came to Cottage 59.

Burr thought the space heaters were a good idea, but all they proved was how foolish it was to stay in Cottage 59 year-round. The grand old house had been built for summer—July and August, the only real summer in Harbor Springs. The exterior walls were the interior walls. Snow ended up on the windowsills inside the house when the wind blew from the northwest—which was where the wind was blowing from today.

Aunt Kitty had woodstoves in the living room, kitchen, two of the upstairs bedrooms, and the master bath, but they couldn't keep out the cold. The pipes froze at least once a year. Burr thought living in Cottage 59 in the winter was like camping in a wall tent at the North Pole.

It was gray outside. Gray sky, gray water. Even the snow was a shade of gray.

What wasn't gray was black. Black tree trunks, black bark, black pavement.

And brown. Brown leaves where the snow hadn't buried them and brown leaves on the oaks. They wouldn't lose their leaves until spring when the new ones pushed them off.

And it was cold.

Today was November 15th, the opening day of firearm deer season in Michigan, about as close to a holiday as Michigan could get without it being official. Businesses were closed, some schools. The deer hunters took the day off, and there were empty seats in every classroom. Six hundred thousand hunters took to the Michigan woods on November 15th, which would be the second largest standing army in the world except for the People's Republic of China.

Burr wanted nothing to do with opening day. He stayed as far away from the woods and the fields as he could on November 15th. He thought he'd probably be safer at the business end of a firing range. Most years he sailed in the Deer Hunter's Regatta on November 15th, the race from Harbor Springs to Charlevoix for lunch and then back. Another exercise in poor judgment. But not this year.

Aunt Kitty sipped her martini.

Burr looked at his martini but didn't touch it.

I'd rather have hot chocolate.

"Aunt Kitty, it's simply too cold to live here this winter."

She took one of her gloves off and wagged a finger at him.

"I will live where I choose, and if that's the only reason you're here, you can leave right now."

Burr started to get up.

"Sit down. I do appreciate your concern."

"There is another reason I'm here."

"I certainly hope so."

"Aunt Kitty, I'm not the one for this."

"For what?"

"This."

"This what?"

"You know. This." Burr took a bigger gulp. The gin warmed him up.

I probably could live here in the winter if I drank enough gin.

Aunt Kitty glared at him. "I've never seen you ever at a loss for words."

Me either.

"Aunt Kitty, I'm not the right one to defend Collin."

She put her hands in her lap. "Of course you are."

"I'm not a criminal lawyer."

"Of course you are," she said again.

"I'm not a criminal lawyer." He said again.

"You haven't lost yet."

"And this Thorne Swift business isn't going well."

"Nonsense. This is just part of the battle."

Burr looked out into the darkness.

"What else is it, nephew?"

He looked at his aunt. "I think I'm in the twilight of a mediocre career."

"You may be a lot of things, but mediocre isn't one of them."

"Thank you, I think."

Aunt Kitty looked in her glass, clear as water.

She can't possibly complain about the vermouth. I didn't put any in.

She looked up at him. "Maybe a drop of vermouth."

He started to get up.

"Never mind," she said. "No one knows this case or the people better than you."

Burr put another log on the fire. It caught right away. The flames licked up the chimney and out of the firebox. Zeke stretched next to the fireplace.

"I have no idea where to start."

She studied her drink. "This is real clear." She looked at Burr. "If you did know where to start, where would that be?"

Burr studied his own drink, cloudy with olive juice. "I'd start at the beginning."

"And where is the beginning?"

"The beginning? The lady's slipper is the beginning," he said, without thinking.

"Start there."

"Where?"

"With the lady's slipper. You just said that."

Burr nodded to himself. "I'd start with Dewey Ballantine. He started it all when he sold the land."

Burr smelled something burning.

One of these damn space heaters has finally caught on fire.

"Something's burning," he said.

"I don't smell anything."

Burr took another breath. "There's something burning."

Aunt Kitty looked around the room, then, "It's Zeke."

"What?"

She pointed at a smoking patch of hair on his back.

Burr, always quick on his feet, threw his martini on the smoking hair. The alcohol in the gin flashed but the fire went out.

Zeke hadn't actually caught on fire, but the tips of the hair on his back near his tail were smoking.

The living room smelled like burning hair. Zeke hadn't noticed he was on fire—except for the smell of gin, which he didn't like.

It was too much for Burr. He mixed his aunt a dividend, put another log on the fire, and left.

He put himself to bed in his fourth-floor room at the Harbor Inn, which wasn't much warmer than Cottage 59. Burr piled on four of Stewart's Hudson Bay blankets. Zeke cuddled with him, and they spent an altogether pleasant night together.

CHAPTER EIGHT

Burr climbed the stairs. He'd counted twenty-three so far, and he wasn't close to the top. They were icy and so was the handrail.

There must be a better way to get there.

He'd left Zeke under Stewart's watchful, but not too happy eye, who told him at least half a dozen times that dogs weren't allowed at the Inn.

He stopped to catch his breath at the landing at the top of the stairs.

This is no place for Zeke.

He knocked on the door. Once. Twice. Three times. He turned around to leave when Dewey Ballantine opened the door. He looked at Burr and tried to shut the door. Burr put his foot in the doorway. It didn't quite get broken when Dewey slammed the door.

"Please, Mr. Ballantine," Burr said.

"I don't have anything to say to you."

"Please, Mr. Ballantine," Burr said again.

"I don't have to talk to you."

"No, you don't."

It was colder and windier than yesterday. And snowier.

"Could you not talk to me inside?"

"No."

"It's freezing out here."

"Go back the way you came," Dewey said. "Watch your step. It's slippery."

Burr slipped inside. "Just a few minutes."

"All right."

Burr followed him into the living room.

Dewey lived in a grand house on Glen Drive. White clapboard on the first floor, forest green shakes on the second, white dormers on the third. The living room had a cathedral ceiling, floor-to-ceiling windows, and looked out on Little Traverse Bay. Everyone who was anyone in Harbor Springs had a view of the bay.

"You may as well sit down." He pointed at a Scotch-plaid upholstered chair big enough for two. "But I don't have to talk to you."

"Of course you don't." Burr pulled his chair closer to the fireplace.

"It's my land. I can do what I want with it."

Burr didn't say anything.

"Did you hear me?" Dewey's face turned red, starting at his chin and working its way up to his forehead.

"I'm not here about the lady's slipper."

"You're not?" He lost some of the red.

"I'm here about Collin Murphy."

"He's the one causing all the trouble with Thorne Swift."

"He's been accused of murder."

"Couldn't happen to a nicer guy," Dewey said. "Helluva temper."

"I'm representing him. I have a few questions I hoped you might be able to answer."

"I don't have anything to say."

Burr walked to the window. The waves crashed on the beach. A deer hung on a buck pole next to the house.

"Did you shoot that?"

"Shoot what?"

"That buck."

Dewey joined him at the window.

"Yesterday at Pleasant View Swamp. South of Robinson Road."

"Looks like an eight point."

"Nine. You can't see the tine on the other side of his rack."

"Good looking deer."

Dewey lost some of the red in his face.

I can be shameless when I want something.

"When you leave, there's a better way out. Not so many steps." Dewey pointed to a hallway on the other side of the house.

I knew he didn't take those stairs.

"I'm here about the murder of Frank Slaughter. I won't ask you anything about the lady's slipper. Or Thorne Swift."

Dewey nodded.

"Do you know if Mr. Slaughter had any enemies? Anyone who might have had a reason to kill him?"

"Other than Collin Murphy?"

I'll make sure not to ask you that at the trial.

"Did he have any enemies?"

"I didn't really know him."

"But he was the caretaker at the preserve."

"I never really had much to do with him."

"Didn't he work for you after you terminated the lease?"

Ballantine didn't say anything.

"It was your property."

"It still is. Not for long, though." Dewey smiled.

"Why are you selling it?"

"Smart gave me a great price."

Time to move on because you're broke.

"I had every right to terminate the lease."

We'll see about that.

Dewey brushed the hair he didn't have off his forehead. "The sale is going through. As soon as that judge dismisses your latest lawsuit."

Burr ignored him. "If Collin had pictures on his camera that would help him save the flower, that would be bad for you."

Dewey started to turn red again.

"Slaughter would know that, wouldn't he? He could have tried to sell the camera and the pictures to you. You could destroy them, and the study couldn't be done in time."

"The pictures didn't matter because that damn flower isn't endangered."

Burr didn't say anything."That damn flower has caused a hell of a lot of trouble." Dewey's face turned fire-engine red. "Are you accusing me of killing Frank?"

"Not at all. I'm just saying that Frank could have offered you the camera."

"It's time for you to go." He opened the door and pointed down the long stairway.

* * *

Burr picked up Zeke at the Inn. He helped him in the Jeep and covered him with a blanket and headed south. He took a roundabout way to Detroit, stopping at Jay's in Clare to buy Zeke a neoprene vest. He didn't think Zeke would be interested in hunting, but it would keep him warm, a little dryer, and he'd float if he fell in.

Burr had another hunt with Victor, but he had important business first. He kept his waders, his parka, and his shotgun in his Jeep during duck season, but he also kept a suit, shirt, tie, and his scuffed-up cordovan loafers with the tassels. He took the downtown Detroit exit for the Fisher Building. He gave the valet a twenty to watch Zeke and told him there'd be another twenty when he got back.

When the Fisher Brothers sold Fisher Body to General Motors in 1928, they built the Fisher Building across the street from GM's world headquarters in the New Center area. Designed by Albert Kahn, the art deco building was faced with limestone, granite, and marble.

Burr's first memory of the Fisher Building was a production of *Mr. Popper's Penguins*, which his mother had taken him to in Fisher Theater.

The elevator clattered and shook, reminding him why elevators made him nervous, but the smell of fresh wax helped a little.

The elevator had just passed WJR on the seventh and eighth floors. Burr's parents had listened to J. P. McCarthy at the breakfast table, and Burr had grown up with him. He felt like he knew J. P., who had said, "Give him my regards but don't tell him where I am."

I've said that more than once. And meant it.

The elevator stopped at twenty-seven, three floors from the top. Burr got out and found Johnson Smart's office. A twentyish blonde sat in the reception area.

"May I help you?"

"I'm here to see Mr. Smart."

"Is he expecting you?"

I can't see why anyone would come up here uninvited.

Burr nodded.

She knocked on the door behind her, went in, and came right back out. She held the door open for him.

"Mr. Smart will see you now."

Burr walked into a plain office. Beige walls, beige carpet, and a dented cherry desk.

Johnson Smart stood and shook his hand. "Welcome, laddie."

Laddie?

Smart pointed at a dented chair in front of his desk. Burr sat.

There was nothing special about Smart's office, especially for someone who was buying, or at least trying to buy, some of the most expensive real estate on Lake Michigan. Smart's office was plain in every way, except one. It had a view that stretched all the way downtown. Burr could see the Renaissance Center from his days at Fisher Allen.

He could see Lake St. Clair to his left, flat and gray, and the Grosse Pointes, naked trees blanketing the homes of the rich, the somewhat rich, and the would-be rich.

"Quite a view." Smart ran his hand through his salt and pepper hair, then rubbed his pencil mustache.

He must have a barber take care of that thing.

"I knew your grandfather, your father, too. A shame what happened." Smart shook his head. "To Colonial Broach. And your father."

This is the last thing I want to talk about.

"Our company bought broaches from them. We were in the stamping business."

Burr's grandfather, Aaron Lafayette, invented the broach, the first tool that could cut a square hole in metal. Aaron was a metalworking genius, and the broach had made the Lafayette fortune. But Burr's father never had a head for business. He'd lost it all—including his life when he ran into a bridge abutment on the Chrysler Freeway. In deference to the family, the crash had been ruled an accident, but they all knew better. Burr's mother died of a broken heart. Burr was left with a University of Michigan law degree, his Aunt Kitty, and precious little else.

"What say we have lunch?" Smart led him to the elevator and took them up to the top floor. Burr did his best to look calm.

They walked out of the elevator and into the Auto Club, one of Detroit's most exclusive clubs, lunch only, and a waiting list longer than a 1965 Fleetwood.

"I have your table ready, Mr. Smart." The maître d' led them to a window table, next to a potted palm.

Burr did his best not to look down.

"Sherry," Smart said. "For two."

I hate sherry.

"We made good money selling parts to GM, but the union made it tough. I sold the business and bought five acres next to Metro. I turned it into a parking lot. It's amazing how much money you can make parking cars next to an airport. Shuttle buses and cashiers. That's all you need." Smart smiled the smile of someone who was smart and knew it.

The waiter brought their sherry.

"We'll each have a Caesar salad and the steak tartare." To Burr, "Best steak tartare in Detroit. They make it when they know I'm coming."

I hate steak tartare.

Smart raised his glass. "To the lady's slipper."

Smart ass.

Burr clinked Smart's glass and took a sip.

It tastes like wet raisins.

The man with the pencil mustache smiled at Burr. "I assume you're here to settle this Thorne Swift business once and for all."

"Not exactly."

"You're going to lose on the lease. You do know that."

"I wouldn't bet on it."

"Of course you're going to lose. We can make this simple. Drop your lawsuit, and I'll set aside some of the property for that flower."

"I'm not here about the lady's slipper."

"Then why on earth are you here?" Smart pulled on his mustache, not that there was much to pull. "This flower nonsense was your way of trying to block the sale of Thorne Swift." Smart smiled a condescending smile. "Clever, but destined to fail. And the lease won't work either. Ballantine had every right to terminate it."

"Thorne Swift is too important for million-dollar cottages."

"If that's why you're here, lunch will be over before it starts." This time, a nasty smile. "I don't have to talk with you, and it's a violation of the bar association's code of ethics to visit with me without my attorney present."

This guy knows everything.

"The only reason I agreed to meet with you was to settle your frivolous lawsuit. If that's not why you're here, I'll have your steak tartare put in a to-go box." Smart finished his sherry.

Burr looked at his sherry but didn't touch it. "Mr. Smart, Collin Murphy has been charged with murder. I represent him."

"How unfortunate. For both of you." Smart sipped his sherry. "Drink up, laddie."

I guess lunch isn't over.

"What can you tell me about Frank Slaughter?"

"I hardly knew him. He worked for Dewey. Nice enough fellow. Followed orders."

"Which included beating up Collin and stealing his camera."

"I highly doubt it."

"He offered it to Mr. Murphy. For a price."

"Is that so?"

He already knew that.

"Did he offer it to you?"

"Me? Of course not. Why would he?"

"The pictures on the camera were crucial to preserving Thorne Swift."

"No one knows who took Mr. Murphy's camera, or for that matter, if anyone did take it." Smart rubbed his mustache again. "For all we know, Mr. Murphy made it up to get more time. Not that it matters now."

"Do you know if Frank had any enemies?"

"Slaughter? Hardly. I think he was a teacher and a family man."

"So, somebody murdered a boy scout who was selling a camera with pictures on it that would ruin your chance to buy Thorne Swift."

"The lady's slipper was of no consequence."

"No one knew that at the time."

"I've had rather enough of this," Smart said.

Burr and his sherry walked to the potted palm next to the window. He poured the sherry into the potted palm pot and sat back down. "It's my job to defend Collin Murphy."

"Of course it is," Smart said. "I have no idea why anyone would want to kill Mr. Slaughter. Other than Mr. Murphy."

* * *

Burr watched the smoke from his cigarette. It rose straight up. Not a breath of wind, but it was cold. Very cold and very clear. "Severe clear," as his grandfather had said. A perfectly beautiful late November day and perfectly miserable for duck hunting.

They'd had to break ice to get into the pond, running the bow of Victor's boat up on the ice, the boat's weight breaking it. Again and again. Burr had dropped Victor and Zeke off at the blind and then ran the boat in circles to open a hole for the ducks to land.

They sat in the stake blind in the cattails on the edge of the Holiday Pond, Victor on one side, Zeke on the dog platform. Burr watched the open water freeze. Not that it mattered. There wasn't a duck in sight.

Burr crushed out his cigarette and poured half a cup of peppermint tea from his Stanley thermos, gray-green and nicely dented. He took a swallow. It had just enough honey to make the peppermint interesting.

Zeke squirmed in his vest, then bit at it.

"He doesn't like it," Victor said.

"It's keeping him warm."

"He doesn't know that." Victor lit a cigarette. The smoke drifted off to the northeast.

"Maybe we'll get a little wind and get a few birds flying," Burr said.

Victor looked at Zeke. "Is he eating?"

"Yes," Burr lied.

"They quit eating when they're getting ready to pass," Victor said.

A snowy owl, pure white with yellow eyes and a black beak, swooped over the pond, fooled by the decoys. It dropped its legs to grab a duck, figured out the game, and flew off.

"That thing is as big as a lawn chair," Burr said.

"Down early this year. Means a bad winter."

Burr looked over at Zeke. His vest covered his ribs, but Victor was right. Zeke wasn't eating much. Only the ground beef and rice that Burr cooked for him.

A colored-out drake pintail appeared from nowhere. Long, white neck, gray-brown body and a long, thin pointed tail. He circled the pond, wary.

Burr stood and pushed the safety. It wouldn't release. He pushed again. "Damn thing is stuck."

Victor poured some of Burr's tea on the safety. Burr pushed it again. It released.

"Not stuck," Victor said. "Frozen."

Burr killed the duck. Zeke didn't move.

"You better think about saying goodbye," Victor said.

* * *

The driveway into Thorne Swift wasn't plowed and neither was the parking lot. Snow piled up, window high, at the nature center.

Burr had gotten stuck twice on the way in. But for the four-wheel drive, he'd still be stuck. He driven past the "closed" sign and parked in front of the "no parking" sign. Burr got out of his Jeep and waded through the snow to Ian Nash.

"There's a reason Thorne Swift is closed in the winter," Ian said.

"That must be your truck on the side of the road."

Ian nodded. He was a member of Friends of Thorne Swift, Burr's client. Late thirties, lean and lithe. He had black hair and blue eyes, a crooked smile, and a pointed nose. He started wading through the thigh-high snow.

Burr had on his Sorels, duck coat, Carhartt bib overalls, gloves, stocking cap, and his secret weapon, a black wool neck warmer.

I have a chance to stay warm.

He followed in Ian's footsteps, literally.

Judge Abbott was going to rule on the lease any day, and Burr was no closer to saving Thorne Swift or Collin than he had been sixty days ago. He didn't have any idea what he might find out here, and he was running out of ideas.

Harbor Springs was always snowy, but this year the snow had started on Halloween and hadn't stopped since. And it was cold. Crooked Lake was already frozen, and there was ice in the harbor.

Ian stopped and waited for Burr to catch up. "I can't see how we could possibly find anything here today that could help save Thorne Swift."

"You might see something that jogs your memory."

"Under three feet of snow?" Ian started down the snowed-in path, Burr in tow.

Ian stopped a hundred yards in. A small creek just ahead. "Watch your step. There's a little bridge under the snow, but it's narrow. You'll get wet if you fall off."

Maybe this wasn't such a good idea.

The path that would have a path if it hadn't been buried in snow, forked. Ian took the right fork past two outhouses. Burr caught up with him, Lake Michigan in front of them. Six-foot waves crashed in from the northwest, a ribbon of sand between the snowy beach and the surf.

"Beautiful," Ian said.

The breaking waves and the wind in the trees drowned out his voice.

"What's that?" Burr said.

Ian shouted into Burr's ear.

Burr nodded, not convinced.

"The *Edmund Fitzgerald* went down on a day like this," Ian said.

That's encouraging.

Burr trudged through the woods behind Ian. The path circled back toward the parking lot. "There's an open spot over there. That's where they grow."

"Under three feet of snow?"

"It's like the legend. When the girl got stuck in the snow on her way back to the village with the medicine. There will be lady's slippers here after the snow melts."

"In my footprints."

Ian pointed with his right hand. "Over there. There's a colony there in the spring."

"Colony?"

"They like to grow in bunches."

"Is this where you saw Collin taking pictures?"

"Yes."

"How do you know?"

He pointed a gloved hand to a beech tree, silver bark, and at least ten feet around. It rose up and through the canopy. "The flowers grow in wet ground. That beech grows in a dry spot."

Burr looked at the tree. There were carvings cut into the bark, black with age.

"What's that?" Burr said.

"It's a beech tree."

I came all this way to see a beech tree?

"What's on the tree?"

"Initials."

"Initials?"

"People carve their initials on it."

"Why?"

"If they're boyfriend-girlfriend. Lovers. It's called the Tree of Hearts."

Ian started back through the snow.

"Just a minute." Burr curled his fingers into fists inside his gloves, then, "Do you come out here very often?"

"I help out at a camp in the summer. I bring the kids out here. My daughter, too. It's a great place to teach kids, and it's safe. No cars, well supervised."

"You have a daughter?"

Ian nodded. "Come on." Ian started off again. "I'm cold."

* * *

Burr spent a frigid night at the Harbor Inn, under as many blankets as he could find, and as close to Zeke as he could get, which wasn't difficult because Zeke was cold, too. He pawed Burr until he put a blanket over him.

The next morning, Burr lifted Zeke into the Jeep and covered him with Stewart's heaviest blanket.

He's fading before my eyes.

They took US-131 south to Grand Rapids. Burr parked at the Amway and tipped the valet in advance.

He walked to the federal building and waited in the lobby where he could see the elevators.

Judge Elizabeth Abbott got off the elevator in a full-length fur coat.

It looks like mink.

She went out the back door and headed west on Bridge Street on foot. Burr followed her. She crossed the river and five blocks up she ducked into the Anchor, one of Grand Rapids' oldest and most famous dive bars.

Maybe they have a lunch special.

Burr counted to twenty-five, then went in. The Anchor was paneled in hardwood, now black, and smelled like flat beer, ashtrays, and too many years. It was dark and mostly empty. He couldn't see a thing, except the red and white Budweiser mirror behind the bar and the Christmas tree in the corner. It was lit up with old-fashioned Christmas lights—red, blue, green, yellow, orange, and white. Big bulbs. The kind that didn't blink.

There's nothing like a string of C9s.

He didn't see Judge Abbott anywhere. Finally, his eyes adjusted. There was only one place she could be. A row of booths with high backs lined the wall across the bar. He couldn't see if anyone was in the far booth.

Here goes.

He sat at the bar stool across from the last booth and ordered a Budweiser.

Labatt was too much to hope for.

He looked at Judge Abbott in the Budweiser mirror. She had her fur draped around her shoulders and what looked like a beer and a shot.

It's a little early in the day for that.

The judge downed her shot and waved for another one.

The bartender delivered the shot. Burr delivered himself into the seat across from her.

She doesn't recognize me.

"Is there something you want?"

I'm not that forgettable.

"Burr Lafayette." He reached his hand across the table.

"What are you doing here?"

"I'm having lunch."

She glared at him.

The bartender came over. "Judge?"

"My usual," she said.

"Another?" he said, pointing at her empty shot glass and her beer.

She nodded.

The bartender turned to go.

"I'll have my usual," Burr said.

"You don't have a usual," the bartender said.

"I'll have her usual." He pointed at the shot glass and the beer.

"You're as big a smart ass outside the courtroom." To the bartender, "Mr. Lafayette was just leaving."

"Right after lunch."

The bartender left.

Judge Abbott pulled her fur up around her shoulders. She wore a navy dress underneath, dangling gold earrings, and pink lipstick.

She doesn't look much like a judge.

"Mr. Lafayette, if you want something from me, file a motion. Or request a conference."

"I thought this might be better."

"Ambushing me at lunch is not better. And it's unethical."

Their drinks came. Judge Abbott sipped her shot, so did Burr.

"Maker's Mark?" he said.

She smiled, just a little, then drank half the shot.

That's her third.

"If you want something, this is a poor way to get it."

Burr chewed on his cheek. "I'm sorry, judge. I'm on my way back from Harbor Springs, and I wanted to see you. I shouldn't have interrupted your lunch."

"No, you shouldn't, but you're here. What is it?"

The bartender delivered their "usuals." A Reuben sandwich with coleslaw and fries.

It's not a whitefish sandwich, but it'll do.

She drowned her fries with ketchup from a plastic squeeze bottle.

It clashes with her lipstick.

Burr squirted ketchup next to his fries and dragged one through a puddle of it. "I was out at Thorne Swift yesterday."

She cocked her head mid-French fry.

"The nature preserve. Where the lady's slipper grows."

She nodded.

"It's beautiful. Even in winter."

"In all that snow?"

"Have you been there?"

She shook her head and started in on her Reuben.

"It was really snowy, but beautiful. It would be terrible to lose it."

The judge put her sandwich down. "Mr. Lafayette, I can't make decisions based on beauty. "

"There's an Ojibwe legend about the lady's slipper."

"If you've got a legal argument for stopping the sale of Thorne Swift,

I'm all ears. Legends aren't going to work. Neither is 'endangered.' Dahlberg has you there."

"Thorne Swift needs to stay Thorne Swift."

"That's not a legal argument."

"Judge, the lease can't be terminated for development."

"Not here. Where you shouldn't be."

"Ballantine can't terminate the lease."

"I am still considering your argument, but I wouldn't get your hopes up."

Damn it all.

"Have you been there?" Burr said again.

"You already asked me that."

"You could make an official visit," Burr said.

She ignored him. "Is there anything else?"

"Just one more thing."

"What is it this time?"

"It's about Mr. Murphy."

She arched her eyebrows and drank part of her shot.

"There have been some extenuating circumstances."

Judge Abbott finished half of her sandwich and went to work on the other half.

"Well …" Burr paused. "Mr. Murphy has been charged with murder."

The proper Judge Elizabeth Abbott's jaw dropped, a mouthful of sandwich in it.

"We need a stay in the proceedings. It's a terrible misunderstanding, but we need a stay. Until the trial is over."

The bartender came over. "Anything else?"

"Spin 'em," Burr said.

"Mr. Lafayette, I really must get back to my office."

You should have done that two shots ago.

"Mr. Murphy can't defend Thorne Swift and himself at the same time," Burr said.

"What does Mr. Murphy's lawyer think?"

"I am Mr. Murphy's lawyer."

"You're not a criminal lawyer."

CHAPTER NINE

"You're not a criminal lawyer," Jacob said.

"That's what she said."

"And you can't go around ambushing judges."

"She said that, too."

"Especially while they're eating lunch."

"The good Judge Abbott mostly drank her lunch."

"She did not."

"She did."

"Stop it. Both of you," Eve said. "We have important business to take care of."

"Such as?" Burr said.

"Such as, how are we going to make payroll?"

"We'll write checks." Burr reached into his drawer for the accursed Lafayette and Wertheim checkbook. Long blue checks, stubs on the left in a black three-ring binder.

I hate that thing.

Except the checkbook wasn't there.

"I have it," Eve said. "Not that it matters. There's no money in it." She tugged on her earring.

"I must be paid," Jacob said.

"Then you're going to have to collect some money," she said.

Jacob's olive complexion turned a whiter shade of pale.

He may be ill.

Jacob, for all his talent as a researcher and writer, was deathly afraid of conflict—any kind of conflict. He had never asked a soul for money, let alone any of their clients.

"Give me the list. I'll call."

Eve handed Burr a scrap of paper. "It's a short list. When you're done with that, find us some more work."

"I have work," Burr said.

"Collin Murphy and the lady's slipper don't count," Eve said.

"You said you didn't want to work for free," Jacob said.

"I don't."

"It doesn't matter who's not paying us," Eve said.

There is that.

"And Truax has a solid case," Jacob said.

"Collin looks guilty," Eve said.

"Stop piling on."

"And he's not very likeable," Eve said.

"You're both right. Collin isn't a sympathetic defendant." Burr looked away, then back at Jacob and Eve. "He may have done it, but he still deserves a defense."

"One of these days you're going to lose," Jacob said.

Burr had driven back to East Lansing after his lunch with Judge Abbott— more like an early cocktail hour.

He sat at his desk, Jacob and Eve in the blue wingback chairs across from him.

This desk is my last line of defense.

"The elevator isn't working right," Eve said.

"If you'd take the elevator, you'd know that," Jacob said.

"Zeke and I took the elevator. It worked just fine, ran right up here," Burr lied.

"Then you didn't take the elevator," Jacob said.

"They had to take the elevator," Eve said. "Zeke can't take the stairs anymore."

"I beg your pardon."

He and Zeke had taken the elevator to his sixth-floor office. Zeke's days of taking the stairs were over. The elevator groaned and clanked all the way up. It had taken the better part of five minutes to get there. He'd have to get the elevator fixed again, but he couldn't get it fixed until he could pay for it, his credit long since exhausted with every elevator company in town.

Jacob turned around and looked at Zeke sprawled on the couch. "That cur is where he always is." Jacob sneezed for effect.

I knew he was going to do that.

"He's only on the couch because Burr lifted him up there," Eve said.

"There's no reason for a dog to be on the furniture in the first place."

* * *

There was no good reason to be out here. None whatsoever. Victor knew it, Burr knew it, and Zeke surely knew it.

No good reason, save one.

It was the last day. The last day of duck season, and Burr always hunted the first day and the last day. And as many days in between as he could get away with.

He'd watched the season change from late summer, with golf ball–sized nuts on the shagbark hickories, green cattails in the marsh with their chocolate-brown heads, and the blue-winged teal.

The nuts had fallen. The cattails had turned brown. The mallards and the pintails had colored out. The teal and the wood ducks had flown south, and the bluebills, redheads, and canvasbacks had taken their place.

Fall and the great migration kept Burr going. But not today.

Today was winter. Twelve degrees, cloudy, northwest wind at twenty, and ice. Ice everywhere. Walpole Marsh was frozen. The cattails knocked down, the muskrat houses sticking up through the snow. They were frozen out of the Holiday Pond.

Victor had tucked into a half-acre bay on the Johnson, just upstream from his house. He'd hidden the boat on the edge of the cattails and thrown out his thirteen decoys, probably just for show.

"Better day to eat sausage, hash browns, and fry bread inside. And drink coffee."

Burr took the cigarette out of his mouth but didn't say anything.

"There's no good reason to be out here."

Burr nodded but still didn't say anything.

"You should be working, and there's no ducks flying."

Burr looked across the river to St. Anne's Island. The tribe had cut the corn two weeks ago, and there was a chance the mallards would fly in for the corn the combines didn't get. A chance. If the snow wasn't too deep.

But that wasn't the reason they were here, and it wasn't because it was the last day.

They were here because Burr was pretty sure that this was going to be Zeke's last duck hunt.

* * *

Burr picked up Zeke-the-Boy after the hunt. The mallards had flown into St. Anne's about eleven. They swirled over the corn stubble like a tornado, spiraling downward and landing. After gorging themselves on the spent corn, they flew across the river to Victor's decoys. Burr shot a limit. Zeke watched.

Zeke-the-Boy sat in the back with Zeke-the-Dog. Zeke-the-Dog had given up riding shotgun. Burr didn't think Zeke-the-Boy was old enough to ride shotgun, although his son didn't agree.

The three of them were off to East Lansing and Burr's sixth-floor apartment for the weekend. It had taken some doing to get permission from the ever-vigilant Grace, a better mother and wife than Burr had been a husband and father.

She had taken a look at Zeke-the-Dog and given permission, grudgingly.

The three of them were off on a boy's weekend of swivel chairs, copy machines, and elevators.

* * *

Zeke lined up his shot, then stood.

"Dad, you're in the way."

Burr walked around behind him.

"Don't stand behind me."

Burr took half a dozen steps to his right. Zeke crouched over the cue and lined up his shot again.

"Twelve in the corner pocket." He stroked the cue. The cue ball hit the twelve squarely, but it glanced off the bumper.

"Damn it," he said.

"Zeke," Burr said.

"That's what you say."

"I'm forty years older than you are."

"Not quite."

Burr walked around the table. "Seven in the side pocket." He scratched.

"Nice shot," Zeke said.

"Zeke, I'm your father, and I would like to be treated with some respect."

They were at Tripper's, a sports bar in Frandor, about a mile from Burr's office and just outside the East Lansing city limits. The walls were lined with televisions, all tuned to sports. It was dark, smoky, and full of pool tables. Burr didn't think Tripper's was an appropriate place for Zeke, but he'd insisted.

I guess the days of copy machines, swivel chairs, and elevators are over.

Zeke took the cue ball out of the pocket and lined up another shot. "Nine in the side pocket." He made the shot and three more before he missed a bank shot. Burr missed his next two shots, and Zeke won his third game in a row. They had just started their fourth game when their food arrived. Zeke put an onion on his cheeseburger.

Chuck E. Cheese is over, too.

Burr ordered another beer.

"That's your fourth," Zeke said.

"It's my third."

"Fourth. I've been counting."

Even three is too many.

Zeke-the-Boy wasn't really a boy anymore. He was tall and skinny and hadn't grown into his body yet. Long, shaggy hair. He had Burr's nose but his mother's eyes, sad and gray. He was going to be tall, taller than Burr and feisty like Aunt Kitty.

Zeke poured a puddle of ketchup and dunked his cheeseburger in it.

"Dad, it's bad enough having Zeke for a name, but it's terrible being Zeke-the-Boy."

That's what Grace says.

"There's no greater honor than being named after Zeke-the-Dog."

"Why did Mom ever let you do that?"

It took everything I had.

The waitress dropped off Burr's beer.

Zeke wanted to come here for the pool. It was Labatt on draft that brought Burr in. He looked at it longingly but didn't touch it.

Zeke dunked his cheeseburger in his ketchup again. He took another bite, then looked at the TVs. The Pistons, Red Wings, and MSU basketball were all on. It was almost Christmas—dark at five-thirty, gray all day, and a foot of wet snow.

"I don't want to be called Zeke anymore."

Burr reached for his beer but thought better of it. "What?"

"I don't want to be called Zeke. Call me Aaron."

"Zeke is your name."

"So is Aaron."

"Zeke is your first name," Burr said. "People go by their first names."

"You don't."

Burr looked at the wall of televisions. The Wings, Pistons, and Spartans were all losing.

Just like me.

Zeke was right. Aaron Burr Lafayette did, in fact, go by his middle name. He hadn't liked his first name, and Zeke didn't like his first name either.

At least it's not Ezekiel.

Burr looked at his beer but still didn't touch it.

"Can I think about it?" he said.

"No. It's my name, and I want to be called Aaron from now on. Mom's fine with it."

Grace didn't tell me.

"What will Zeke think?"

"He's a dog."

"Zeke knows you as 'Zeke.' He won't know what's going on."

"He'll learn."

"Zeke-the-Dog is old. He may be going to heaven soon."

"It's Aaron," Zeke said. "You mean he's going to die?"

"He's had a great run, but he's old. I'm not sure he's going to last much longer."

"Are you going to put him down?"

When did he grow up?

* * *

"Mr. Lafayette, the last time I saw you I said that I would consider it a personal favor if you never appeared before me again."

"Yes, Your Honor," Burr said.

"And here you are."

"Yes, Your Honor."

"Is it absolutely necessary that you be here?"

"Yes, Your Honor." Burr started to straighten his already straight tie.

"Stop that. If you must be here, you may not do that silly preening in my courtroom."

Gillis had been the trial judge at a murder trial that Burr had somehow managed to win. He thought he may have been more lucky than smart.

A win is a win.

Judge Gillis still looked like he hadn't missed any meals, and if he was trying to grow hair on his head, it wasn't working. He had a round head, a round face, a round nose, and a fringe of black hair above his ears. He was somewhere in his sixties.

Burr thought Gillis was living proof that you didn't have to be smart to be a judge. All you had to do was get elected, which Gillis had managed to do, time and again.

"Do you have a reason for being here? Or is it just to show off your thousand-dollar suit? Which I've seen more than once."

"Yes, Your Honor," Burr said again.

I'm losing and I haven't even started.

The courtroom of the Honorable Benjamin R. Gillis was a step above the courtroom of the not-quite-so-honorable Paul Bailey. All things being equal, which they weren't, the pecking order of the Michigan judicial system required that the courtroom of the circuit judge be above that of a district judge, but just one step, because the court of appeals and the supreme court each had their own steps.

Not that there was anything fancy about Gillis's courtroom. It had the same pews in the gallery and the same tables and chairs for the litigants as Judge Bailey's district courtroom. But the varnish on the pews was a little fresher, the tables didn't have quite as many initials scratched in them, and the chairs didn't wobble as much. Gillis's desk was higher and there was a window—not a big window, but a window just the same.

Both courtrooms smelled like Ajax and Spic and Span, but the janitors may have used a little more of each in the circuit courtroom. In the pecking order hierarchy, the circuit court was on the third floor of the courthouse, the district court on the second floor, the police department on the first floor, and the jail in the basement.

He looked out the window. It was snowing again. Actually, it was still snowing. Burr thought that the snow that had started in October had never stopped. The snow was piled so high that the drivers had put orange ribbons on their antennas so they could be seen. Burr had run into a snow squall in Grayling and he'd had to drive the rest of the way to Petoskey in four-wheel drive. He'd made it to the court just in time, but there was no time to drop Zeke off at the Inn. He'd left Zeke under a blanket in the Jeep, but he couldn't leave him there for long. Luckily for Zeke, the way this had started, it didn't look like this was going to last very long.

"What is it that you want?" Judge Gillis said.

Burr took a step closer. "Your Honor, I'd like to enter an appearance in the matter of State versus Murphy."

Gillis groaned. "I might have known. Couldn't you be here on a bank robbery? Or a kidnapping? Your appearance is granted. And you needn't have come all this way to enter an appearance. In a snowstorm to boot. You could have done it by mail."

"There is one other thing, Your Honor."

"Of course there is."

"I object, Your Honor."

Burr looked across the aisle at Calvin Truax, now standing.

"Calvin," the judge said, "how can you possibly object? Mr. Lafayette hasn't said anything yet."

"I know what he's going to say, Your Honor," Truax said. "It's in his two motions." Truax shuffled through the papers on his table and picked up a file. "It's all in his motion. Which is poppycock."

"Poppycock?" Burr said.

"What motions?"

"I filed them with the clerk a week ago, Your Honor."

"You most certainly did not," the judge said.

The court stenographer, a short, dowdy, middle-aged woman with the longest fingers Burr had ever seen, shuffled through her papers. She found what she was looking for and handed Gillis a file.

"I suppose it is motion day," the judge said.

Tuesday was motion day in the Emmet County Circuit Court. The courtroom was full of lawyers, but there were virtually no clients. Motion day was the day the lawyers argued about substance and procedure, but mostly procedure. Should the case be dismissed? Should the trial be postponed? Should bail be revoked? All sorts of issues to rule on. Some easy, some not so easy.

Burr loved motion day because he loved arguing. He loved standing in front of a judge.

He was pretty sure he was going to lose on his motions, but that's why he was here.

Gillis flipped through the motions and the twenty-page brief ably written by Jacob, under protest. Something about getting paid.

Maybe if I thought about getting paid more often, we might get paid more often.

Gillis flipped through the motions, then set them down in front of him, side by side. "You may proceed, Mr. Lafayette."

There's no way he read them.

"Thank you, Your Honor. There are two motions before the Court. If the Court were to grant the first motion, there would be no need for the second."

Gillis nodded.

Burr walked around his table. "Your Honor, as I'm sure you're aware, my client, Collin Murphy, has been charged with murder."

"And you're defending him?"

"Yes, Your Honor."

"Saints, preserve us."

Another good Catholic.

"Your Honor, my client has been charged with murder without the slightest shred of evidence."

Truax bounced to his feet. "That is absolutely not true, Your Honor.

"It's not your turn."

"I'll decide whose turn it is, Mr. Lafayette."

"Yes, Your Honor," Burr said. "The fact of the matter is that no one saw Mr. Murphy kill Mr. Slaughter. Mr. Murphy had no reason to murder Mr. Slaughter. Moreover, Mr. Murphy was nowhere near the scene of the crime when Mr. Slaughter was murdered."

I may have stretched the last part.

"None of that is true," Truax said.

Burr looked over at Truax again. "Be quiet." To the judge, "For these reasons I ask that you dismiss the charges against Mr. Murphy."

"Now it's your turn, Calvin," Gillis said.

"Thank you, Your Honor." Truax picked up his file and opened it.

That's all for show.

"Your Honor, Judge Bailey held a preliminary exam on this matter. As I'm sure you'll agree, he is extremely competent. He found that it was more likely than not that Mr. Murphy murdered Mr. Slaughter. As you know, the standard for a murder charge is much lower than the standard for conviction, which is beyond a reasonable doubt."

"I know what the standards are," the judge said.

Truax inched closer to Gillis. "Furthermore, Your Honor, Mr. Lafayette's statements are patently false. Mr. Murphy believed that Mr. Slaughter had stolen his camera. He was seen arguing with Mr. Slaughter before he was killed. He threatened Mr. Slaughter, and he followed him after he threatened him. Means, motive, opportunity." Truax smiled at Burr.

I hate it when he smiles.

"Moreover, the murder weapon belonged to Mr. Murphy."

"That has not been proved," Burr said.

Yet.

"Means, motive, opportunity."

"Your Honor—"

Gillis cut him off. "Mr. Lafayette, I have great respect for Judge Bailey. He is a most able jurist. If he thinks there is probable cause, then I agree with him. He sent this case up from district court, and I intend to try it."

"Your Honor—"

Gillis cut him off again. "It is these very disputes of fact that will be sorted out during the trial. That's what a jury of Mr. Murphy's peers will do. Motion denied." Gillis banged his gavel. "Next case."

"I have another motion."

"Motion denied. Whatever it is." The judge banged his gavel again. "Next case."

"Your Honor, I request a delay in the trial date."

Gillis flipped through Burr's second motion. He found what he was looking for and read it, lips moving. "We'll start our trial on February 14th. Valentine's Day." The judge smiled at Burr. "Next case."

"Your Honor—"

Gillis pointed to the door at the back of the courtroom. "Out."

CHAPTER TEN

Burr sat at his favorite table at Michelangelo's, a window table that looked out on downtown East Lansing. Michelangelo's was a very good but very expensive Northern Italian restaurant on the first floor of Burr's building. It had red and white checkered tablecloths. Burr knew they were a cliché. And boring. Which was why he liked them.

Sometimes boring is good.

Zeke lay at his feet, panting on one of the Hudson Bay blankets Burr had taken from Cottage 59.

Scooter, the restaurateur with a pasty complexion and not a drop of Italian blood, hurried to Burr's table. "Mr. Lafayette, there are no dogs allowed in Michelangelo's."

"Zeke is a seeing-eye dog."

"He isn't a seeing-eye dog, and you're not blind."

I think we just had this conversation for the last time.

"Scooter, about the rent."

Scooter scooted off.

He was Burr's only tenant, but he rarely paid his rent. Rather than evicting the restaurateur in arrears, Burr took the rent he didn't get in cash out in trade, but no matter much he ate or drank, he couldn't eat enough pasta or drink enough Chianti to come out close to even, much less ahead.

Scooter came back to the table. "Are you ready to order?"

"Where's the waitress?"

"She comes in at five. I'm cutting back during the day. A martini?"

Burr shook his head.

"We have a new Chianti. Very smooth."

Burr shook his head again.

Scooter turned even pastier. "Is there something wrong, Mr. Lafayette?"

"Yes. And no." He bent down and scratched Zeke's left ear. "I have some terrible business this afternoon, and I need to keep my wits about me."

"That's never stopped you. And you could take a nap."

"Not today." Burr smiled at his tenant in arrears. "I'd like two orders of the clam linguine with red sauce. Extra clams on one of them."

"Are you expecting someone?"

"No."

"Then why … never mind."

Scooter scurried off. Burr looked out the window. It was three o'clock and the sun was already low in the sky.

"Zeke, I really need my lights. They're in the closet somewhere."

Who am I going to talk to after today?

Scooter brought the plates of linguine. He took a place setting from the next table over and set it across from Burr.

"We won't be needing that."

"Is your guest going to eat with his fingers?"

"My guest doesn't have any fingers."

"I beg your pardon."

Burr set the plate with the extra clams in front of Zeke. He sniffed it once but didn't eat any.

Scooter's jaw dropped. "Mr. Lafayette, it's one thing to bring your dog in here. It's quite another to put a plate of my linguine and clams with red sauce on the floor in front of him." Scooter put his hands on his hips. "With extra clams."

"Not today, Scooter." Burr pointed to the kitchen. Burr reached down and picked a clam off Zeke's plate and held in in front of Zeke's mouth. Zeke turned away.

* * *

Burr spread the blanket on the floor, then carried Zeke in from the Jeep and laid him on the blanket. He sat down and scratched Zeke's left ear.

Dr. Nolan came in five minutes later. She was about forty-five and had soft brown eyes, shoulder-length hair to match, and a quiet smile. She had been Zeke's vet since he was a puppy. She sat down next to Burr.

"I'm so sorry."

Burr didn't say anything.

"Are you sure it's time?"

Burr put his arm around Zeke's neck and nodded at her.

"I'll be right back." The vet walked out of the room and came back with two syringes. She sat down next to Burr. "Are you sure?"

Burr looked at her but still didn't say anything.

"We have to talk about this," she said. "Just a little."

"I'm not sure I can talk about it."

She took Burr's hand. "Is he eating?"

Burr shook his head.

"Can he get up on his own?"

Burr shook his head again.

"Is he starting to have accidents?"

Burr nodded. "I don't think he's having fun anymore. When he stopped wanting to hunt, I knew it was coming. He'd rather fetch a duck than eat. He stopped eating, and he's getting weaker and weaker." Burr looked away, then, "He's my best friend."

Dr. Nolan looked at Zeke, then at Burr. "They get to a point where they're ready to go, but they won't die on their own. I've seen dogs linger for months when their owners didn't have the courage to do what needed to be done. What the dog really wanted."

"It's time." Burr started to cry, a quiet cry. "It's what he wants."

Dr. Nolan stroked Zeke's back, then picked up one of the syringes. "This is a tranquilizer. It will relax him. It takes about five minutes to work. Then I'll give him the other shot." She wiped Zeke's hip with alcohol, then took the cover off the needle.

"Just a minute." Burr hugged Zeke. "Goodbye, old friend." He nodded to Dr. Nolan. She gave him the first shot. Burr held Zeke in his arms. He felt the old Lab relax. Dr. Nolan picked up the other syringe. "This will stop his heart. He'll stop breathing and pass peacefully."

Burr started crying again.

"I do this almost every day, and it's never easy. He needs you to do this for him." She put her hand on Burr's shoulder. "Do you want me to leave you alone with him? I can come back when you're ready."

"No, it's time." Burr held Zeke in his arms. He nodded at Dr Nolan. She gave the second shot.

"Goodbye, old friend. I love you."

Zeke looked up at Burr one last time, then he closed his eyes and dropped his head. Burr held him in his arms. He felt Zeke's breathing become shallower and shallower. Then it stopped. Burr sobbed.

Dr. Nolan put her arm on Burr's shoulder again. "Stay with him as long as you want." She stood and left.

Burr covered Zeke with the blanket, then laid down beside him.

* * *

Burr spent a sleepless night alone in his apartment for the first time since he'd had Zeke. Almost fourteen years. He didn't like it.

His apartment was one of the few things that had turned out with his otherwise disastrous building. His living quarters had two bedrooms, two and a half baths, living room, dining room, galley kitchen, and a patio facing west. It was the perfect size when Zeke-the-Boy came to visit, but too big for Burr and Zeke-the-Dog, and much too big for just him.

Burr made it to his office at eight sharp the next morning, about two hours earlier than usual. His office was just across the hall, not much of a commute. He couldn't stand being in his apartment, and his office wasn't much better. He looked at his couch where Zeke should be napping, but wasn't, and never would again.

Burr looked out at the gray January morning. He still hadn't found his light. He'd made it through the solstice, just barely, and January wasn't much better than December. He looked up the time of the sunrise and sunset every morning in the *Lansing State Journal*. If anyone ever asked him when sunrise and sunset were, which no one ever did, he could tell them to the minute.

Downtown East Lansing was gray like the sky, gray sidewalks, gray snow piles, gray people. He turned back around and tap, tap, tapped his pencil, then broke it in two.

"I heard that." Eve came in, followed by Jacob. They took their assigned seats. "I didn't see you come in," she said, "but there's nothing like the sound of a breaking pencil to announce your presence."

Burr handed her what were now two pencils.

"Only one of them has an eraser," she said.

"I've never seen you do anything with a pencil. Other than break it," Jacob said.

"He taps them," Eve said.

"When do you think we'll get a decision from Judge Abbott?" Jacob said.

"I have no idea," Burr said.

"What do we need to do to get ready for Collin's trial?" Eve said.

"Burr," Jacob said.

There's an elephant in the room.

Burr put his hands on his desk, palms down. He looked over at the empty couch and did his best not to tear up. "I miss him. I can't believe he's gone. I keep looking over at the couch, but he's not there." He stopped, then, "And he's never going to be there again."

"I'm so sorry," Eve said.

"I am, too." Jacob ran a thumb and forefinger on the crease of his midnight blue slacks.

"You never liked him," Burr said.

"I did like him."

"You called him a cur."

"No, I didn't."

"You did. Every time you saw him."

"I did not."

"All you ever did was complain about his shedding."

"That's not true."

"Zeke liked you."

"I liked him," Jacob said.

"You didn't like him, but it's all right," Eve said.

Jacob took his freshly pressed, snow-white handkerchief from the breast pocket of his midnight blue jacket and wiped his eye. "You're right. I didn't like Zeke. You're right about that." He looked at his hands, then at Burr. "I didn't like him, but you did. You loved him. That's what matters." Jacob let all his breath out. "I'm sorry for your loss. I truly am." Jacob started to cry. So did Burr. Eve wiped tears from her eyes. Burr turned to the window.

How am I going to get through this?

No one said anything. Burr looked out at the empty downtown. Finally,

"There's nothing to do but get on with it," he said, still looking out the window.

* * *

Burr didn't get on with it.

He came to his office later and later each day, and when he was there, he didn't get anything done. He sat at his desk and looked at the empty couch or looked out his window. He broke all his pencils. Eve wouldn't buy him another box.

"If you want to break something, break sticks. They're free."

He couldn't bring himself to take a nap on his couch. He loved that couch, but it smelled like Zeke. He couldn't even sit on it.

January gave way to February, and he quit coming to his office altogether.

He stayed in his apartment, rarely ate, slept most of the time. He quit shaving, then quit getting dressed. Eve ran the office as she'd always done. Jacob wrote the briefs, but the work was running out.

Finally, Eve couldn't stand it any longer. She knocked on Burr's door. No answer. She waited a minute, then knocked again. Still no answer.

"I'm coming in." She took the key to his apartment out of her purse. She'd insisted on having a key, not because she wanted one, but because she was sure Burr would lose his. Which he had. Time and again.

"I'm coming in. Are you decent?"

He was sitting in his La-Z-Boy looking out the window, not that there was much to see. There was an urn on the end table next to him.

"It's me. Eve."

Burr nodded but didn't say anything. She walked over to him and kissed him lightly on the cheek. His whiskers scratched her chin. "You haven't shaved in days. Or showered." She pulled up a chair from the dining room table and sat next to him.

"How are you?"

He nodded.

"Is that Zeke next to you?"

No response.

"Let me get you a cup of coffee."

Burr had left the Mr. Coffee on. The coffee had burned out of the pot. There was a black crust on the bottom.

"This is disgusting. I'll be right back. Don't go anywhere. Not that it's very likely."

She came back ten minutes later with a cup of coffee, freshly brewed from the Lafayette and Wertheim coffeemaker, made just the way he liked it. Strong with cream. She handed it to him, but he wouldn't take it.

"I'm going to put it here, next to Zeke." She set it down next to the urn and sat back down.

They sat there, quietly, silently, neither one saying anything. Finally, Eve got up and left. She came back with another cup. "I'll join you." She sipped her coffee.

Burr's cup was half empty. "That's a good sign," she said, mostly to herself.

"We miss you at the office, and we need your help."

Burr nodded again but still didn't say anything. Eve drank more of her coffee. She looked around the apartment. There were newspapers on the floor, dishes in the sink, and piles of clothes on the furniture. "This is a disaster." She looked at Burr. "I'm sorry for your loss. Very sorry. Zeke was a good dog."

"He was my best friend," Burr said, not looking up.

"I thought I was your best friend."

Burr smiled, just a little smile.

"Jacob and I miss you, and we need you. We're running out of work."

"I'm not feeling much like working."

"I can see that. How about if I fix you some eggs and you take a shower."

"I'm fine."

"You've got to eat something. And you smell like a locker room." She stood. "I'm going to run the shower and scramble some eggs."

She did the dishes, which had enough mold to culture penicillin. The eggs were spoiled, and the bread was moldy. She made him oatmeal with cream and sugar from the office.

"Eat," she said.

She finished cleaning the kitchen, then walked back to Burr and Zeke.

"You ate your oatmeal. That's a start." She jumped up. "Damn it, I forgot about the shower."

The water still ran hot. "The hot water is the only thing that works in this building. Go take a shower."

"I don't feel like it."

"You *can* speak."

Burr smiled a little again.

"I'm really sorry about Zeke. He had a great run. You had great adventures. You took wonderful care of him, but it was his time. That's what you said. You said he was ready." She put her hand on his knee. "It's fine to grieve. I get it, but you need to start living again. Just a little."

"I just can't seem to get going."

She took his hand. "Would another dog help? A puppy? A new best friend?"

"I can't bear the thought of outliving another dog."

"At the rate you're going, that's not very likely."

He turned away.

"We're all in this together. We all have responsibilities. You're being too self-absorbed. Even for you."

He didn't say anything. Again.

"How is Zeke-the-Boy doing?"

"He doesn't want to be called that anymore."

"There's no reason to call him that now."

"No, there isn't."

"How is he doing?"

"I haven't seen him."

Eve shook her head. "Burr, it's one thing to sit here by yourself and mope. Maybe not mope. Mourn or grieve, I guess. But you have a son who needs you. Especially now. He loved Zeke, too."

"He did."

"You named him after Zeke."

"I did."

"Yes, you did. And we have work to do across the hall."

Burr didn't say anything for at least the fifth time.

"We're going to get a decision from Judge Abbott soon, and there's the small matter of the murder trial." She stood. "It's okay with me if you want to be by yourself. I get it." She started for the door. "But you need to rejoin the land of the living."

* * *

Burr stayed in his chair all day, but he did get dressed. He took a shower every once in a while. Eve made him breakfast and lunch every day. She was his only visitor until Jacob barged in unannounced.

"It happened."

Burr arched his eyebrows.

"Does that mean you actually want to know what happened?"

"Not really."

"We just got Judge Abbott's decision."

He kept on not saying anything.

"If you're not going to ask, I'll tell you." Jacob sat. "Judge Abbott said Ballantine was within his rights to terminate the lease. She dismissed us. We lost. Ballantine is free to sell Thorne Swift to Smart. It's terrible. Terrible. That's what it is."

Burr nodded.

"Don't nod at me. What should we do?"

"Whatever you think best."

"What I think best? What I think best? I want to know what you think."

"I don't really care."

"Damn it, Burr. We need to save Thorne Swift, and we need more clients."

* * *

Jacob appealed.

Aunt Kitty came to see Burr. She was sympathetic at first, but it didn't end up that way. "You have work to do." She left in a huff.

Burr was glad to see Victor, not to mention surprised. He rarely left Walpole, and he never came to the states. He didn't have a passport. Burr thought he must have come over by boat and borrowed a car at Algonac. It was nervy, and Burr was grateful.

He brought a hand-carved drake mallard decoy, hollow on the inside. He put Zeke's ashes in it.

There's no place Zeke would rather be.

Maggie came with Finn. He didn't know if he was happier to see her or her dog. He hadn't seen much of her in the past year. He'd missed her, but she wanted to get married, and he wasn't ready for that.

Not now. Probably not ever.

Then Zeke-the-Boy showed up unannounced.

Burr sat up straight in his chair.

"What are you doing here?"

"I came to see you. Because you won't come see me."

"Where's your mother? How did you get here?"

"I took a cab," Zeke said.

"A cab?"

"I don't have a driver's license."

"A cab?"

Zeke opened the refrigerator. "There's nothing to eat."

"You took a cab? How did you pay for it?"

"I didn't. He's waiting downstairs."

Burr got out of his chair. "I'll pay him."

"How will I get home?"

"Does Mom know you're here?"

"No."

"What were you thinking?"

"That I wanted to see you. See how you're doing."

"I'm fine. I'll go pay him."

"How will I get home?"

"I'll take you."

The taxi was waiting at the curb. Burr and Zeke-the-Boy. Or was it Aaron? The two of them walked over to the cab. The driver was snoring softly, his forehead on the steering wheel.

Zeke opened the back door. Burr slammed it. "You're not going anywhere."

The driver jumped in his seat.

"I'm going home."

"You just got here."

"Now that I can see you're all right, I'm going home."

"The first thing we're going to do is call your mother. Then we're going to get something to eat and figure out what to do."

Zeke grabbed the door handle. Burr put his hand over Zeke's.

"You're not in charge of me."

"I'm your father."

"Then why did you leave?"

I deserved that.

"I left your mother, not you."

"You left both of us."

The taxi driver rolled down his window. "The meter's running."

"How much?"

"Won't know until we get back." He scratched the black stubble on his chin.

"It's a round trip. That's what the kid said."

"I don't care if you keep the meter running for the rest of your life. I'm paying you for a one-way trip. How much?"

The driver scratched his ear this time, then, "One fifty."

"One fifty what?" Burr said.

"Hundred and fifty dollars." He smiled at Burr. "Cash."

Damn it all.

Burr pulled a handful of cash from his pocket and paid the driver two hundred even.

"Let's call Mom. We'll get something to eat, and I'll drive you home. Unless you want to spend the night."

CHAPTER ELEVEN

"This is outrageous, Your Honor," Truax said.

Gillis shook his head. "Mr. Truax, have you ever noticed that virtually everything is outrageous to you?"

"Things are only outrageous when he's involved." The prosecutor glared at Burr.

We're right back where we started.

"Mr. Lafayette, what exactly is it that you want, and why do you want it?" Gillis said.

After paying the cab driver, Burr and Zeke had taken the stairs back up to his apartment. He called Grace who was not delighted to hear from him and most certainly not delighted to hear that Zeke had skipped school and taken a cab to East Lansing. Burr took Zeke for a late lunch at Tripper's, with pool but not Labatt. They went sledding on the hill behind Frandor, then spent the evening with pizza and Coke in front of the television with an MSU basketball game. The Spartans won, as they usually did. Burr thought it was good for Zeke to root for a winner.

I'm not sure I'm a winner. At least not at the moment. I was, though.

The next morning, he drove his son back to Grosse Pointe, dropping him off at school and avoiding Grace—and the lecture he so richly deserved.

That afternoon he filed a motion with Judge Gillis. Now, a week later, he'd driven to Petoskey. He looked over at the passenger seat for Zeke at least two dozen times on the way, but Zeke wasn't there. Zeke, his son— formerly Zeke-the-Boy, now Aaron, at least for now—had jolted him back to the land of the living. It was one thing to ignore his practice, but it was quite another to ignore his son. He'd been derelict and he knew it. He knew his divorce had affected Zeke, but he hadn't known how much. He should have known. He'd done his best, but his best was probably a C+. He was going to do better, and part of that was getting back to work.

And here he was, back in court.

"Your Honor, it is not outrageous to ask for a delay, especially under the circumstances."

"And those circumstances are?"

"Your Honor, there has been a death in the family."

"Whose family?" the judge said.

Here goes.

"Mine, Your Honor."

"Who died?" Truax said.

"You're not asking the questions," Burr said.

"Who died?" Gillis said.

Burr ran his hands through his hair. "A close relative, Your Honor."

"Who?" Truax said.

Gillis glared at Truax.

"Who?" the judge said.

"My nephew," Burr said.

My nephew, Zeke-the-Dog.

"And who might that be?" Truax said.

Burr walked up to Gillis. "Your Honor, is it so much to ask for a delay? What is the possible harm?"

"Counsel is abusing the judicial process," Truax said.

Burr turned toward Truax. "Not only are you totally lacking in any sense of human decency. You must have been sick on the day they taught turn-taking in kindergarten."

Gillis tapped his gavel in the palm of his hand. "Mr. Lafayette, I am going to grant your request, but I want you to provide me with a death certificate. We are adjourned." He tapped his gavel on the desk.

* * *

"You don't have a nephew," Jacob said.

"That's right," Burr said.

"You don't have any relatives at all. Except for Aunt Kitty and Zeke-the-Boy."

"Aaron," Burr said.

"What?"

"He wants to be called Aaron."

"Who?"

"Zeke."

Burr had returned, triumphant from Judge Gillis's courtroom. He'd gotten an extension and felt like he had gotten on with things, or at least he was heading in the right direction.

Eve sat back in her blue chair. "Just to review the bidding, you did get the trial postponed, but you have to produce the death certificate of your nephew."

Burr nodded.

"And you can't produce a death certificate because you don't have a nephew, and if you did have a nephew, he's not dead."

Burr nodded again.

"And Zeke-the-Boy doesn't want to be called Zeke."

Burr nodded a third time.

"He wants to be called Aaron," Eve said.

"This is a fine mess," Jacob said.

"Let's move on," Burr said. "We need to get going on trial prep."

"How can you possibly produce a death certificate for a nephew you don't have?"

"I was hoping Gillis would forget about it."

"He might forget but Truax won't," Jacob said.

Probably right.

"So, what are you going to do?"

"We're going to find ourselves a couple of suspects, just like we always do."

"That dog of yours has caused all of these problems."

Burr looked over at the blue leather couch where Zeke wasn't.

"You gave up on life, on all of us, and if it weren't for Zeke-the-Boy—"

"Aaron."

"Whatever. If it weren't for your son, you'd still be in bed with two weeks of whiskers," Jacob said.

"Burr shaved once a week," Eve said. "Most of the time."

Thank you.

Jacob picked an imaginary dog hair from his slacks.

"You do not have a dog hair on your slacks, and if you did, it would be an honor," Burr said

"That cur."

"I love that word."

"That dog is ruling from the grave. I can't get away from him," Jacob said. "No matter what I do."

Burr stood and looked out the window, his back to Jacob and Eve. Another gray day in East Lansing. Thirty-five and slushy.

"Maybe the sun will come out someday."

"What's that?" Jacob said.

"Burr needs his light," Eve said.

Jacob stood. "I give up."

"What we need are a few suspects." Burr turned back to Jacob and Eve. "Let's start with Frank."

"While we're looking for suspects, there's also the little matter of Thorne Swift," Jacob said. "Smart can buy it now."

Burr ignored his partner. "Let's find out who Frank Slaughter was. What he was like."

Jacob left in a huff.

* * *

"Zeke, we need the four-wheel drive." Burr pulled off on the shoulder of M-68 and put the Jeep in neutral. He shoved the lever on the floor and shifted into four-wheel drive. Nothing happened. He wiggled it back and forth. Still nothing. He looked in the rearview mirror and saw the snow piling up on the back window where the windshield wiper would have been if he hadn't broken it off.

"The damn thing never worked right."

Burr pushed and pulled and pushed again. The transmission clunked. He put the Jeep in gear. It groaned, and off they went, at all of twenty miles an hour.

There were flurries at Grayling, light snow at Gaylord, and now, just outside Indian River, the snow was falling like it meant it. That, and the wind was blowing at twenty-five from the northeast.

"Zeke, old friend, is it ever going to stop snowing?"

Burr had always talked to Zeke. The dog wasn't much of a conversation-alist, but he was a good listener, and as long as Zeke was close by, no one thought Burr was crazy when he was talking to himself.

"That's probably not true about talking to ashes in a decoy."

Burr looked at what was left of Zeke in the hollowed-out drake mallard decoy Victor had carved. Zeke had always ridden shotgun, and Burr had always talked to him. He couldn't get used to looking at the passenger seat without Zeke in it, and he couldn't stop talking to him. Talking to Zeke's ashes was a poor substitute, but it was all he had, and he didn't feel as sad talking to the decoy full of Zeke.

"I am definitely not on my game."

The Jeep groaned through Alanson and Oden, past Crooked Lake, not that he could see it through the snow. At Pleasant View Road, he turned north, then west on Quick Road, Boyne Highlands to his right. The plows hadn't made it out yet and the snow drifted across the road. He turned into a driveway just past the nursery, pines and spruce covered with snow, the rest of the trees bare. He swerved and just missed the riding snowplow.

"This driveway is at least half a mile long."

The driveway was clear to the house. The snowplow followed him. Burr parked in front of the garage. The snowplow pulled up alongside him. The driver rapped on Burr's window. He pushed the switch, but the window didn't budge.

"Frozen." Burr cracked open the door.

"You're late."

"It's snowing," Burr said.

"That's why I'm plowing."

Why don't you wait until it stops.

"It's best to plow with the snow."

A mind reader.

"Follow me." The plow drove up the sidewalk to the front door. The driver got off and went inside, leaving the door open.

Burr left the remains of Zeke in the Jeep and walked into the house. The driver had stripped out of her orange snowsuit, her back to Burr, her blonde hair hanging over her shoulders. She turned toward Burr, red cheeks and red nose. She wore a blue turtleneck sweater over jeans stuck into a pair of

Sorels. She had a thin face, a pointed nose, and bags under her eyes. Pretty in a thin, tired way.

"You're late," she said again.

Burr ignored her. "Thanks for taking the time to meet with me, Mrs. Slaughter."

She stepped out of her boots and her snowsuit and walked off. "Take your shoes off and come with me." She marched off. "Don't get snow on the floor. It gets slippery."

Burr took off his boots and followed her into the kitchen. She started boiling water in a teakettle.

"Tea?"

"Do you have peppermint?"

"What kind of lawyer drinks peppermint tea?"

She rummaged around the cupboard. "I drink Earl Grey." She took out two mugs, filled them with boiling water, and dropped a tea bag into each one and took them to a table by a double window. Burr pulled out her chair.

He walked to the other chair and stuck out his hand. "Burr Lafayette."

"I know who you are," she said, not shaking his hand. Burr looked at his hand, put it in his pocket, then sat across from her.

"Thank you for seeing me," he said. "I'm so sorry for your loss."

"Thank you." She dunked her tea bag. "I still can't believe he's gone."

"I'm so sorry," he said again.

She sipped her tea. "It's hot. Be careful. What is it that you want?"

Burr looked out the window. Emmet County was filling up with snow. *Is it ever going to stop?*

Burr sipped his tea.

This is terrible.

"Frank wanted to live way back here. He got an easement from the nursery. It's our driveway, but it's their ground, and now I'm the one who's got to keep it plowed. It's not my idea of a good time."

Burr looked out the window. The driveway was already covered in snow. He couldn't see the road.

"I hope the bus gets the kids home. There's no such thing as a snow day in Harbor Springs." She sipped her tea again. "It's cooling off."

Burr smiled at her and sipped his tea.

I only like peppermint.

With Victor and Zeke. Now it will only be Victor.

"Mrs. Slaughter—"

"Call me Jill."

"Jill," he said, "it's very nice of you to see me."

"Let's get on with it."

"As you may know, I represent Collin Murphy."

She nodded.

"I'd like to learn a little more about your husband."

"Why do you need to know anything about Frank?"

"It may help me defend Mr. Murphy."

"That self-righteous bastard killed my husband."

He may have.

"Mrs. Slaughter, I'd just like to learn a little about your husband."

"Jill," she said again.

"Jill."

"Like what?"

"Did he have any enemies? Anyone who might have wanted to harm him?"

"You mean stab him with a Swiss Army knife and hide him in a swamp in another one of those stupid preserves?"

"Did your husband have any enemies?"

She looked out the window, then at Burr. "Everybody loved Frank. I did, too."

She doesn't look like she's going to cry.

"He was the caretaker at Thorne Swift in the summer. He could have upset someone."

"It was just a summer job. Something to do when school was out."

"It seems like your husband got upside down with Mr. Murphy. He said Frank beat him and took his camera."

"Frank would never do that." She looked out the window, then back at Burr. "If that's what you think, you can leave right now."

I'll never get past the end of the driveway.

"I'm sorry, but I have a client."

"And I have two teenagers to raise. By myself." She stood and walked to the refrigerator. "They're going to want a snack after ski practice." She opened the refrigerator, picked through the shelves, then took out a

Tupperware container. "Hamburger, noodle, and onion. Joey's favorite. Allie doesn't like it much, though." She closed the refrigerator. "This house isn't much by Harbor Springs standards, but it's ours. Ours and the bank's."

"What about the camera?"

"What about it?"

"Mr. Murphy said your husband knocked him unconscious and stole his camera. Then he tried to sell it back to him."

"It's time for you to go."

"I'm sorry, but I have a client to defend."

And a swamp to save.

"Frank wouldn't hurt a fly."

"Who then?"

"We had a nice life here. Frank had a good job at the school. He coached the ski team. We could just about afford for me to be a stay-at-home mom." She paused. "Those days are over.

"I have to go back to work." She walked to the window. "Here comes the school bus. I guess they called off ski practice. Because of the snow." She shook her head.

"I'm really sorry about your husband, but if Frank didn't have the camera, who did?"

"Maybe it just got lost."

She's not telling me everything.

The widow Slaughter started toward the door. "How about Dewey Ballantine? Or Johnson Smart? They had all the reason in the world."

Burr nodded. "Anyone else?"

"I've got to go. The bus will be here any minute." She disappeared into the entryway. Burr followed her. She was putting her snowsuit back on. "The kids like me to pick them up at the end of the driveway. They love to ride on the plow." She zipped up. "They're getting too old for it, but it's what we have together. Without Frank." She put her pink snow hat back on and her leather mittens. "What about Ian?"

"Ian?"

"He never liked Frank."

"Ian?"

"Put your coat on. Follow me so you don't get stuck."

Jill and the plow started down the driveway, Burr following. The bus stopped in front of the driveway. Her kids got out and climbed on the plow. Burr skidded the Jeep into the tire tracks of the bus and trailed behind it.

"Zeke, this is the only way we're going to get out of here."

I've got to stop doing this, but I miss him.

The bus turned south at State Road and Burr followed it to Harbor High, the hundred-year-old, three-story brown brick building on the bluff. It had a spectacular view of Little Traverse Bay. The developers thought it was wasted on high school students and had been trying to buy it for years. The school board always said "no."

Burr parked and went into the school. He wandered around the halls until he found the principal's office.

He walked past the open-mouthed secretary, past the sign that said *Lynne Sheffield, Principal.*

"Do you have an appointment?" a voice from behind him said.

He knocked twice, then walked in.

"Do you have an appointment?" a voice in front of him said.

"I thought I'd just drop in."

Burr stood in front of the desk of *Lynne Sheffield, Principal.* "The only way I could get here was to follow your school bus, and I did want to meet you."

"Me?" The principal, about thirty-five, bundled up in some kind of floor-to-ceiling sweater, didn't smile. She pushed the stocking cap back on her head. She had creamy skin, doe eyes, and no smile.

"Do you have an appointment?" said the voice behind him.

"No, he doesn't, but I think it's all right. I'll scream if he gets out of line."

Finally, someone with a sense of humor.

The secretary left.

"And you are?" the principal said.

"Burr Lafayette."

"Is that supposed to mean something to me?"

A biting sense of humor.

Burr stuck his hand out. She didn't shake it.

"Burr Lafayette. I represent Collin Murphy, and I was hoping I could learn something about Frank Slaughter."

"No, you can't."

"Ms. Sheffield—"

"It's 'Miss,' and I have nothing to say to you."

Burr ignored her. "It will only take a few minutes."

"No."

Burr sat. Miss Sheffield didn't.

"Miss Sheffield, I was just with Mrs. Slaughter. She told me Mr. Slaughter was a teacher here."

"'Was' is the correct tense."

"What did he teach?"

"Math."

"Algebra?"

"And geometry, trigonometry, calculus. This is a small school."

"And he coached?"

"He coached the ski team."

"Thank you so much, Miss Sheffield. I represent Collin Murphy."

"You said that."

"I'm trying to find out if Mr. Slaughter had enemies, someone who might want to kill him."

"Other than your client?"

Here we go again.

She stood and looked out her window. The snow kept falling. "All it does is snow. Especially this year. Never stops. But it's good for Nub's and the Highlands."

"Miss Sheffield, did Frank have any enemies?"

"You already asked me that." She turned to him. "Call me Lynne." Her hand appeared from her full-length sweater, an altogether pleasant hand with rose fingernail polish that matched her lipstick.

"Enemies? Not that I know of. Everyone loved Frank, and he was a good teacher."

"Is there someone who might have had a grudge?"

"Your boots are making puddles on the floor."

Burr looked down at his boots. "I'm sorry."

She sat and swiveled back around to her window. "It doesn't snow like this in Novi. Where I'm from."

"It doesn't snow like this here very often."

"It has ever since I've been here." She turned back to Burr. "We all loved Frank. All of us. Teachers, students, staff."

"Surely there must have been someone."

"This is a small school. We're close to each other. We pride ourselves on our academics."

"My client said Frank beat him, took his camera, and tried to sell it back to him."

She shook her head. "I can't believe Frank would do that. I just can't."

"Did he need money?"

The principal balled her hands into fists. "Frank? Not that I know of."

"Who else at the school could I talk to?"

"Here?" She unclenched her fists. "No one. They'd all say the same thing. We all loved Frank, and we all miss him."

This isn't going anywhere.

"What about Dewey Ballantine? Or Johnson Smart?"

She cocked her head. "Who?"

"Dewey Ballantine is trying to sell Thorne Swift to Johnson Smart."

"I hope he doesn't."

"Could there have been something on Mr. Murphy's camera they wanted?"

"How would I know?" She cocked her head again.

Zeke did that.

Burr looked down at his feet.

"Is there something wrong?" she said.

"A memory."

* * *

Burr sat in Nub's Pub, his second Labatt in front of him.

I'm a big fan of any bar that has Labatt on tap.

He had a table by the plate-glass window that looked out on the slopes, the green four-seat chair lift in front of him, the yellow chair to his right. The blue lift wasn't running. Nub's only ran it when they were busy, which wasn't today. The blue lift was the original chair at Nub's. Old but fast, *Smooth Sailing* on the right, *Birch Run* on the left. It was just after 4:30, skiing over for the day, the ski patrol making one last run to make sure the slopes were clear. The Tucker Sno-Cats had just started up, towing the groomers behind them. Nub's Pub was packed, even on a Tuesday.

The snow is good for Nub's.

A tap on his shoulder. Burr stood. "Thanks for meeting me."

Ian nodded and sat. Burr waved at the waitress.

"That'll take forever." Ian picked his way to the bar and came back with a clear rocks glass full of ice and an olive.

"Man after my own heart," Burr said.

"Vodka," Ian said.

"Never mind." Burr took a swallow of his beer. "How's the ski business?"

"Ski school is full every day. We can't keep up."

"How long have you run it?"

Ian sipped his vodka. "Six … no, seven years. Good money as long as there's snow, which we've gotten plenty of this year."

"You make your own snow."

Nub's had the best snow-making machines in Michigan, maybe in the Midwest. More importantly, Nub's had the best snowmakers. They were particular. Fussy would be a better word, and they worked at night. Eccentric was an understatement.

"You run the ski school?" Burr said.

"I own the ski school. I have a contract with Nub's. They get a cut."

"When does the season end?"

"Did you drive out here in this snow to talk about ski school?"

Burr looked around the bar. Packed with skiers, ski jackets on the backs of their chairs. Hats, mittens, and goggles next to their drinks. The windows started to fog up. A bartender cracked the door to the deck.

Burr shivered.

They're all dressed for it.

"I can tell you all you want to know about the ski school in two minutes."

"I'm trying to figure out who might have wanted to kill Frank."

"No idea."

"Did he have enemies?"

"I don't know."

"I thought everybody loved Frank."

"Someone loved him enough to kill him."

There is that.

"How about Dewey Ballantine or Johnson Smart?"

"I don't think so. Frank worked for them."

"I thought he worked for the Conservancy."

Ian ran his finger around the turtle part of his turtleneck. "That's right, but at the end he worked for Dewey."

Burr waved at the waitress. She ignored him.

"If you want another beer, you're going to have to get it yourself."

Burr stood. Ian handed him his glass. "Stoli on the rocks with a twist."

Ian is an expensive date.

It was Burr's turn to snake his way to the bar. It was surrounded by good-looking women in ski clothes. He felt decidedly out of place in his khakis and Irish setters.

I'm sure they think I'm the help.

Back at the table, "It seems like the trouble started with Collin's camera."

Ian nodded.

"Why would Frank steal it?" Burr said.

"To screw up Collin's study." Ian took a swallow of his drink.

"The camera didn't matter, because the lady's slipper isn't endangered."

"No one knew that at the time."

Burr looked out the window. It was getting dark. The Sno-Cats had their lights on. He looked back at Ian. "Maybe there was something else on the camera."

Ian shook his head. "It doesn't matter what was on the camera."

Burr coughed. The bar was filling up with cigarette smoke. It hung in the wet air.

"It just seems like murder is a bit of an overreach for a stolen camera."

Ian twisted the twist in his drink. "Collin is a hothead. Who knows what he might do if he lost his temper."

"Was he that passionate about the lady's slipper?"

Burr finished his beer.

I should stop at three.

"Are you passionate about the lady's slipper?" Burr said.

Ian leaned toward Burr. "Do you think I killed Frank?"

Burr leaned back in his chair. "No. Of course not. I'm stuck. No suspects and a trial coming up."

CHAPTER TWELVE

Burr pulled the space heater closer to his feet. "I don't have any suspects."

"It's that awful Dewey Ballantine. I know it is," Aunt Kitty said.

He pulled the Hudson Bay blanket around his shoulders.

"Don't get too comfortable." She handed him her glass, but he didn't take it.

I can't go through the martini ritual today. It's too late, and I'm too cold.

She pushed her glass into his hand but didn't say a word.

Burr came back from the kitchen with the closest thing a martini could be to straight gin.

"Where's yours?"

"I've had enough."

"I can't believe my ears," she said, sipping.

"I'm out of suspects," he said.

"And you're going to be out of luck when Gillis finds out your nephew was a dog." She sipped her martini, made a face, but didn't say anything. "Does Dewey have an alibi?"

"No one knows exactly when Frank was killed. So, everyone has an alibi, and no one has an alibi."

"I still think it's Dewey. He had the most to gain."

"So did Smart."

Burr inched his chair closer to the heater. "You really can't stay here. You couldn't get out of here if you had to. There's too much snow, and it's too cold."

"I have a snowmachine."

"I don't think you should be driving one of those things."

"Nonsense. I can't get my car out here."

"Exactly." Burr looked out the front window of Cottage 59. The snow had drifted up to the windows. It was dark and still snowing. He didn't have to see the harbor to know it was frozen. Burr patted Zeke and the mallard decoy on the head.

Aunt Kitty squeezed her eyes shut. "It gives me some comfort that you've returned to the land of the living, but you can't be carrying a decoy with Zeke's ashes everywhere you go."

"I didn't want to leave him in the car."

"My point exactly."

"There must be someone who had a reason to kill Frank."

Aunt Kitty ate her olive.

"There is so much passion around Thorne Swift and the lady's slipper," Burr said.

"Does that make me a suspect?"

Maybe I should have a martini.

"Claire was passionate about it," Burr said.

"You think Claire killed Frank?"

"She could have."

"I'll tell you who was passionate about it," Aunt Kitty said. "Collin. I hate to say it, but he might have done it." She wrapped her blanket a little tighter around her shoulders. "And he was, is, passionate about Claire."

"Claire?"

"Have you seen the moon eyes he makes at her? I don't think she feels the same way. Or at least, not as much."

"I never should have left Fisher and Allen."

"Stop that. You've made yourself a fine life."

"I should have married Maggie when I had the chance."

"Stop feeling sorry for yourself." She looked out the window, then back at Burr. "If Collin didn't do it, who did?"

"I have no idea. Ian? Jill?"

"I doubt it, but it would be helpful if you could find that camera," Aunt Kitty said.

"I think it's gone forever. Not that it matters. We just lost for the last time."

Aunt Kitty stood. The Hudson Bay blanket fell off her lap, but she still had one wrapped around her shoulders. She came over to Burr and put her hand on his shoulder. "Nephew, this is just a minor setback. Go tell Judge Abbott that the Friends of Thorne Swift will match Smart's offer."

"I beg your pardon."

"You heard me."

* * *

Burr spent the night at Cottage 59. He didn't want to stay, but he couldn't leave his aunt by herself in the snowstorm. Not that she wouldn't be by herself tomorrow. Maybe it would stop snowing by then. It had to stop sometime.

His aunt didn't allow space heaters to be plugged in while they slept so he covered the bed with the Hudson Bay blanket, two quilts, and the throw rug from the floor next to his bed. The covers crushed him, and he was still cold. Zeke slept on the nightstand.

* * *

"Mr. Lafayette, as you know, I declined your motion to prohibit the termination of the lease. Which you appealed. Your appeal has now been dismissed by the Court of Appeals. Which you must also know." She waved the motion at him. "What more could you possibly ask me for?"

"Your Honor—"

"And one more thing. The fact that Mr. Murphy is on trial for murder has absolutely no bearing on the right of Mr. Ballantine to sell his property. It is unfortunate for Mr. Murphy, but it has absolutely nothing to do with the matter at hand." She bit her lip. "Unless, of course, he did it. In which case it's not unfortunate."

"Your Honor—"

"Mr. Lafayette, I'm told you're an able, if lucky, criminal lawyer. I wish you all the best."

"There is one thing, Your Honor."

"I don't want to hear it." She raised her gavel.

"Thank you, Your Honor." This, from the freshly pressed Roy Dahlberg.

"Your Honor," Burr said. "There is a group that would like to buy the property from Mr. Ballantine."

"That's ridiculous," Dahlberg said.

It is ridiculous, and I can't believe I let Aunt Kitty convince me to ask for it.

"Your Honor, if the preserve must be sold, why not sell it to a group that will preserve it?"

Dahlberg stepped around his table. "Your Honor, this is ridiculous."

Burr looked over at Dahlberg "You already said that."

She wagged her finger at Burr.

"My client would like to buy the property."

"There already is a buyer," Dahlberg said.

"Your Honor, this is a fair way for everyone to get what they want."

"We already have what we want," Dahlberg said.

"What's the harm?" Burr said.

Dahlberg stepped around his table. "If they were serious about buying the property, they could have done it before all this started."

"I didn't think we'd lose," Burr said, mostly to himself.

Judge Abbott leaned toward Burr. "What did you say?"

"Nothing, Your Honor."

"He said—"

Burr cut Dahlberg off. "I said my client doesn't want to lose the preserve."

"That's not what he said."

"It most certainly is."

"Respectfully, Your Honor, Mr. Ballantine has a binding agreement with Mr. Smart. You can't overturn it."

"Enough." The judge glared at him. "Mr. Lafayette, I'm going to give you thirty days to match the offer Mr. Ballantine has."

"Your Honor, we may need a little—"

"Thirty days. And don't darken my door ever again." She smashed her gavel.

* * *

Burr drove to East Lansing under clear skies.

"Zeke, this is unbelievable," he said to the remains of his aging lab in the decoy urn.

I've got to stop this, but I don't want him to hear me say it.

"This is really silly," Burr said out loud.

He looked out the window at the snow on the cut corn fields.

"At least the freeway is clear and dry."

I'm just talking to myself. That's all I'm doing.

Burr, with Zeke under his arm, climbed the six flights to his office. He put Zeke on his couch and waited for Jacob and Eve to come in, which didn't take long.

Burr told them the tale of Judge Abbott's courtroom.

"You what?" Jacob said.

"It seemed like a good idea at the time."

"I expect Smart will have something to say about this," Jacob said.

"I'm sure he will," Burr said.

"Has anyone given you the slightest inkling that they were interested in raising the money to buy Thorne Swift?" Jacob said.

"Not exactly."

"Does 'not exactly' mean 'no'?"

Eve smiled at him.

"Yes. 'Not exactly' means 'no.'"

"Then all you've done is get yourself into more trouble."

"I bought us a little time."

"You're tilting at windmills again," Eve said.

Jacob looked at Eve. "I beg your pardon?"

"Burr is the Don Quixote of law," Eve said.

"Jacob, that makes you Sancho Panza." Burr smiled at Eve. "You're much too good looking to be Dulcinea."

"Thank you. I think," Eve said.

"Jacob, I need you to find out all you can about Frank Slaughter."

"I am absolutely not going to work on another murder case with you."

"You already are."

"Not anymore."

"We have work to do," Burr said. "I need you to find out what you can about Frank Slaughter. And Claire Fisher."

"I don't work for free."

"I'm going back to Harbor Springs." Burr started for the door.

"You can't keep driving around Robin Hood's barn," Jacob said.

I haven't heard that in a month of Sundays.

"If you're not going to do your job, I'll do it myself."

"All right. I'll do it. Just this once."

"You might as well let him go," Eve said.

"I said I'd help."

"It doesn't matter." Eve looked at Burr. "Judge Gillis wants to see you."

Burr stopped.

"About the death certificate."

"The death certificate?"

"Your nephew."

* * *

Burr looked out at his Jeep. It was cloudy, but at least it wasn't snowing.

The city had yellow front-end loaders and orange dump trucks piling the snow in any open space they could find. There was a twenty-foot-high pile in the park next to the tennis courts, and a thirty-foot pile next to the deer park. But the plows kept Main Street open. Burr parked in front of the real estate office and found Claire Fisher at her desk.

"I'm so glad you're helping us, Mr. Lafayette."

Now that I'm not fired.

"I'm not sure how much help I've been."

"Thorne Swift hasn't been sold yet."

The snow was melting off his boots onto the carpet. He stepped out of the puddle. "We have about a month to come up with the money."

She frowned. "We don't have the money."

"This is our last chance."

"The plan was to stop the development. Not to buy Thorne Swift. It's much cheaper that way."

It's really cheap if you don't pay me either.

"Claire, you sell real estate. At the end of the day, Thorne Swift is going to be sold. To somebody."

"It doesn't have to be that way."

It's always easy when it's somebody else's money.

Burr leaned back in his chair. The front legs came off the floor.

"Thorne Swift belongs to Dewey Ballantine. The judge said he had the right to terminate the lease. He can do what he wants."

"Thorne Swift needs to stay the way it is."

"Unless you raise the money to buy it, Dewey has the right to sell it."

"You can stop it."

"It's his property."

"But the lady's slipper is endangered."

"No, it isn't."

"That's what you told the judge."

"That was at least five motions ago."

"That's what you told the judge," she said again.

"That's how it started. That's not where it is now."

"You have to do something."

Burr ignored her. "Claire, about you and Collin."

"What?"

"You and Collin."

"What do you mean, 'me and Collin?'"

"You know. Are you …" Burr leaned forward. The chair came down on all four legs. "An item?"

"An item?"

"You know … together. Boyfriend and girlfriend."

"Collin and me?"

"I've seen the way he looks at you."

"We're friends." Claire put her hands on her desk, then she put the right hand over the left and squeezed.

"If Collin has anything to say about it, I'd say you're more than friends."

"What does that have to do with anything?"

"Is that why you hired him?"

"I didn't hire him. The Conservancy hired him. And he's the best there is."

She squeezed both her hands together.

Your hands are giving you away.

"I'm just trying to understand how all this fits together."

"What you need to fit together is how to save Thorne Swift."

"Should I save Thorne Swift or Collin?"

Claire squeezed her hands together again. "Collin," she said. "Save Collin."

I'm not sure Collin is her first choice.

* * *

Half an hour later, Burr was in Judge Gillis's chambers. The judge sat behind a walnut desk that must have taken the better part of a woodlot to build. Burr sat in a wobbly, straight-backed chair.

This thing is made of toothpicks.

Gillis wore a heavy, dark brown suit that looked like a throw rug. Burr sat quietly. Finally, "I was wondering where Mr. Truax is."

"I haven't the faintest idea."

"I thought you wanted to see us."

"Just you."

"Your Honor?"

"This is between the two of us." He pointed at Burr, then poked his chest with his forefinger. "You and me."

"Your Honor?" he said again.

"The death certificate."

"The death certificate?"

"Where is it?"

"Where is what?"

"You have no idea what I'm talking about?" Gillis picked up his gavel, thought better of it, then set it back down.

Burr smiled at Gillis, weakly.

"Mr. Lafayette, I granted you a delay because you said you had an urgent family matter. A death in your family. That's what you said."

Damn it all.

"The death certificate?"

"You heard me. That's the only reason I granted you a delay. As you may recall, Mr. Truax was furious." The judge fondled his gavel. "As a show of good faith, I did not ask Mr. Truax to be here today." Gillis put his hand out. "Please give me the death certificate."

Burr reached into the breast pocket of his jacket for what he knew wasn't there. His hand came out empty. "I'm sorry, Your Honor, I didn't know that's why you wanted to see me."

"Don't come back to this court without it." Gillis slammed his gavel on his desk.

* * *

Burr drove back to Harbor Springs, then took State Road north about two miles. He turned into a gravel driveway with shoulder-high snowbanks on each side.

He looked over at the decoy. "What am I going to do about a death certificate?"

He got out of his Jeep and walked up to a pole barn with an office tacked onto the front. The daylight was fading, but in late February there was still light at six o'clock.

He knocked on the door. No answer. He knocked again. Still no answer. The doorknob turned in his hand, and he walked in. A desk and matching chair, harvest brown. The desk had a finish so bright he could see himself in it. A grain with streaks and swirls that looked like they'd been drawn on the wood. He ran his hand on the desktop. It was smooth and slippery.

The rest of the office wasn't much. Off-white walls, a file cabinet, a refrigerator, a door to the pole barn, and sawdust everywhere, except on the desk.

How does he keep it so clean?

Burr heard the whine of a saw on the other side of the door. Inside, Ian Nash, his back to Burr, wore safety glasses at a table saw, doing, of all things, sawing. A teenaged girl, also wearing safety glasses, stood next to him, watching him work. She had blonde hair and was almost as tall as he was. Behind them, the skeleton of a sailboat in a cradle. Burr walked in between the half-built sailboat and the saw, where they both could see him. The girl looked up at him—Ian kept sawing.

I don't want to scare him into cutting his finger off.

Ian worked at the saw.

He's lost in his work. I could probably learn something from him.

Burr turned around and looked at what was going to be a sailboat. The keel was about a foot off the concrete floor. Then came the hull. The planks fastened to the ribs like so many bones on a skeleton. The deck would be on top of that, three feet above Burr.

This boat is going to draw at least six feet.

The girl tapped Ian on the arm. The saw stopped. "She's going to be an NM," the girl said.

They both pushed their safety glasses up on their foreheads.

They look like they've got four eyes.

"I wondered if that's what she was."

"Most of an NM is underwater," Ian said.

They were the fastest boats on Little Traverse Bay in their day. There were faster boats now, but none as beautiful.

Ian wiped his hands on his jeans. "I don't suppose you're here to commission me to build you a boat."

Burr shook his head. "This is my daughter, Megan," Ian said.

The girl stuck her hand out to Burr. "Meg."

They shook hands, then Burr ran his hand along the planks of the hull. He stuck himself with a sliver. "Damn it all." He sucked on his finger.

"You're going to need a needle to get that out," Ian said.

"I'm here about Collin and the murder trial."

"Let's get that thing out before it gets infected." He went over to the cabinet next to the wall and came back with a first aid kit.

"I can take care of it later."

"Let's do it now. Before it gets used to being in there." He fished around inside the first aid kit and came out with a bottle of hydrogen peroxide and a needle.

"Meg, would you go get a Band-Aid for Mr. Lafayette?"

"There's Band-Aids in the first aid kit."

"They're all shriveled up."

She made a face at her father and left.

Ian held Burr's finger. He started poking.

"Ouch."

"Hold still."

Burr wiggled again. Ian stopped.

"I build boats when I'm not running the ski school, which is most of the time. Nub's is closing soon. Right now, I've got both jobs. I'm good at building boats, but it seems like I'm always one boat away from being out of business.

Just like me.

Ian held Burr's finger with one hand and poked him with the other. It was all Burr could do not to jerk his hand away.

"Ian." Burr gritted his teeth. "It seems like you spent a lot of time at Thorne Swift with the kids. Why?"

"Megan goes to camp, and they need help."

"Why you?"

"What do you mean, 'why me'? I'm her father. I work for myself. I take a little time off and help. She likes it. I like it." He poked again. "This thing is really in there."

I can't look at this.

"What about Thorne Swift? Is it as simple as it seems?"

"As simple as it seems? A fight over real estate and an endangered flower that isn't. What's simple about that?" He stopped poking and looked at Burr. "We talked about this at Nub's."

"Does her mother help out, too?"

"Her mother?"

"With the camp."

"Megan's mother is dead."

"I'm so sorry. How did it happen?"

Ian looked out the window, then back at Burr. "She died during childbirth." He poked Burr's finger again. Deeper this time. "There it is." He dug it out.

"Ouch."

Ian held up the sliver. "An inch long."

Burr's finger bled.

* * *

"This is another fine mess," Jacob said.

"Not really," Burr said, sitting behind his desk.

"Not really? How can you possibly say 'not really'?"

"I've had bigger problems."

"Like when?"

"How about when Burr was thrown out of court for having two thousand dollars in parking tickets?" This from Eve, in her place, as were Jacob and what was left of Zeke, lounging on the blue couch.

"It wasn't two thousand," Burr said.

"It was more than two thousand," Eve said. "Or when you were arrested for drunk driving."

"It wasn't drunk driving."

"It most certainly was." Eve looked at Jacob. "Or when he spent the night in jail because you were growing marijuana on the roof?"

Jacob lost his color. "There is very good sun on the roof."

"Jacob, old friend, nothing bad has happened yet."

"There will be the next time you see Gillis."

"I'll figure something out."

"You do not have a death certificate of a close family member. You don't have close family members."

"He has Zeke and Aunt Kitty," Eve said.

"You can't wish them dead over this."

"Right," Burr said. "Now, where were we?"

"We haven't gotten past your silly story about the death of a close relative."

"I couldn't think of anything else to say."

"You've made it worse."

"I was distraught. I'm still distraught."

"Burr bought himself some time. While he got back on his feet."

Thank you, Eve.

Burr looked at the couch. "We've got to get on with it."

Jacob shook his head. Eve nodded.

Burr drummed his fingers on his desk. "I don't think a camera is a good enough reason to kill someone."

"Maybe there was something on the film that Collin had to have," Jacob said. "And he killed Frank to get it back."

"There wasn't any film. It was a digital camera," Eve said.

"Whatever."

"Stop it," Burr said.

"Maybe Collin is lying," Jacob said.

"Maybe there was something else on the camera." Burr started drumming again.

"Would you please stop that," Jacob said.

"We've got to try something else."

"Don't include 'me' in 'we,'" Jacob said.

"Don't say a word about not getting paid. I'll figure that part out."

"Just like you always do."

Burr ignored him. "Jacob, see what you can find out about our cast of characters. Ballantine, Smart, Ian, Claire. Jill, too. Any one of them could have done it."

"I thought you already talked to them," Eve said.

"I did, and I didn't get anywhere."

"If you didn't get anywhere, what in the world am I supposed to do?"

"I don't know what else to do. We're at the 'grasping at straws' stage."

"We always end up here," Jacob said.

"I have never met anyone so positive. Why do I put up with you?"

"Because I'm the best researcher and writer in the universe."

"And modest," Burr said.

"Don't forget cheap," Eve said.

Jacob scowled at Eve. "I'm not cheap. I charge a fair rate. It's just that I don't get paid." He gave Burr a half smile. "Burr, old man, I know you abhor the simple solution—and the obvious one—but it's conceivable that Collin did kill Frank.

"If Frank stole Collin's camera, and then tried to sell it back to him, Collin would be really angry. Anyone would. And Frank was murdered with Collin's Swiss Army knife. And Collin has a bad temper."

"Occam's razor," Burr said.

"I beg your pardon."

"Sometimes, the obvious answer is the right one," Eve said.

CHAPTER THIRTEEN

Burr parked in the "No Parking" spot in front of the greenhouses at Michigan State University. Row after row with translucent glass above waist high brick walls. They sparkled in the sun.

There must be fifty of these things.

Burr tried to open the door of the closest greenhouse. It was locked. As was the one next to it, and the one next to that.

The greenhouses were on the south side of campus, and it was only a ten-minute drive from his office, but it didn't matter how close they were if he couldn't get into them, let alone find Collin.

Just as he was about to give up, Burr found a doorknob that turned.

"It must be eighty in here."

"Shut the door. You'll kill the plants."

There were rows and rows of waist-high racks full of plants. Burr looked around but couldn't see a soul.

"You're going to kill everything in here."

"I beg your pardon?"

A face popped up, a young woman with a smudge on her cheek that matched the smudge on her forehead. "Shut the door."

"I'm looking for Collin Murphy."

"He's not here."

"I can see that."

"Try number twenty-seven. It's that way," she said, pointing. "Shut the door on your way out."

Burr found building twenty-seven. The doorknob turned in his hand. He opened and shut the door behind him.

"I am trainable. After a fashion."

An arm wrapped around his neck, choking him. Burr grabbed for it, but a hand wrenched his arm behind his back.

"Let me go. It's me, Burr."

Burr couldn't breathe, and felt like he was going to pass out. He kicked behind him. The hands let go. Burr sprang forward.

His attacker was doubled over. Burr picked up a flowerpot and was about to smash it on the attacker's head when the man stood up.

It was Collin. Collin in a white lab coat with a torn sleeve and a smudge on his nose.

"You almost killed me," Burr said.

Collin held his groin. "You may have ruined my ability to have children."

"If you keep this up, you're not going to have the chance."

"What?"

"You'll be in jail."

"I didn't know who you were."

Burr rubbed his neck. Collin rubbed his groin.

"Do you attack everyone you don't recognize?"

"I'm not supposed to be here."

Burr looked around the greenhouse. Rows and rows of tables, all filled with plants, just like the other greenhouse. But there was a difference.

"What's that smell?"

"Orchids."

"They smell so …"

"Sensual," Collin said.

"And …"

"Exotic."

"I was thinking more like …"

"Erotic."

"I can finish my own sentences." Burr rubbed his arm. "You've got to calm down. If you keep fighting with everyone, Gillis will revoke your bail. And there won't be a thing I can do about it."

"I thought you were an intruder."

"Don't be such a hothead."

Collin walked over to one of the tables. He plucked dead leaves from the base of one of his orchids. It had a pink and white flower the size of a man's fist. He stroked the flower, lovingly. "It's getting too much water. That's why the bottom leaves are dying."

Of course.

"That's what happens when grad students take care of things in here." Collin pulled the bottom leaves off the next plant. "They're fragile."

I was thinking 'fussy.'

"The university put me on administrative leave."

"Because of the murder charge?"

Collin nodded. "These orchids will all die if the grad students take care of them."

He loves his orchids.

"All my research gone to waste."

"Research?"

"I've got three grants. The first one is—"

Burr held up his hand. "Collin, you've been charged with murder. If you're convicted, you and these orchids won't see each other again for a very long time. If ever."

"These orchids are all I have."

"What do you mean?"

"I don't have any family."

"I'm sorry."

"Maybe Claire. Someday."

Burr nodded.

"And I didn't kill Frank."

I'm not so sure.

"I know you didn't, but it doesn't look good. Frank beat you up, then he took your camera. That's what you said. And that's a bad start. Then he offered it back to you. For a price. You were seen arguing with him."

"Anybody would do that."

"That's the problem. Not everyone would. And hardly anyone would start a fistfight over it."

"I didn't start a fistfight."

"That depends on who you ask."

"I may have given him a little push."

Collin took a step toward Burr who took a step back.

"You have a temper, and that has a lot to do with why you've been accused of murdering Frank. And then there's your alibi. Which you don't have."

Collin moved to the next plant. "Whose side are you on?"

"Are you listening to me?"

Collin plucked.

"And there's the small matter of the murder weapon."

More plucking.

"Frank was murdered with your Swiss Army knife. Which, at some point, Truax is going to figure out."

Still more plucking.

"Damn it all. Stop whatever it is you're doing and look at me."

Collin stopped plucking and looked at Burr. "I've told you over and over again, Frank took my knife after he knocked me out. I didn't have it."

"You could have taken it from him when you followed him down Fourth Street. Or maybe you had it all along." Burr looked at Collin's smudge.

I'd really like to rub that off.

"Whose side are you on?"

"I'm on your side but Truax has all the cards."

Collin moved to the next plant.

"Stop it. No more plucking."

Collin kicked at a foodball-sized pile of dirt.

"It seems like Frank was part saint."

Collin looked at the next plant. He put his hands in his pockets.

It's all he can do to stand there.

Burr walked over to Collin and looked at one of the orchids.

The bottom leaves are dead.

Burr pulled off a brown leaf. "Is this what happens when they get too much water?"

"That's why I have to be here. To save them."

"What does Claire think?"

"She hasn't been here since I was suspended."

"About the case."

"She's beside herself."

It didn't seem that way to me.

"She wants this over so we can get on with things."

"Saving Thorne Swift?"

"That. And the two of us."

* * *

Burr sat across from Truax. Neither one of them said a word. Burr did his best to avoid looking at the plaques, certificates, and trophies that covered his desk, the walls, and the shelves that marked a mediocre career.

I'm sure he's got a Kiwanis Club award in here somewhere.

Burr looked at the prosecutor's desk.

At least he's got some family pictures. Unless they're fake.

Truax cleared his throat but still didn't say anything.

The first one to say anything loses.

Burr looked over at Truax who looked away, then made a show of reading through a file.

Not a word from either of them.

This is silly, but I'll be damned if I'll be the first one to say anything.

They sat there. And sat there. Burr memorized the inscription on Truax's Lions Club service award.

He's really something.

Burr looked over at Truax again who was looking at him. The prosecutor looked back down at his file.

The clock ticked. Minutes passed. Neither said a word.

We're off to a good start, and we haven't even started.

More of the same. Finally, "I suppose you'd like to know why you're here."

"Not really."

"I invited you here so you could plead this."

"Plead what?"

"Come on, Lafayette. You'll never get Murphy off. He's guilty as sin and you know it. I've got everything I need to convict him of first-degree murder."

"I hardly think so," Burr said, who did think so.

"He was seen arguing with Frank. He was seen following Frank, and he had a motive. Plus, he has no alibi."

"Neither does anyone else."

"There is no anyone else."

He's right about that.

"His knife is the murder weapon."

Did he figure it out?

Burr crossed his legs, then uncrossed them.

"He's not exactly a sympathetic defendant. What with his temper." Truax smiled at Burr.

He's right about that, too.

"Calvin, I take it you lost your run for the state senate."

The prosecutor didn't say anything.

"You didn't even get the nomination, did you?"

Truax turned red.

"I'm surprised you got reelected prosecutor."

Truax turned even redder.

Truax pointed to the door. "Get out."

"Why don't you drop this? You're going to lose." Burr tapped his feet. "All right. We'll plead."

"You will?"

"To disorderly conduct. A misdemeanor."

"You've got to be kidding."

"No jail time."

Truax pointed at the door.

Burr started for the door. "See you in court."

* * *

Burr sat at the defense table, Truax across the aisle, Gillis at the bench. No one else in the courtroom except for Swede and Miss Longfingers.

Burr had made a point of not inviting Jacob, Eve, or Aunt Kitty. He certainly hadn't invited Collin.

There's no one to stop me.

He didn't want to be here, and he didn't think this needed to happen. He had hoped that Gillis had forgotten about it or was letting it go. Until Truax filed his motion.

It's my own damn fault.

Gillis looked at the prosecutor. "You may proceed, Mr. Truax."

Burr stood. "Is this really necessary, Your Honor?"

"That's not for you to say," Truax said.

"I wasn't talking to you."

"Mr. Lafayette, it is entirely your doing that we are here today."

"Your Honor, it doesn't seem that we need a court proceeding for this."

"Sit down, Mr. Lafayette." To Truax, "You may proceed."

Truax cleared his throat. "Thank you, Your Honor." Truax walked around his table and stood in front of it. "As the court knows, Mr. Lafayette asked for and was granted a continuance." The prosecutor looked at Burr. "Because of a death in his family. A close relative, I think he said."

The judge nodded.

"We are here today for proof of that death."

Burr stood again. "Your Honor, you granted the continuance. We're about to have a trial." Burr looked over at Truax. "Unless the prosecutor comes to his senses and dismisses this frivolous motion."

"Lafayette," Truax said, "there's nothing frivolous about murder."

"You don't have any proof, and you know it."

Gillis banged his gavel. "Stop it. Both of you." To Burr, "Mr. Lafayette, I asked you for a death certificate."

"Respectfully, Your Honor, this was a personal tragedy. What business is it of Mr. Truax?"

"It is my business and the business of the state. You have delayed these proceedings."

"What on earth is the harm?" Burr said.

"The delay costs the taxpayers money, and time always makes what happened less clear. Witnesses forget. People die."

"It's been all of two months."

Gillis rapped his gavel again. "Whether or not this is any of Mr. Truax's concern, Mr. Lafayette, I do recall asking you for a death certificate. Please produce it. Now." Gillis held out his hand.

Damn it all.

"Your Honor."

Gillis held his hand out. "Now."

Burr sat. "Nuts," he said, mostly to himself but not quite enough to himself.

"I beg your pardon?"

"I didn't say anything, Your Honor."

"I could have sworn I heard you say something."

It was Truax's turn to smile. "He said 'nuts,' Your Honor."

"Nuts?"

"Nuts."

This is a good time for me to be quiet.

"Please produce the death certificate, Mr. Lafayette." Gillis held out his hand again.

"Yes, Your Honor." Burr shuffled through his papers, then he looked up at Gillis. "I was sure I brought it but I can't seem to find it."

"The death certificate is the only reason we're here. Look again."

Burr made a show of searching for it, but he knew exactly where it was. "I'm sorry, Your Honor. I was sure I had it, but I can't seem to find it."

Gillis shook his head. "Bring me the file. The court reporter will look for it."

That won't work.

Burr rummaged through the file again. He took out a piece of paper and handed it to Miss Longfingers.

"Let me see that." She handed Gillis the death certificate.

Maybe he won't notice.

Gillis studied the death certificate, his lips moving. "Here it is. Zeke, age fourteen." Gillis looked at Burr. "Mr. Lafayette, I'm sorry for your loss. I truly am. Court is adjourned." Gillis lifted his gavel.

"Your Honor," Truax said.

"Mr. Truax, we are adjourned."

"May I look at the death certificate?"

"I hardly think that's necessary," Gillis said.

Burr ran to the bench. He snatched the paper from Gillis. Truax ran up and snatched it from him. Burr tried to take it back, but Truax was too quick for him. Burr lunged. Truax ran back to his table. He studied the death certificate.

"Stop it. Stop it. Both of you," Gillis said.

Burr started for Truax.

"Mr. Lafayette, sit down. Mr. Truax, hand me the death certificate."

Truax came around to the front of the bench and handed Gillis the death certificate.

"Your Honor, you are quite right. This is indeed a death certificate." Truax looked at Burr, then back at Gillis. "And Zeke did die at age fourteen."

"A tragedy," Gillis said, nodding at Burr.

"Zeke was a dog," Truax said.

* * *

Burr sat at a four-top with Aunt Kitty, Jacob, and Eve in the Chart Room, two steps down from the bar at the Pier. It was, for all intents and purposes, a basement. Burr didn't like basements to begin with, and to make matters worse, the Chart Room was known for its salad bar.

Eve loved a good salad bar. So did Aunt Kitty. Jacob was happy, as long as he could get a grilled cheese on white bread with the crusts cut off.

Eve sat down next to him with two plates from the salad bar—one overflowing with cottage cheese, potato salad, and pickled beets, the other with lettuce, cucumbers, green peppers, and cherry tomatoes.

I hate cherry tomatoes almost as much as I hate salad bars.

Eve popped one in her mouth.

"How can you eat those things?" Burr said.

"They burst in your mouth."

"They don't taste like anything. In fact, they taste like nothing."

"This is the best salad bar I've ever seen." She popped another cherry tomato in her mouth. "You really should try it."

"I don't come to restaurants to make my own salad."

"It looks to me like you came here to drink your dinner again," Jacob said.

"I'm having the seafood chowder. And an olive salad." He ate one of the olives in his martini.

Aunt Kitty looked at Burr. "You've managed to make things even worse."

"I had to come up with a death certificate."

"For a dog?"

"My grief was real. And it still is."

"I hope you didn't bring that silly urn into court with you," Jacob said.

When the Honorable Benjamin R. Gillis found out Burr's close personal relative had, in fact, been a dog, he had, not unsurprisingly and unceremoniously, thrown Burr out of his courtroom.

"How long are you kicked out for?" Eve said.

"Gillis didn't say."

"How long do you think?" Jacob looked nervous.

"If I had to guess, I'd say that Gillis doesn't ever want me back in his courtroom."

"You've got to get back in court," Jacob said. "Jury selection is next."

"That's right," Burr said.

"What are you going to do?"

Burr finished his martini and ate the other three olives.

"What are you going to do?" Jacob said again.

"I told Gillis that you'd be taking my place."

* * *

Burr insisted on giving Aunt Kitty a ride back to Cottage 59, cars not allowed on the Point except in the off season, which was now.

She wanted to walk. It wasn't far and the sidewalks were clear, but it was dark and there were patches of ice. Now he wished he hadn't.

"You just can't stay out of your own way," she said.

Burr didn't say anything.

"You keep making things worse for yourself. And everyone else."

He turned into Harbor Point but still didn't say anything.

"Trying to pass Zeke-the-Dog off as a person is too much. Even for you."

Still nothing from Burr.

"What do you have to say for yourself?"

"My seafood chowder was a little cold."

"Your seafood chowder? Have you heard a word I said?"

Every word. Unfortunately.

"You just can't go on like this."

Burr pretended to concentrate on his driving.

"Answer me," she said.

"I'll do my best to coach up Jacob, but I think you'll have to be in court with him."

"Nonsense."

Burr put the Jeep in park. "He almost threw up his grilled cheese."

"I'm not going to court."

"He can't do it by himself."

"He can't do it with me, either. He just can't do it. When it comes to court, he's afraid of his own shadow."

"You've been in court dozens, hundreds of times," Burr said.

"I'm not a criminal lawyer."

"Neither am I."

"Touché." She rolled her window down and looked out into the night. "A 'death in the family' was a stupid thing to say."

"Zeke was family. He was my best friend."

She looked in the backseat. "There he is." Aunt Kitty shook her head. "Collin will be convicted if you don't find a way to make peace with Gillis."

"He may be convicted anyway."

"I love your optimism."

Burr reached into the backseat and scratched the back of the decoy's head.

"Stop that." Aunt Kitty slapped his hand. "You're still in Judge Abbott's good graces, aren't you?"

"We have to make our written offer to Dewey by Wednesday."

"Offer?"

"To match Smart's. This was your idea."

"Go ahead and make the offer."

"With what?"

"A piece of paper, I suppose."

"Have you raised the money?"

Aunt Kitty rolled up the window. "No."

* * *

The seal on the Jeep's valve cover blew somewhere around Cadillac. By the time he got to Manton, the Jeep was burning oil almost as fast as it burned gas. The oil sprayed under the Jeep, over the exhaust pipe, and then up the back window, covering it with a smoky, black film.

He looked in the rearview mirror but couldn't see anything out the back. "This is just ducky."

He had to stop in Big Rapids for three quarts of oil, but he managed to get to Judge Abbott's chambers, more or less on time.

The judge wore a knee-length gray suit with a white blouse, her blonde hair pulled back, and, as always, her pink lipstick. She offered Burr a side chair across from the couch in her office where Ballantine and Smart were sitting. Ballantine was as wrinkled and disheveled as Smart was starched and pressed.

I didn't know they'd be here.

The judge sat in a wing chair.

It looks like a throne.

"Have you been in a fire?" she said.

Burr sniffed the sleeve of his jacket.

I smell like I've been standing downwind of a campfire.

"Just a little car problem."

"Mr. Lafayette, today is the day for you to present your offer."

"Yes, Your Honor."

"Are you ready to make your offer?"

"Yes, Your Honor."

"How much is it?"

"The Conservancy is matching Mr. Smart's offer."

The judge nodded. "May I see it?"

This is where it gets tricky.

"Your Honor, we are matching Mr. Smart's offer."

"Mr. Lafayette, I'm sure you are familiar with the statute of frauds."

"I am."

"Then you must know that an offer for this amount of money must be in writing."

"Yes, Your Honor."

"Then please let me see it."

Neither Aunt Kitty, Claire, Collin nor anyone else had managed to raise the money to buy Thorne Swift. Burr had told them he couldn't go see the judge without a written offer. His aunt had told him to go anyway. "You're the master of legal-sleight-of-hand. You can do it," she'd said. He refused. She insisted. Back and forth they went. Burr was going to ask for more time, but Aunt Kitty put the offer in his hand just as he was leaving. He read the offer. It did match Smart's price, but there was no provision for an earnest money deposit.

"Is this legit?" he'd said.

"Of course it is."

"What about the deposit?"

"We'll figure that out later."

She sounds like me.

"If we commit a fraud on the court, I could go to jail," Burr said.

"You've already been thrown out of Gillis's courtroom. Jail would be the next logical thing."

"That isn't funny," he'd said.

"Is everything all right, Mr. Lafayette?" Judge Abbott said.

"Yes." Burr said. "Quite."

"Where were we?" she said.

Burr cleared his throat. "Your Honor, as you know, I represent the Friends of Thorne Swift. They have matched Mr. Smart's offer."

"May I see it?" she said.

"See it?"

"It is customary to produce a written offer."

"A written offer?"

"Yes, a written offer."

I was on thin ice. Now I've fallen through.

Smart cleared his throat. "If he doesn't have a written offer, it's no good."

"Your Honor, you gave my client thirty days to match Mr. Smart's offer, which I have just done."

Smart looked at Burr. "As I'm sure you're aware, the statute of frauds requires any transaction of this amount to be in writing."

Burr looked back at Smart. "I am familiar with the statute of frauds."

"Then you most certainly have your offer in writing."

It's not going to help if I have to show it to her.

"Judge Abbott said we had to match your offer. She didn't say what form it had to be in."

"If it's not in writing, it's not valid. If it's not valid, it's not an offer." Smart smiled a steely, tight-lipped smile. "You lose."

"I didn't know you were in charge," Burr said.

"You've dithered, dallied, and delayed for over a year. This must stop," Smart said. "Now."

"Mr. Smart, it is for me to decide if Mr. Lafayette's parole offer is valid. Not you."

"What's a parole offer?" Ballantine said.

He looks like he just came out of the spin cycle.

"It means oral as opposed to written," Smart said. "It's a verbal offer."

"Mr. Lafayette, I must see a written offer."

"Respectfully, Your Honor, Mr. Ballantine has already accepted my offer. All we need to do is close. I don't believe it was proper for you to allow Lafayette to have thirty days to merely match my offer. I didn't raise a more forceful objection at the time, because I was certain he wouldn't be able to come up with the money. Which he hasn't."

Judge Abbott looked at Burr. "If you can't produce a written offer, I am going to allow Mr. Smart to purchase Thorne Swift from Mr. Ballantine at the agreed upon price."

Burr sat back in his chair, hands on his knees. He smiled at Judge Abbott. She didn't smile back. She tapped the fingertips of both hands against each other five or six times, then, "Mr. Lafayette …"

Burr smiled at her again.

"Your silence is deafening." To Smart, "Very well. In the absence of a written offer from the Friends of Thorne Swift, I am going to allow Mr. Ballantine to accept Mr. Smart's offer. Mr. Smart, please have your counsel prepare a motion for me to sign. Include a 'dismissed with prejudice.'"

"Thank you, Your Honor." Smart smiled his condescending smile at Burr.

I hate that smile.

"Thank you, gentlemen. You may leave."

The pressed Smart and the wrinkled Ballantine stood.

I was hoping I wouldn't have to do this.

Burr reached into his jacket pocket and took out a piece of paper. He unfolded it and set it in front of Judge Abbott.

"What's this?"

"This is the matching offer for Thorne Swift." To Smart, "In writing."

Judge Abbott picked up the piece of paper, studied it, then put it down. "You would have spared me a lot of trouble if you'd given me this when I asked for it."

Giving you that piece of paper was the last thing I wanted to do.

"May I see that, Your Honor?" Smart said.

She handed the piece of paper to Smart. He read it, then dropped it in

Burr's lap like it was yesterday's grocery list. "Your Honor, there is no provision for an earnest money deposit. Without that, there is no consideration, and without consideration, the offer isn't valid."

"I didn't know you were a lawyer," Burr said.

"I don't have to be a lawyer to know a fraud when I see one."

Smart stood. Burr got to his feet and stood nose to nose with him.

"Sit down. Both of you," the judge said.

Smart stepped a nose closer to Burr.

"Sit down, I said."

I'll be damned if I'm going to be the first one to sit.

The judge clapped her hands together. "Enough of this testosterone, I'm going to count to three. On 'three,' both of you sit. If either one of you gets cute, the other one wins." She looked at Burr, then Smart. "Is that clear?"

They both nodded.

"One, two, three."

Neither one moved. They glared at each other.

"I said 'sit.'" Burr started to sit but stopped halfway. Smart sat. Burr grinned at Smart, then sat.

"You are an ass," Smart said.

"And you are a liar and a thief."

Judge Abbott walked to her desk, picked up her gavel, and pounded it on her desk. "Because the offer of the Friends of Thorne Swift does not have an earnest money deposit, it does not match Mr. Smart's offer. Therefore, it fails. Mr. Smart, you may proceed with this purchase."

"Your Honor—" Burr said.

"No more 'Your Honors.' Get out. All of you." She slammed her gavel.

CHAPTER FOURTEEN

"Have you been in a fire?" Eve said.

Burr smelled his sleeve.

I smell worse than before.

"No," he said.

"It's that broken-down car he drives," Jacob said.

"It's a Jeep."

Burr had had to add two more quarts to make it back from Grand Rapids. He didn't want to talk about his Jeep, which was going to cost at least a thousand dollars to fix—for the third time—but talking about his Jeep was better than what they had been talking about.

"So, you lost again," Jacob said.

I've lost every step of the way.

"Not exactly."

"Not exactly?" Jacob twirled a curl. "You said that Judge Abbott ruled that Smart could buy Thorne Swift. What about that isn't a loss?"

"She didn't rule. Nothing is going to happen until there's a motion."

"Dahlberg will have it on her desk tomorrow," Jacob said.

"Why wasn't Dahlberg there?" Eve said.

"I'd say Smart and Ballantine did just fine without him," Jacob said.

"We can appeal," Burr said.

"We're out of appeals," Jacob said. "We lost. That's it."

This isn't going well, and it's about to get worse.

"We'll figure out what's next with Thorne Swift. We have to get ready for Collin's trial."

"My dear, Burr, we can get as ready as we want, but it won't do any good. You've been thrown out of Gillis's courtroom."

There is that.

"You're going to have to find someone to try the case for you," Jacob said.

"How about Aunt Kitty?" Eve said.

"Aunt Kitty isn't a criminal lawyer," Jacob said.

"Neither is Burr."

"There's a pretrial conference with Gillis and then jury selection," Burr said. "I need to figure out how to get back in court, but I've got to get the Jeep fixed before I can go anywhere." He turned around and looked out his window. It was late afternoon. The sun was below the buildings to the west, but it hadn't quite set so there was still some daylight.

I'm just about past the time of year when I need my lights, which I can't find. So I guess it doesn't really matter.

He turned back around. "Jacob, while I figure out how to get back into the good graces of the Honorable Benjamin Gillis, you're going to have to take over for me."

Jacob turned the color of his freshly pressed white shirt.

* * *

Burr parked at the Northwood Inn across from Crooked Lake.

He pulled on his duck coat, stocking cap, and gloves, and crossed US-31. He stood on the beach and looked out at the lake. "There it is." He slogged through the snow, knee deep, crusty on top, slushy underneath. The ice seemed firm enough, but it was the middle of March, and it could go out any day. He could break through on any step. Who would rescue him? Who even knew he was here? For that matter, who would care?

"I need to stop feeling sorry for myself," he said out loud. "I've had a great run. Plenty of people care about me. Zeke-the-Boy took a cab to see me. That was a bit much."

Burr stopped to catch his breath. "Why couldn't he fish closer to shore?"

He slogged on. He stopped two more times before he made it to the shanty. It was the size of an outhouse with a coat of fresh white paint and forest green trim.

I've seen plenty of cottages that don't look this good.

A bright red snowmobile was sinking in the snow beside the shanty.

Burr knocked on the door.

"Go away."

Burr knocked again.

"Go away," again.

Burr started to knock again, thought better of it, then pulled the latch and stepped inside the shanty. He couldn't see a thing.

"Get out of here."

Burr took another step.

"I said 'get out.'"

"It's a long way out here."

"I don't care if you crawled on your hands and knees. I threw you out of my courtroom. Permanently."

"Your Honor, you did remove me from your courtroom. You didn't say I couldn't see you in your ice shanty."

"You know what I meant. Shut the door. The light spooks the fish. Shut the door with you on the outside."

The not-too-happy Judge Gillis wore a black-and-red checked wool Mackinaw, the old-fashioned kind, over brown Carhartt bib overalls, extra-large. He had on a Stormy Kromer hat with the earflaps pulled down. A sucker minnow the size of a hot dog swam in the hole, hooked through the back. The judge had a spear in his hand.

He could kill somebody with that thing.

Burr shut the door, standing inside. There was just enough light to see.

"How did you find me?"

"It was just luck. I took a chance that you'd be here."

"Nonsense." The judge jigged the minnow in the hole. "How much did it cost you?"

"I beg your pardon?"

"My secretary. She's always broke."

"Twenty."

"Twenty? She usually charges fifteen." Gillis looked in the hole. He picked up his spear, three dangerous looking barbs on the end.

There was a lawn chair leaning against the wall of the shanty. Burr opened it and sat across the hole from the judge.

Gillis jigged his minnow. "What do you want? As if I didn't know."

"Your Honor—"

"Your partner didn't look too good." Gillis made a face. "He threw up in my weeping fig. I think he's got the flu."

"It's not the flu."

"I can hold off on jury selection until he's better."

"Thank you, Your Honor, but he's not going to get better."

"Is he that sick?"

It had been all Burr could do to get Jacob to go to the pretrial settlement conference with Gillis and Truax. Burr had driven him to the courthouse and taken him inside. Jacob's olive skin had turned white again, and his hands shook. Burr waited for him outside the judge's chambers. About ten minutes later, Burr heard a terrible retching. Jacob staggered out. He wiped the corners of his mouth with his handkerchief. He smelled like yesterday's cat food. Burr drove Jacob back to East Lansing, where he took to his bed.

That had been a week ago. He refused to get out of bed as long as he was the one taking Collin's case to trial. Eve took him his meals.

"He sure didn't look too good." Gillis jigged the minnow again. "I guess we can wait a while longer."

"Respectfully, Your Honor, I don't think Mr. Wertheim is going to get better."

Gillis looked over at him. "Is it fatal?"

"As it relates to litigation, I'm afraid it is."

"I've read the briefs, which I'm sure you didn't write. He's a fine lawyer."

"He is, Your Honor, but he's terrified of courtrooms."

"What kind of lawyer is that?"

"Your Honor, I think the best solution would be to allow me back in your courtroom."

Gillis looked down in the hole. "Why on earth would I do that?"

Burr inched his chair closer to the hole and looked down at the minnow. *He doesn't look like he's got much life left in him.*

"Your Honor, Mr. Murphy's best chance for a fair trial is if I defend him."

"You should have thought of that before you lied to me." Gillis peered into the hole again. A dark shape swam a lazy circle below the minnow, which was trying to swim away.

"Zeke was family to me, Your Honor."

"He was a dog."

"He was my best friend."

The shadow came to the surface. A Northern pike as long as a baseball bat and as fat as a football. It lunged at the minnow. Gillis threw the spear.

* * *

"Mr. Wertheim, approach the bench," Judge Gillis said.

Jacob didn't move.

"Mr. Wertheim, please approach the bench."

Jacob started his chameleon-like color change.

"Are you going to be ill?"

Jacob shook his head.

"Come up here." Gillis pointed at the floor below his desk. "Now."

Jacob shook his head.

"Do I have to throw you out, too?"

He's going to be sick again.

Burr stood.

"Sit down, Mr. Lafayette. This isn't about you."

"I object, Your Honor. This behavior is making a mockery of your courtroom."

"This isn't about you, either, Mr. Truax."

"Front and center, Mr. Wertheim."

Jacob didn't budge. Burr stood. He took Jacob by the shoulder and dragged him in front of Judge Gillis. Jacob started to shake.

The judge shook his head. "Mr. Wertheim, I thought you were gravely ill." Gillis shook his head again. "How you could make it this far as a lawyer with a fear of litigation is beyond me."

Jacob looked at his shoes, still shaking.

"You're like a bird who's afraid to fly."

"He does the writing. I do the fighting," Burr said, cheerfully and hopefully.

"Quiet, Mr. Lafayette." The judge looked down at Jacob. "It's only because of my high regard for your writing and research abilities that I am, against my better judgment, allowing Mr. Lafayette back in my courtroom."

"Thank you," Jacob said, mumbling.

"Thank you, Your Honor," Burr said, not mumbling.

"I object, Your Honor," Truax said. "Not only did Mr. Lafayette demonstrate a callous disregard for the court's schedule, not to mention my own, he lied to the court. Blatantly."

Right on cue.

"It was all lies," Truax said.

"I had a death certificate," Burr said.

"Of a dog," Truax said. "A dog."

"A dog can be part of a family," Gillis said.

* * *

"Mr. Supinski, have you ever been to the Thorne Swift Nature Preserve?" Burr said.

"Never heard of it."

"Are you familiar with the Little Traverse Conservancy?"

"Nope."

Burr put his hands in his pockets and looked up at Matthew Supinski. He was about fifty and had a square head, a square face, and a square jaw that looked like it couldn't wait to get punched.

"Mr. Supinski, do you believe in protecting land from development? Building houses or cottages on wild, undisturbed land."

"As long as it percs."

"Percs?"

"As long as you can put a septic tank on it."

"Septic tank?"

"Where have you been all your life?"

I might as well let him hang himself.

"It's fine with me to build as long as the bathroom part of things works right. What else are you going to do with it?"

"So, you approve of developing wild places?"

"Are you one of them tree huggers?"

Burr looked up at Gillis. "Your Honor, I move to excuse Mr. Supinski."

"Whatever for?"

Isn't it obvious?

"Your Honor, Mr. Supinski is quite obviously opposed to land conservation. My client can't get a fair trial with a juror opposed to conservation."

"I ain't opposed to conservation. I never shoot any more deer than I got on my license."

You're the next Aldo Leopold.

"Your Honor, I move to excuse Mr. Supinski," Burr said again.

Truax stood. "Your Honor, Mr. Supinski is a most qualified juror. He is a resident of Emmet County. He has a family. He's gainfully employed. He has no criminal record, and he is an outdoorsman."

"Mr. Supinski does not believe in conservation," Burr said.

"I do, too."

Gillis looked up at the ceiling, then, "I rue the day I let him back in my courtroom."

"I beg your pardon," Burr said.

"Mr. Lafayette, we've been at this since ten this morning. We have two jurors. At this rate, the ice will be out, the leaves will be on the trees, and it will be morel season before we have a jury."

"Respectfully, Your Honor, I believe Mr. Supinski is a fine man, a model citizen, but he is prejudiced against land protection which is at the heart of this case."

"This happened the last time you were here. I should have known better."

"My client deserves a fair and impartial jury."

"I'm fair. I umpire my kid's baseball games. Nobody ever complains."

"Please excuse Mr. Supinski," Burr said.

"Your Honor, Mr. Supinski is the epitome of a qualified juror," Truax said.

Epitome?

Gillis tapped his fingers on his desk, then he looked at Truax, then Burr, and finally at the prospective juror. "Mr. Supinski, I am going to seat you on the jury."

"Your Honor, I am going to use one of my preemptory challenges."

"What?"

"I am going to use one of my preemptory challenges," Burr said again.

"If you didn't want him on the jury, why didn't you do that twenty minutes ago?"

"I didn't want to waste one on a juror who was so obviously partial."

Gillis turned red.

"Your Honor," Truax said, "counsel for the defense has used all of his preemptory challenges."

"I have not," Burr said, who had and knew it.

"Yes, you have," Truax said.

Gillis thumped his forehead. He looked down at Miss Longfingers. "See how many preemptory challenges Mr. Lafayette has used."

She rewound her machine. Gillis drummed his fingers.

Burr tapped his foot.

However this turns out, it isn't going to be good.

Five minutes later, Miss Longfingers stopped her machine. She folded her hands together.

"What did you find?" Gillis said.

She looked up at the judge. "Mr. Lafayette has used seven preemptory challenges." She smiled at Burr.

"Who's counting?" Burr said, mostly to himself.

"This is an outrage. Counsel is entitled to five. Mr. Lafayette has abused the court. Again."

Another outrage.

Gillis thumped his forehead again.

"But for Mr. Lafayette, we'd have a jury by now," Truax said.

"No, we wouldn't."

"We would."

"Mr. Lafayette, I am sorely aggrieved. You are, in fact, abusing the court."

"I'm sorry, Your Honor," Burr said, who wasn't. "I must have lost count. On the other hand, I should think Mr. Truax would be keeping track of my challenges." He looked at Truax. "I've been keeping track of his."

"I haven't used any."

"I know. I've been keeping track."

Gillis pounded his gavel. "Mr. Supinski, you are hereby impaneled."

Supinski cocked his square head.

"It means you're on the jury," Truax said.

"You are excused," Gillis said. "For now. Bailiff, bring in the next prospective juror."

* * *

Gillis had his jury by lunchtime the next day. Five men and seven women. Burr had done his best to keep realtors, bankers, developers, and the construction trade off the jury. He wanted a jury of conservationists, environmentalists, and the well-heeled. He mostly succeeded.

* * *

The next morning, Burr sat at his desk, Jacob and Eve across from him, all three of them in their assigned seats.

"It's one thing to poke holes in Truax's case. It's quite another to have our own suspects," Jacob said. He'd made a remarkable turnaround since Burr had been reinstated.

"It's so nice that your health has been restored. Along with your boundless optimism," Burr said.

"I haven't been able to find anyone who might have wanted to kill Frank."

"Other than Collin," Eve said.

Burr ignored her. "Frank seems like a small-town hero. No enemies."

"If he was such a great guy, why did he beat up Collin and steal his camera?" Eve said.

"Maybe he didn't," Jacob said. "Maybe Collin made it all up."

"We have to believe someone," Burr said.

"We don't have to believe Collin," Jacob said.

"Collin is our client," Eve said.

Thank you.

"Lawyers lie. Witnesses lie. Most of all, clients lie." Jacob smiled at Burr. "That's what you always say."

Burr took a yellow pad out of his desk. "Who else could have killed Frank?"

"Other than—" Jacob said.

Burr cut him off. "No more of that. Who have we got?" Burr looked at Eve, then Jacob, then Eve. Neither of them said a word.

"All right, I'll start. Smart? Ballantine?" Not a word. "Ian?" Still nothing. "How about Claire?"

"Claire?" Eve said. "Why would she kill Frank?"

"She's as passionate about the lady's slipper as Collin," Burr said.

"That's no reason to murder Frank," Jacob said.

"I could say the same thing about Collin. How about Jill?"

"Frank's wife?" Jacob said.

"You said they had a good marriage," Eve said.

"There's always Aunt Kitty," Burr said.

"Good God, man. She's your aunt," Jacob said.

"But for her, I wouldn't be involved in this disaster."

"Not you. We," Eve said.

"Who then?" Jacob said.

"The trial starts tomorrow," Eve said.

"I'd say we're euchred."

* * *

"Ladies and gentlemen. The taking of a life is a heinous, hateful act. It's called murder. It's the worst crime a person can commit. The State of Michigan views it so seriously that it imposes the most severe punishment for someone convicted of murder." Truax paused and looked at the jury, left to right, one by one, including that champion of the environment, Matthew Supinski. "In Michigan, first degree murder is punishable by life imprisonment." Another pause. "Without the possibility of parole."

The prosecutor walked to the corner of the jury box and put his left hand on the railing. "And that, ladies and gentlemen, is what we have here." He pointed at Collin, who looked away.

That's exactly what I told him not to do.

Burr leaned toward Collin. Under his breath, "Don't do that. When he looks at you, look back at him. Meet his eyes. Don't smile. Don't frown. Look him in the eyes. Just like we practiced."

Burr sat at the defense table, Collin to his right in a navy-blue suit with a white shirt and a red, white, and blue striped tie, a textbook defendant's wardrobe. Jacob and Aunt Kitty, who'd insisted on being of counsel, were to the right of Collin. Eve and Claire, behind them in the first row of the gallery.

Ballantine and Smart sat together behind Truax. Judge Abbott sat by herself in the back of the courtroom.

What's she doing here?

Burr loved being in court. It was his favorite place, a place where he could forget about himself and live in the moment with the matter at hand. He felt alive whether he was winning or losing, more so when he was losing, which wasn't very often.

This might be the time.

He smelled the courtroom smells, the varnish on the tables and the pews, the wax on the tile floor, the freshly scrubbed faces.

Truax pointed at Collin again. "The defendant killed Frank Slaughter in cold blood. He snuck up on him, in the dark, and stabbed him with a knife. He stabbed him in the back. Again and again." Truax paused. "Then he stabbed him in the eye."

The jury cringed, as one.

"It was no accident. He did it on purpose. He had a plan to murder Frank Slaughter, and he carried out his plan.

"The deceased, or as I should say, the victim, had no part to play in any of this. He wasn't a criminal. If anything, he was a model citizen. He was a faithful husband, a good father. He and his wife, Jill, had two teenaged children, and she's left to raise them by herself. She's here in court today, but she wouldn't let her children come."

Truax put his hands in his pockets and nodded to Jill.

The widow Slaughter sat in the first row just behind the prosecutor's table. She wore a long-sleeved, high-necked, knee-length black dress, two-inch heels, no makeup, and looked every bit the grieving widow. She put her hands on her lap, showing a gold wedding band, her only jewelry. She looked at Truax, then down at her hands.

She's been well-coached, and she's following directions.

Truax wasn't finished singing Frank's praises. "Not only was Frank Slaughter a family man, he was a pillar of the community. He taught math at Harbor Springs High School. He coached the Harbor Springs Ski Team. He was a parishioner at the Holy Childhood Catholic Church."

He should be up for sainthood.

Truax looked out at the gallery again, this time at a priest with a clerical collar and a frock coat.

I'm sure he's a war hero.

Truax put his hands in his pockets and looked at his shoes.

Just polished.

He looked up at the jury. "Did you know that Mr. Slaughter was a war hero? Mr. Slaughter served in Vietnam. He led a platoon during the Tet offensive. He was wounded and received a purple heart."

I'm going to have to be careful about what I say about him.

Truax nodded to Smart, in yet another black suit with a starched white shirt, and this time, a club tie. Dewey sat next to him in a wrinkled tweed jacket and slacks that didn't match.

Truax walked halfway between the jury and Collin. He stared at Collin who met his gaze this time.

Much better.

The prosecutor looked back at the jury. "It wasn't enough for the defendant to murder Frank Slaughter in cold blood. Collin Murphy murdered Frank Slaughter under the cover of darkness and then snuck away. Mr. Slaughter's body wasn't found for almost a week. Frank always came home at night. He never stayed out. He was missing, a family man missing all that time. Can you imagine how his wife and children must have felt, a husband, father, and provider missing? It must have been terrifying."

This has to stop.

Burr stood. "I object, Your Honor. Mr. Slaughter wasn't missing for a week. He was found after three days."

"That doesn't matter," Truax said.

"It most certainly does."

Judge Gillis rapped his gavel. "Overruled. You may continue, Mr. Truax."

I knew I'd lose, but I had to slow him down.

Truax cleared his throat. "Let me go back to the beginning of this horrible crime, this murder. Mr. Slaughter worked in the summer as the caretaker at Thorne Swift. It's private property owned by Dewey Ballantine and marked with a 'No Trespassing' sign. Yet, the defendant repeatedly and forcibly entered Mr. Ballantine's property without permission, time and time again. Mr. Slaughter politely asked the defendant to leave. He refused. Again and again. This angered the defendant who is known to have a violent temper and who attacked Mr. Slaughter."

Burr jumped up. "I object, Your Honor. The prosecutor is making this up. It's simply not true. It's a lie, and he knows it." Burr glared at Truax.

"I never lie."

"Call it what you like. Mr. Murphy never attacked Mr. Slaughter. Never."

"Your Honor, it is a well-known fact that the defendant has a violent temper."

"It is not well known that he attacked Mr. Slaughter."

Gillis looked at Burr. "Overruled," he said, then to the prosecutor, "Mr. Truax, I will permit a little puffery in your opening statement. I will not permit fabrication."

"I am not fabricating, Your Honor."

"You're not fabricating," Burr said. "You're lying."

"Be quiet, Mr. Lafayette." It was Gillis's turn to glare. "You're on thin ice, and we just started."

"Your Honor—"

"Sit down, Mr. Lafayette."

Truax took a step toward the jury box. "The Harbor Springs Police finally found his truck, tucked back in a turnaround, but they couldn't find Frank. They searched and searched. Nothing." Truax held his hands out, palms up. "Finally, they got the state police and a tracking dog to help in the search. The police gave the dog something of Frank's so it could get his scent. The dog searched and searched. Nothing." Palms out again. "Finally, the dog led them down a boardwalk at a preserve where Frank's car had been found. Still nothing." Palms up again.

Stop that.

"The dog led them off the boardwalk and into the swamp the boardwalk cuts through. They all got soaked. The dog searched and searched." Truax paused. "At last, the dog found Frank, face down in the swamp. He'd been stabbed to death. They searched and searched the area and finally found the murder weapon." Truax looked at Collin again. "It was a knife, a Swiss Army knife that belonged to the defendant, Collin Murphy."

Collin started to stand. Burr held him down, then jumped to his feet. "I object, Your Honor. This is speculation and hyperbole. No murder weapon has been introduced into evidence. Nothing. Much less that it belonged to Mr. Murphy."

"The state will make its proofs, Your Honor," Truax said.

"This is speculation and hyperbole."

"You already said that."

Burr stepped around his table toward Truax.

"Not one more step," Gillis said. "Or you'll find yourself out in the hall, and Mr. Wertheim will take your place." Gillis pointed at Burr's chair. "Sit."

Burr backed up, slowly.

"As for you, Mr. Truax, this is supposed to be an opening statement, not a filibuster. Are you quite through?"

Truax looked up at Gillis. "No, Your Honor. Not quite."

"Then finish up. Spit spot."

"Spit spot?"

"Get on with it," the judge said.

Truax turned back to the jury. "Ladies and gentlemen, unfortunately we have a body. We have a murder weapon. We have a motive. We have witnesses who saw the defendant arguing with Mr. Slaughter. We have witnesses who saw the defendant follow Mr. Slaughter that night. We will prove all of these things during the course of the trial." Truax took a breath. "It goes without saying that we have the three requirements for first-degree murder."

Truax held up a finger. "Motive. The defendant believed that Mr. Slaughter beat him and stole his camera. He wanted it back."

The prosecutor raised a second finger. "Means: the murder weapon, the defendant's Swiss Army knife."

The third finger. "Opportunity: the defendant followed Mr. Slaughter to the end of Fourth Street and onto the boardwalk."

He's proud of himself.

"Ladies and gentlemen, first-degree murder requires a killing, which we have. It must be intentional—stabbing in the back and in the eye cannot possibly be accidental. And finally, it must be premeditated, which means there must have been a plan. Nothing could be more premeditated or according to plan than following Mr. Slaughter and stabbing him to death.

"When you have seen the evidence, there is no doubt in my mind that you will find the defendant, Collin Murphy, guilty of first-degree murder." Truax pointed at Collin again, then sat. "Nothing further, Your Honor."

Truax repeated himself, but it worked.

"Mr. Lafayette?" Judge Gillis said.

If the trial ended right now, I'd lose.

Burr didn't move.

"Surely, you have something to say, Mr. Lafayette."

Still nothing.

I want the jury to pay attention to me.

"If you don't make your opening statement this instant, you will waive your right."

Burr studied his pencil du jour. He took his time. He turned it over in his hand, studying it like it was a treasure. He put it behind his ear, put it back in his hand, then put it on his table. The jury watched his every move.

Now I have them.

He walked to the end of the jury box, where he could see the jury, Truax, the gallery, Collin, and his team, if his sorry group of misfits could be called a team.

He put his hands in his pockets and rocked back and forth on his feet, heel to toe.

"Ladies and gentlemen, it's true that Frank Slaughter was murdered. He was horribly murdered. Stabbed to death, as Mr. Truax has said. It's tragic. It truly is."

Burr put his left hand on the railing of the jury box. "Someone murdered Frank Slaughter." He looked at the jury, one at a time. Fresh faces, sincere faces, wanting to do the right thing. Finding the truth. Some of them met his eyes. Some didn't.

"Frank Slaughter was murdered, but that doesn't mean Collin Murphy did it." Burr looked at Collin, who nodded at Burr.

Just like we practiced.

Burr looked at the jury again. "It doesn't mean that at all. Someone murdered Frank Slaughter, but it wasn't Collin Murphy." He walked to the other end of the jury box. The jury followed him with their eyes. He stopped and looked at them again. Then he walked to the witness stand and wiped a smudge off the railing.

Truax stood. "Your Honor, we are supposed to be having opening statements, not theater."

It's all theater.

"I listened politely to your far-fetched and preposterous prattling. You can at least have the decency to afford me the same courtesy."

"I would hardly call your behavior—"

"Mr. Lafayette, you are allowed some theater but not Shakespeare."

"Yes, Your Honor."

So far, so good.

He turned back to the jury. "The most important thing about the prosecutor's opening statement is what he didn't say. He was quick to say that the murder weapon was Mr. Murphy's knife, which he hasn't proved. And if he does prove that Mr. Slaughter was killed with Mr. Murphy's knife, that doesn't mean that Mr. Murphy was the one who killed Mr. Slaughter with it. The prosecutor was also quick to say that Mr. Slaughter and Mr. Murphy were seen together at Bar Harbor. He said that they were seen together the night Mr. Slaughter disappeared. But we don't know when Mr. Slaughter disappeared. Someone may have seen him. We simply don't know, and it doesn't look like Mr. Truax looked very hard."

Burr turned to Truax, who had turned one shade of red less than a boiled lobster.

Back to the jury. "The prosecutor also said that Mr. Murphy was angry with Mr. Slaughter. For once, I agree with Mr. Truax." Burr smiled at the seething prosecutor.

He's not smiling back.

"But just because someone is angry doesn't mean they'd murder someone. This wasn't a case of rape, theft, or even drunkenness. Is that a reason for murder?" Burr paused. "I don't think it is.

"Mr. Truax is quite right to bring up Mr. Slaughter's character. He seems to have been a fine husband and father. Certainly, his service to our great country is commendable. Unfortunately, many fine people are killed. But that doesn't mean Mr. Murphy killed Mr. Slaughter."

Burr walked back to the jury box. "And, of course, there are plenty of people who could have killed Mr. Slaughter. Who, you ask?" Burr turned to Truax who had lost some of his lobster coloring.

He's about to get it back. And then some.

"Mr. Truax failed to mention that Mr. Murphy was doing critical research at Thorne Swift. Critical research. Mr. Murphy has a PhD in botany from Michigan State University. He is extremely well respected and held in high regard. He was doing research at Thorne Swift to save it from developers. He was there under a court order. He had the express permission of the

Federal District Court of the Western District of Michigan. Mr. Slaughter's actions were not only unwarranted, they were illegal."

Burr looked at the jury again, one by one.

"It is notable that Mr. Truax failed to bring that up." Burr looked over at Truax who had gone from sunburn to Santa Claus suit, to fire truck red.

Back to the jury. "There's one more thing, and this is the most important thing. No one saw who killed Mr. Slaughter. No one. There were no witnesses. None. It may be convenient for Mr. Truax to try to pin this on Mr. Murphy. But that's all it is. Convenient. Any number of people could have killed Mr. Slaughter. But it wasn't Mr. Murphy."

Burr walked back to his table and stood next to Collin. "Ladies and gentlemen, Mr. Murphy did not kill Mr. Slaughter. This is a case that should never have been brought. Never. Charging Mr. Murphy with the murder of Mr. Slaughter is convenient. It's nothing more than that. Mr. Truax is making Mr. Murphy a scapegoat because he doesn't know who else to charge. It's nothing more than that."

CHAPTER FIFTEEN

The opening statements had gone past noon and Gillis, never one to miss a meal, dismissed them for the day. They all met for lunch at the City Park Grill. Collin, Claire, Eve, Jacob, and Aunt Kitty. They were all hungry, and Burr knew they all expected him to buy lunch.

I hope there's room on my credit card.

"You did well, nephew," Aunt Kitty said. "In spite of yourself."

"I beg your pardon."

"You should have told the jury about Collin getting beat up by Frank."

I just killed it with my opening statement, and this is what I'm getting.

"Did you forget?"

"I purposely didn't bring it up. That would give Collin a reason to kill Frank. We don't need to give the jury any reason to think Collin had a reason to kill Frank."

Burr looked at Collin who was staring at what was left of his cheeseburger. He put his hand on Claire's. She took it off.

"The beating is going to come up in due course, but my opening statement wasn't the place for it."

"Is that why Truax didn't bring it up?" Claire said, well into her own cheeseburger.

Burr chewed on his whitefish sandwich, then, "It's a little more complicated for Truax. If he tells the jury that Collin wanted his camera back, because Frank took it from him, and he killed Frank to get it back, that helps Truax. But …" Burr took another bite of his sandwich. They all watched him chew.

Let's let the suspense build.

"But that means that Frank took Collin's camera without Collin's permission. And that takes away from the All-American image Truax painted."

Burr took another bite of his sandwich.

"The camera is going to come out. I'll make sure it does."

"Thank you for all you've done," Claire said.

We have a long way to go.

* * *

Burr turned off M-119 onto Beach Drive, then drove through the woods, still full of snow, until he came out on the bay. It was frozen all the way to Petoskey, but there was open water on the big lake.

"The ice will be going out soon," he said to the decoy riding shotgun.

Burr looked back at the bay. The late afternoon sun, much higher in the sky, lit up the ice. He squinted.

"I wonder where my sunglasses are."

He turned into the Harbor Inn. He'd made reservations for Jacob and Eve, not that they needed reservations. It was late March, and Harbor Springs was deserted.

He'd decided to stay here, too. He couldn't face another night with space heaters and a mountain of blankets at his aunt's.

Stewart would charge for all three of them. Burr wouldn't pay, and they'd start over.

* * *

Truax started where Burr would have started. With the body.

He may be a jerk but he's a good lawyer.

The prosecutor called Officer Kyle Stone from the Harbor Springs Police Department.

"Were you the officer in charge of finding Frank Slaughter?" Truax said.

"I was."

"Would you please tell us, in your own words, how you became involved, what you did, and what you found?"

Here goes nothing.

"Your Honor, this information is in the transcript of the preliminary examination. I ask that the transcript be used instead of Officer Stone's testimony. Not only will it save the court's valuable time, it is already a written record."

"That's ridiculous," Truax said. "The jury needs to hear what happened. Firsthand."

That's what I'm worried about.

Gillis exhaled. "Overruled. You know better than that Mr. Lafayette. The triers-of-fact need to hear what happened."

"Thank you, Your Honor." Truax scowled at Burr. "As I was saying," then to the witness, "Officer Stone, please tell us, in your own words, about the events surrounding the disappearance of Frank Slaughter and the subsequent location of his body."

The jury cringed at "body."

The policeman nodded. "We received a call from Mrs. Slaughter, Frank's wife. She said her husband hadn't come home last night. She said he was home every night. She was worried sick."

"Please continue."

"We said we'd keep a look out for him. None of the patrol officers saw any sign of him. She came over at the end of the day. In tears. Our policy is to wait twenty-four hours before we issue a missing person's report. She still hadn't heard from him by the next morning, so we issued the missing person's report. The other jurisdictions—Petoskey, Pellston, the Emmet County Sheriff's Office—didn't turn up a thing. We stepped up our search, too." He paused.

The jury leaned toward Officer Stone.

Do you have to make it so suspenseful?

"Please continue," Truax said again.

"We looked and looked. It took us two more days, but then we found his truck. Pretty much right under our noses. It was parked at the end of Fourth Street, off the road. Out of the way. By the turnaround where Bull Moose Hill starts. Not great police work on our part."

This is killing us.

"One of the patrol officers found his truck, a white Ford F-150. There were no signs of a break-in or violence or tampering, but it was a start."

"And?" Truax said.

"We searched the area, talked to the neighbors. There's no one really close. Some houses back down Fourth Street, few over on Glen Drive, but no one had seen him." The cop folded his hands on his knees.

Truax looked annoyed. "What did you do next?"

"We called the state police in Petoskey and asked for help. They sent an officer with a tracking dog, a German Shepherd. Her name was Belle. Nice dog." Officer Stone smiled again. Truax didn't again. Stone got the message.

"It had rained since Mr. Slaughter disappeared. The scenting conditions were poor, but there were a few footprints near the truck. We'd gotten a pair of Mr. Slaughter's shoes and a shirt from his wife. Sergeant Gillespie, Belle's handler, let Belle have a good sniff. Then he showed her the footprints. She had a little interest, but not much. He let her use her nose. She circled around the truck a couple of times, then started down the path into the preserve. The footprints petered out, but Belle kept going down the path." Stone nodded to himself, remembering. "She trotted down the path, head down, sniffing. She didn't move very fast. Sniffing at the ground the whole time." The cop paused again.

"Please continue," the prosecutor said.

I don't think he cares much about the blow-by-blow of the canine nose patrol.

"Belle goes down the path, back and forth. She goes a long way, sniffing all the time. Then we get to the boardwalk. It's swampy there. The boardwalk cuts right through it. Wet on both sides. She stops and sits. Right where the boardwalk starts. I thought we were all done." Stone put his hands on the railing of the witness box. "Sergeant Gillespie gave Belle another sniff of Mr. Slaughter's shoes. That's all it took, and off she went, nose down." Stone sat back in his chair. The jury leaned forward.

Truax was about to say something but instead looked back at the jury. He smiled to himself, then, "Please continue, Officer Stone. In detail."

"Belle keeps going down the boardwalk. I was sure she'd lost the scent. It was so wet, and I didn't think the boardwalk could hold the scent like soil would."

Stone shook his head. "She got interested about two-thirds of the way down the boardwalk, but then she kept going. All the way to the end, where it comes out on Second Street. I figured we were done." He paused. "Was I wrong. She turned around and sniffed her way back down the boardwalk. She stopped right where she stopped before, then she started off into the swamp."

Burr looked at the jury.

If they lean in any further, they're going to fall out of their seats.

"It's really wet there, some standing water. I'm not dressed for it, but I figure we have to follow her. Her handler has hip boots on so he's the one. Off we go. I'm soaked to my knees after the first step."

Collin squirmed in his seat.

I've got to do something.

"We slug on out there, maybe a hundred yards. One of my boots came off in the muck. It was already wet through, so it didn't really matter. Belle stops. She sniffs, paws at the water. I go up to her and—"

Burr jumped up. "Objection, Your Honor. Hearsay."

Truax looked back at Burr. "Nonsense."

"Nonsense, yourself." Burr turned to Gillis. "Your Honor, this was not Officer Stone's dog. The dog's handler should be the one testifying."

Truax looked at Gillis. "Counsel's understanding of hearsay shows he has no understanding of hearsay. Officer Stone was present the entire time. He is relating what he personally saw. That is not hearsay under any interpretation of the rules."

It didn't take Gillis long. "Mr. Lafayette, your objection is not only overruled, it's ridiculous. Sit down."

"Your Honor—"

Gillis pointed at Burr's chair. "I said, sit. So. Sit."

Burr sat.

It was a stupid objection, but it broke up the story.

Truax took a step toward the witness. "Please continue, Officer Stone." Truax looked back at Burr. "In detail."

"Where was I?" Stone said, mostly to himself.

That helps.

"Right. Well, Belle sniffs up a storm. Then she dunks her head in the water, and …"

The jury was hypnotized.

"And she comes up with a sleeve."

"A sleeve?" Truax said.

They practiced this.

Stone nodded. "Yes. A sleeve. I try and get there as quick as I can, but I fell in. Belle's handler, Sergeant Gillespie, grabs the sleeve. He pulls on it, but he can't budge the body. I finally make it there, and we both pulled. Finally, it breaks free of the muck. It was the most horrifying thing I've ever seen, and I've been on police work long enough to have seen a few things. The face is swollen and blue, the eyes popped out. One of them was bloody. It didn't look like a man at all. More like a monster. I let go of him and threw up." Stone turned pale.

The jury gasped. One of the jurors fainted.

"Bailiff, help that woman," Gillis said.

Swede rushed over and propped the woman up.

Her eyes fluttered, then opened.

"Are you all right?" Gillis said.

"I think so," she said, softly.

"Can you continue?"

She nodded.

"Would water help?"

She nodded again.

"Mr. Olsen, give her some water. From my pitcher. Then we'll continue."

Swede handed a glass to the stricken juror. Her color came back.

"Are you all right?" Gillis said.

"Yes, thank you."

"Mr. Truax, you may proceed."

It's going to get worse.

"Thank you, Your Honor." To the witness, "What happened next?"

Burr stood again. "Your Honor, must we hear all this? The defense will accept that Officer Stone found Mr. Slaughter's body."

"Your Honor," Truax said, "it is important for the jury to hear what Officer Stone has to say, including the details—however gory—because they show the heinous nature of the murder."

"You may proceed."

This is just what I don't want.

"Please continue, Officer Stone."

"This time both of us tried to get the body up. We each grabbed an arm and pulled. We leaned it against a tree. It was Mr. Slaughter, but you could hardly tell. He was so bloated and discolored. He was really disfigured. But it was him."

"What did you do then?"

"I radioed for EMS and the crime scene guys."

More practicing.

"Did you examine the body? Look for any wounds?"

"Mr. Slaughter was fully dressed. There was nothing obvious. Except his eye. No gunshot wounds. No bruises. He was horrible to look at."

Burr looked at Collin, who was staring at Officer Stone.

"What did you do then?"

"We didn't want to disturb anything, so we waited for the experts."

"Of course you did. Did you notice anything? Anything at all?"

The cop sat back in his chair. "We got the body out of the water as best we could. It flopped over and then we saw it."

"What did you see?"

Here it comes.

"Rips. There were rips in the back of Mr. Slaughter's shirt."

"Rips?"

"It was torn."

"What did you do?"

"We didn't want to disturb anything, but we did look."

Truax tapped his foot.

This is getting dragged out. Even for Truax.

"What did you find?"

The jury leaned in again. So did everyone else in the gallery.

"Mr. Slaughter had been stabbed in the back."

Groans, sighs, and a shriek from the gallery. The faint juror looked like she would faint again.

"How many times?"

"I counted six."

More upset sounds from the gallery.

Gillis banged his gavel. "Quiet."

"Mr. Slaughter had been stabbed?" Truax said, wide-eyed.

As if he didn't know.

"Yes."

"Was there anything else?"

Stone squirmed in his chair, then, "There was something wrong with one of his eyes. It was all bloody. Like he'd been stabbed in the eye."

The jury gasped.

"What did you do then?"

"We waited for the crime team and EMS."

"And when did they get there?"

"The crime team taped off the area where we found the body. With yellow tape. I'm sure you've seen it."

"Yes," Truax said.

"They examined the body. EMS put it in a body bag and removed it."

"Then what?"

"The crime scene officers searched the area."

"Did they find anything?"

"They found a Swiss Army knife."

"Really?" Truax stepped toward Collin and looked at him. "They found the murder weapon?"

Burr stood. "I object, Your Honor. The witness said a Swiss Army knife. He did not say murder weapon."

Gillis sighed. "Sustained. You're getting a little ahead of yourself, Mr. Truax."

Truax sighed. He walked back to his table, picked up a brown envelope, and walked back to the witness stand. He opened the envelope and took out a red Swiss Army knife. "Is this what they found?"

"Yes," Officer Stone said.

Burr stood again. "I object, Your Honor. The witness has no idea if that knife is what was found."

"Your Honor, the evidence department of the Harbor Springs Police Department provided me with this knife. I have their affidavit that this is the knife found at the crime scene and is, in fact, the murder weapon."

Burr stepped around his table. "Your Honor, we have heard no testimony that indicates that this knife is the murder weapon. For that matter, we don't know if Mr. Slaughter was murdered."

Truax looked at Burr. "He didn't stab himself in the back. The prosecutor turned to Gillis. "Your Honor, we have an expert that will identify this as the murder weapon."

"Until you do that, this is a knife that was purportedly found at the crime scene. That's all it is."

"Mr. Lafayette, must you always be so argumentative?"

"Your Honor, I am merely requesting the prosecutor to follow the rules of evidence."

Truax opened a blade on the knife and showed it to the jury. Then he turned to Gillis. "Your Honor, the state would like to introduce the murder weapon into … excuse me, the knife found at the crime scene."

"Counsel?" Gillis said.

"I would like to review the affidavit and examine the knife. With the blade closed."

"Come up here, Mr. Lafayette."

Burr walked up to Gillis.

"Do you ever accept anything?"

"Yes, Your Honor."

"I'd like to know when." Gillis pointed at the defense table. "Sit down and stop with the frivolous objections."

"Your Honor, I would like to examine the knife with the blade closed," Burr said, still standing.

"Give him the knife, Mr. Truax," Gillis said, "with the blade closed."

Truax held out the knife where Burr could see it. He closed the blade and handed it to Burr. Burr turned it over in his hand. He opened up all the blades one by one, then the scissors and the broken corkscrew.

He turned it over in his hand again. "CM" was scratched on the red body of the blade. Very small. Very neat.

Damn it all.

He handed the knife back to Truax.

"Please close the blades," Truax said. "All of them."

Burr set the knife down, blades opened, on the prosecutor's table. "I have no objection to this knife being entered into evidence."

"Bailiff, mark this knife as Prosecution Exhibit One."

"As long as it is referred to as the knife found at the crime scene," Burr said.

"Your Honor, this is the murder weapon," Truax said.

"It's not the murder weapon until you prove it is. Which you haven't done."

"There is one more thing, Your Honor. The knife has the initials 'CM' scratched on it. Right here." He touched the knife and offered it to Gillis. "Which stands for Collin Murphy."

I knew they'd find the initials.

"I object, Your Honor. There are millions of people with those initials."

"Like who?" Truax said.

"How about Charlie Maxwell?"

"Who?"

"He played outfield for the Tigers." Burr looked at the jury. "Everybody knows that."

Gillis pounded his gavel. "You are out of order Mr. Lafayette."

"Your Honor—"

"Whatever you're about to say, it's overruled. Bailiff, mark this knife as the knife found at the crime scene."

To Truax, "Do you have any further questions of this witness?"

Truax walked to the jury box.

"Ladies and gentlemen, we have shown that Mr. Slaughter disappeared. We have shown that his body was found after a long and arduous search. We have shown that he was murdered." Truax looked at Gillis. "I have no further questions, Your Honor," Truax said.

"Mr. Lafayette?" Judge Gillis said.

Burr walked up to the policeman. "Officer Stone, how long have you been a police officer?"

"Fifteen years," he said, smiling.

He's pleased with himself.

"Fifteen years," Burr said. "And how many murder investigations have you been involved in?"

"Well, I ..."

"Yes?"

"One," the cop said.

"That would be this one?"

"Yes."

"So, you've been involved in one murder investigation in your entire career. And this is the only one."

"I object, Your Honor," Truax said. "Officer Stone's record and qualifications are above reproach."

"Mr. Lafayette, you will consider Officer Stone qualified in this matter, and you will not question his credentials. Is that clear?"

"Your Honor, the record and qualifications of a witness are always relevant."

"They are indeed, and his are not to be questioned."

"Your Honor—"

"Move on, Mr. Lafayette."

I may have sown some doubt.

"Officer Stone, were you acquainted with Mr. Slaughter?"

"Objection," Truax said. "Irrelevant."

"Your Honor, this is the most relevant part of the witness's testimony."

"Enlighten me," Gillis said.

Burr looked at the judge, then the jury. "Harbor Springs is a wonderful place. I keep a boat here."

The jury nodded at him.

"It is a charming, small town where everyone knows everyone. My question is relevant because if Officer Stone knew Mr. Slaughter personally, it could influence, even prejudice, him against Dr. Murphy."

"You may answer the question," Gillis said.

Stone looked at Truax, who shook his head.

"I did know him," the cop said.

"Thank you, Officer Stone. Were you friends?"

"Probably."

"Probably?"

"We knew each other. Not socially."

Burr put his hand on the railing of the witness box. "Officer Stone, could your friendship have prejudiced your investigation?"

"No."

"Could your friendship with Mr. Slaughter have influenced your investigation?"

"Your Honor, I object."

"I have no further questions." Burr walked back to his table and sat.

Jacob leaned behind Collin. "We know that's the murder weapon."

"The jury doesn't."

Truax looked out into the gallery. "The State calls Lawrence Van Arkel."

"They're about to," Jacob said.

"Truax has to make his own case. I'm not going to help him."

Van Arkel shuffled to the witness stand. He wore the same gray suit that didn't quite fit, the same white shirt, and the same solid black tie he wore at the preliminary exam. His chest still looked like it had sunk into his stomach. His ears looked like they were pasted onto his head, but they did hold up his wire-rimmed glasses. His skin matched his suit.

He looks like he's been up all night. Maybe he has.

Swede swore him in.

He looks older than the last time I saw him. Maybe I do, too.

Truax walked up to the witness. "Dr. Van Arkel, please state your occupation."

"I am the medical examiner for Emmet County."

"Is that the same as the coroner?"

Van Arkel sat straight up. "That's an old-fashioned term. But yes."

They didn't practice that.

"Of course," Truax said. "Dr. Van Arkel, you are a medical doctor, an MD. Is that correct?"

"Yes."

"Did you perform an autopsy on the body of Frank Slaughter?"

"I did."

"And why did you do that?"

"An autopsy is always performed if foul play is suspected."

"Foul play?" Truax said.

As if you didn't know.

Van Arkel looked at Truax but didn't say anything.

"Dr. Van Arkel, you said you performed an autopsy on the body of Frank Slaughter. Were you able to determine the cause of death?"

"Mr. Slaughter drowned."

Truax looked like he'd just been stabbed. "Drowned? I thought Mr. Slaughter had been stabbed."

Definitely not practiced.

"I object, Your Honor," Burr said. "It is for the witness to say what the cause of death was. Not Mr. Truax." Burr looked at the jury. "I believe Dr. Van Arkel just said that Mr. Slaughter drowned." Burr smiled at Truax, who didn't smile back.

This is going better than I thought it would.

"Sustained," Gillis said. "Mr. Truax, please ask the questions. Don't supply the answers."

Truax turned red but didn't say anything. "Dr. Van Arkel, was Mr. Slaughter stabbed?"

"Yes."

"How many times?"

"Six."

"Six." Truax looked at the jury. "Mr. Slaughter was stabbed six times." Back to Van Arkel.

"Where was he stabbed?"

"In the back."

"In the back," Truax said. "Anywhere else?"

"Mr. Slaughter was also stabbed in his right eye."

The jury groaned.

"Dr. Van Arkel, did the stabbings contribute to Mr. Slaughter's death?"

Van Arkel rolled his eyes. "That's what killed him."

"I thought you said the cause of death was drowning."

Van Arkel looked over his glasses at Truax.

I'd say he's annoyed.

"He died from drowning, but the stab wounds punctured his lungs and his heart. He'd have died from the stab wounds if he hadn't fallen into the water face first."

Nuts.

"Objection, Your Honor. Speculation."

Truax looked up at Gillis. "Your Honor, Dr. Van Arkel is a highly respected member of the medical community. This is his expert opinion. It is hardly speculation."

"Overruled."

Truax put his hand on the railing of the witness stand. "Dr. Van Arkel, is it your considered opinion that Mr. Slaughter died from being stabbed?"

"Yes."

"Thank you." Truax picked up a file from his table. "Your Honor, the state would like to introduce the autopsy performed by Dr. Van Arkel as Prosecution Exhibit Two."

Burr stood.

"Surely, you can't have an objection to this, Mr. Lafayette."

"I'd like to review the autopsy, Your Honor."

"You can review it on your own time." To Swede, "Bailiff, mark this as Prosecution Exhibit Two."

"Your Honor—" Burr said.

"Sit down. It's not your turn." To Truax, "Do you have anything further?"

"Dr. Van Arkel, were you able to identify the murder weapon?"

"I was."

"And how did you do that?"

"The Harbor Springs Police Department gave me the knife they found at the crime scene. I matched the wounds on Mr. Slaughter's back with the blades on the knife."

"Is this the knife?"

Van Arkel turned it over in his hand. He ran his fingers across the case, stopping at one of the corners. "This is the murder weapon."

"Objection," Burr said. "We don't know if this is the murder weapon."

"Dr. Van Arkel just said it was."

Truax didn't give Judge Gillis any time to rule. "Dr. Van Arkel, how do you know this is the murder weapon?"

"The knife I was given by the police department had these markings." He touched the edge of the knife.

"And what do they say?"

Van Arkel read from the knife. "It's marked with two letters, 'CM.'"

"As in Collin Murphy?" Truax glared at Collin.

Collin jumped up. "Frank Slaughter stole my knife."

Burr pulled Collin back to his chair.

Whatever doubt there was about whose knife it was is gone.

Truax turned around and looked at Collin. "So, it is your knife, Mr. Murphy," Truax said, triumphantly.

Burr jumped up. "Your Honor, it is absolutely forbidden for the prosecutor to question the defendant."

"You know better than that, Mr. Truax."

Those initials are going to be the end of me.

It was Gillis's turn to glare at Collin. "As for you, Mr. Murphy, you will not speak to this courtroom. Unless you are called as a witness." Under his breath, "Which I think very unlikely." Louder, "You may continue, Mr. Truax."

"Thank you, Your Honor. Dr. Van Arkel, you have positively identified the knife you are holding as the murder weapon. Is that right?"

"Yes."

"And you are quite certain, because of the markings on the knife, the initials 'CM.'" Another look at Collin.

Burr put his hand on Collin's knee.

"Yes, this is the knife the police gave me."

Truax took the knife back from Van Arkel.

"Mr. Lafayette?"

The best thing for me to do is nothing.

"No objection, Your Honor."

"I can't believe my ears," Gillis said, mostly to himself. Then, "Bailiff, so mark the knife."

Swede came up to Truax.

"Excuse me, Your Honor. There is one more thing." Truax opened one of the blades of the knife, the biggest blade, three inches of polished steel. The blade gleamed, like a silver dagger. "Dr. Van Arkel, is this the blade that was used to stab Mr. Slaughter?"

"It is."

Truax waved the knife at the jury. The blade caught the light and cast a silver ray across the faces of the jurors. They blinked, covered their faces, or turned away.

Nice touch.

"Ladies and gentlemen," Truax said, "this is the murder weapon, a red Swiss Army knife that belonged to, excuse me, has the initials 'CM' scratched on it." He handed the knife to the bailiff. "I have no further questions, Your Honor."

"Mr. Lafayette?"

Burr walked up to Van Arkel.

Those initials are killing us.

"Dr. Van Arkel, you are an MD. Is that correct?"

"Yes."

"Do you practice medicine?"

"No."

"I see," Burr said, who knew the answer before asking the question.

"Is your work as the county coroner a full-time job?" Burr said, also knowing the answer.

"No."

"So, it's part-time."

"Yes."

Burr rocked back and forth, heel to toe. "What is it that you do?"

"I am a mortician."

"A mortician." Burr looked at the jury. "So, you're an undertaker?" Burr turned back to Van Arkel. "So, rather than help people get better, or cure them, you bury them. Is that right?"

Truax shot to his feet. "I object, Your Honor, this is shameful. Dr. Van Arkel's qualifications are first rate, and his reputation is impeccable."

Burr looked up at Gillis. "Your Honor, the qualifications of an expert are always subject to examination."

The judge shook his head. "Mr. Lafayette, we have already plowed this ground. With this very witness. I take judicial notice that Dr. Van Arkel is well-qualified. There will be no further questions along this line. Is that clear?"

"Your Honor—"

"Is that clear?"

Burr looked at the jury and mouthed "undertaker."

"Your Honor, Mr. Lafayette is taunting you."

"I most certainly am not."

"Mr. Lafayette, you are insufferable."

I take that as a compliment.

Burr picked up the knife from the evidence table. He turned it over in his hand, then held it in the palm of his hand so the jury could see it. "Dr. Van Arkel, is this a common knife?"

"Common?"

"Are there very many of these knives in existence?"

"I have no idea."

"Dr. Van Arkel, I could go to virtually any hardware store in the United States and buy a knife just like this."

Van Arkel didn't say anything.

"There must be thousands of knives just like this. And with this very blade."

Van Arkel still didn't say anything.

"Isn't it possible that Mr. Slaughter could have been stabbed with a knife just like this one, but not this particular knife?"

"This was the knife that was found at the crime scene."

"That's not what I asked you. I asked you if Mr. Slaughter could have been stabbed by another knife."

"I suppose so," Van Arkel said.

"I object, Your Honor," Truax said. "This knife was found at the crime scene and the wounds match the blade on the knife."

"Ladies and gentlemen, based on the evidence before you, it is up to you to determine if this is the murder weapon," Gillis said.

That's as close to a win as I'm going to get.

"Dr. Van Arkel, did you find Mr. Murphy's fingerprints on the knife?"

Van Arkel looked at Truax, then, "No, I did not, but the knife had been under—"

Burr cut him off. "Thank you, Dr. Van Arkel. I have no further questions."

Truax stood "The prosecution—"

"Stop right there, Mr. Truax. I've had enough, more than enough, for one day. We're adjourned." Gillis rapped his gavel and escaped.

CHAPTER SIXTEEN

After Gillis adjourned them, Burr drove to the three-story Victorian on Mitchell Street. The last time he'd been here, he'd cracked the windows and left Zeke in the Jeep. It was too cold to crack the windows today. And Zeke, in the decoy, probably didn't need them cracked. Burr cracked them anyway.

"For old time's sake."

He walked up the sidewalk and into the foyer of the Van Arkel Funeral Home. He'd been here once before, and it hadn't been a great visit then.

"I'd rather be somewhere else."

"I beg your pardon?"

Burr jumped, Van Arkel right behind him. "I didn't see you."

"I guess not."

I'm off to another good start.

"You just cross-examined me. What more could you possibly want?"

"I had a couple more questions that weren't appropriate for the courtroom."

"As rude as you are, I can't imagine why you think I'd help you."

I can't either.

"I'm sorry Dr. Van Arkel, but I have a client to defend."

"And that makes it acceptable to attack my profession?"

"I'm sorry," Burr said again.

Van Arkel looked out the window. "Is your dog in your car?"

The only reason Van Arkel helped me last time was because of Zeke.

"Zeke passed," Burr said.

"I'm so sorry."

"Thank you."

"Did you have to put him down?"

Burr nodded.

"It's terrible, but it's almost always the right thing to do."

"Do you still have your shorthairs?"

"I do." Van Arkel shook his hand. "How can I help?"

This is the only good thing that's come from losing Zeke.

"Dr. Van Arkel, I'm trying to find something, anything, that can help me with Collin."

"How does that involve me?"

"Did the police bring Mr. Slaughter's body here?"

"They did."

"I know you did the autopsy, but I was wondering if you might have found anything about your examination or any of his possessions that might help me. Was there anything in his pockets?" Burr put his hands in his pockets.

"I don't really remember." Van Arkel looked up, then back at Burr. "Nothing stood out. The usual things, wallet, keys, change."

Nuts.

"Do you have them?"

Van Arkel shook his head. "The police took everything."

* * *

"We got his stuff here."

"Can I see it?"

Sergeant George Maples scratched his chin. He was a short, wiry man in his fifties with a gray flattop and a pushed-in nose. He stood behind the window in the evidence cage in the basement of the courthouse. Burr had met him once before, too.

I hope this goes better than the last time.

"What do you want?"

"Can I see what you have in the Frank Slaughter case?"

"I suppose so." Maples disappeared, then came back with a wire basket about the size of a pizza box. He set it on the counter. "You didn't get this from me."

Burr rummaged through the basket. Wallet, car keys, change.

Van Arkel was right. There's nothing here.

Then he found it. He picked up a single key. A single key with a knob on the end and '36' printed on it.

"What's this?"

"Looks like a key."

"For what?"

"Looks like it goes to some kind of locker."

"Locker?"

"Like a bus station or a gym."

Burr ran out to his Jeep.

* * *

Burr parked as close as he could to the Nub's ski rental building and dodged the potholes on foot. Nub's wasn't closed for the season, but almost. Only a few skiers for what was left of the afternoon. There was plenty of snow, but most of the skiers had turned their attention to spring, which was at least a month away.

He walked into the building. A counter in the front, racks of skis and boots behind it. Ski poles on the far wall. He found what he was looking for: a wall of lockers.

He ran his hand across the lockers. Some had keys in them. Some didn't. He turned the key in number thirty-seven. The locker opened. It was empty. He turned the key in thirty-five. It opened, also empty. There was no key in thirty-six. He shook the door. It didn't budge.

"Damn it all."

He shook the locker again. Still nothing. Burr looked around the room. The Nub's employees were all busy. Burr took his own Swiss Army knife out of his pocket. He opened the blade and stuck it in the lock. He worked at the lock. Nothing. He changed blades and wiggled it in the lock. The locker popped open.

"Sir, is that your locker?"

Burr turned around. A young woman with rosy cheeks and a Nub's Nob jacket smiled at him.

"Yes. Yes, it is."

She smiled again and walked away.

He opened the locker. It was empty. Except for a camera.

* * *

"What is it?" Jacob said.

"It's a camera," Eve said. "What else would it be?"

"With Burr you never know."

Burr turned the camera around, slowly. It was five o'clock, and they sat at a window table in the dining room of the Harbor Inn.

Cocktail hour, and the Inn was empty, just like every March. Burr looked out at the bay. There was ice close to shore, but it had broken up out in the bay and was blowing around in the wind.

"It won't be long now. An east wind will blow it all out."

"You may have just found the most important piece of evidence in this case, and you're talking about ice," Jacob said.

"Burr has his priorities," Eve said.

Jacob reached for the camera. Eve slapped his hand.

"What was that for?"

Burr picked up the camera.

"Do you think it's Collin's?" Jacob said.

"Who else's would it be?"

She's in rare form.

"Let's get the film developed," Jacob said.

"It's a digital camera. There's no film."

"No film?" Jacob said.

"We talked about this before." Eve took the camera from Burr. "The pictures are inside." She turned the camera around. "Here's the viewfinder. We can look at the pictures right here."

"Shouldn't Collin be here for this?" Jacob said.

"For now, I think it's best if we're the only ones who know about this." Burr drummed his fingers. "We need to see if there's any pictures in here. There may be something that hurts Collin. And we don't know if he could keep quiet about it." He turned the camera over in his hands. "The camera was in Frank's locker, but that doesn't prove Frank put it there. And we still don't know if this is Collin's camera."

"Let's find out." Eve took the camera from Burr.

The bartender came over. "Can I get you something to drink?"

"I'll have …" Jacob said.

"Give us a few minutes," Burr said. "What's on that thing?"

Eve fiddled with the camera, then, "Here's a picture of the lady's slipper. Here's another one."

"It is Collin's camera," Jacob said.

Burr took the camera from Eve and scrolled through the pictures. Jacob looked over his shoulder. "Did he have to take all these flower pictures?"

"That's the reason this whole mess started." Eve took the camera back from Burr and scrolled through the files. "There's other pictures here." She pushed the camera to Burr. "Look."

Burr scrolled. "A frog sunning itself in a pond. The same frog eating a water bug. Then the frog gets torn apart by a turtle." Burr made a face.

He kept scrolling. "There're pictures of that beech tree. The Tree of Hearts, that's what Ian called it. Closeups of some of the carvings, initials mostly. Then pictures of Ian with the kids on the field trip, his daughter next to him. A picture of a man and a woman. I can't tell who they are. The last picture looks up through the trees, but it's out of focus."

"What does that mean?" Jacob said.

"That must be when Frank started beating him." Burr put the camera down and made another face.

"What?" Jacob said. "What is it?"

"This is Collin's camera. It looks like Frank took it, just like Collin said. I just don't know what to do with it." He waved at the bartender.

* * *

Burr was the first one in the courtroom, just the way he liked it. He sat Zeke on the chair next to him. "You'll have to move when they all get here."

He took his files out of his briefcase.

He smelled the smells of the first-in-the-morning courtroom: wax, furniture polish, bleach.

"It's the best time of the day."

It wasn't going to stay that way.

Jacob came in, along with Eve, Collin, Claire, and Aunt Kitty. Then Truax. Burr put Zeke on the floor next to his chair. "Sorry, old friend."

The gallery filled up. Smart and Ballantine were there again. So was Judge Abbott.

Gillis made his grand entrance. Swede called them to order.

The great smells are gone.

"Mr. Truax, you may call your next witness."

"The state calls Dewey Ballantine."

Swede swore in the rumpled, overweight, balding, soon-to-be former owner of Thorne Swift.

He looks like he slept in that suit.

"Mr. Ballantine, you are the owner of the property known as Thorne Swift. Is that correct?"

"Yes."

"And you leased the property to the Little Traverse Conservancy. Is that also correct?"

"Yes."

Truax nodded. "Would you please tell the court your arrangement with the Little Traverse Conservancy?"

It was Ballantine's turn to nod. "I leased it to them for a dollar a year."

"Did they have any right to buy it?"

Ballantine shook his head. One of his chins followed the other across his face.

"Mr. Ballantine, please answer the question. In words."

Words would be much better than shaking his head.

"No, the Conservancy did not have the right to buy the property."

"Thank you, Mr. Ballantine. Did you have a right to terminate the lease?"

"Yes."

"And what was that right?"

"I had the right to terminate the lease at any time after providing thirty days written notice."

Truax nodded.

My most recent loss.

"Mr. Ballantine, did you terminate the lease?" Truax paused. "If so, please tell the court what you did."

"I gave the Conservancy written notice almost a year ago. Last April."

"What happened?"

"They fought me on it. Tried to stop me from selling it." Ballantine tightened his tie.

It looks like a noose.

"Really?" Truax said, incredulous.

Please.

"What did they do?"

"They sued me. Said there was a flower there that was endangered. That it couldn't be disturbed, and I couldn't sell the property."

"Do you recall the name of the flower?"

"The lady's slipper. How could I forget. That damned flower has caused me nothing but trouble. It's called the lady's slipper. They said it was endangered, but it's not."

Burr stood slowly.

I've got to be careful.

"Your Honor, respectfully, the litigation is ongoing and has not yet been resolved."

"Nonsense," Ballantine said, raising his voice. "You lost. You lost every step of the way. Every time. I've spent a fortune with lawyers, but I've got the green light to sell, and, by God, that's what I'm going to do."

Gillis slammed his gavel. "Mr. Ballantine, you are not to respond to Mr. Lafayette's comments, no matter how wrong-headed they may seem."

"Your Honor—" Burr said.

"Mr. Lafayette, you're in the wrong courtroom if you think we're here to argue about the sale of Thorne Swift." Gillis looked at the prosecutor. "Mr. Traux. I am struggling to see how any of this pertains to your case. This is a murder trial, not a do-gooder's lawsuit."

"I will connect the dots, Your Honor."

"See that you do."

"Yes, Your Honor." The prosecutor looked back at his witness. "Mr. Ballantine, please tell us how this flower relates to the murder charge against the defendant." Truax pointed at Collin. Collin started to stand. Burr held him down.

"He got a court order stopping me from selling the land until a study was done about that damn flower."

"Excuse me, Mr. Ballantine. Who is him?"

"Him." Ballantine pointed at Burr. "Lafayette."

"That's Mr. Lafayette," Burr said.

Another rap of the gavel. "Quiet, Mr. Lafayette."

"So, everything stops." Ballantine pointed at Collin. "Murphy is supposed to do the study. He goes on my property after I ended the lease and takes pictures. He says Frank, Mr. Slaughter, beat him up and took his camera."

"Objection, Your Honor. Mr. Murphy was there legally."

A bang of the gavel. "Mr. Lafayette, as I said, that is a matter for a different court on a different day." To Ballantine, "Please continue."

The tubby witness cleared his throat. "Murphy said Frank, Mr. Slaughter, took his camera. Which I doubt. So, Murphy tracks Frank down. He accuses him of taking the camera. And then he kills him."

This isn't the right time to bring up the camera.

Burr jumped to his feet. "Mr. Ballantine has no idea what happened. I move that his testimony be stricken."

Gillis thumped his forehead.

I hope he gives himself a headache.

Gillis turned to the jury. "Ladies and gentlemen, you will disregard Mr. Ballantine's comments about Mr. Murphy tracking down and killing Mr. Slaughter. You may consider Mr. Ballantine's comments about Mr. Slaughter asking Mr. Murphy to leave Thorne Swift."

The damage is done.

Truax put his hands in his pockets. "Mr. Ballantine, is it your opinion that Mr. Murphy was on your property illegally?"

"Yes"

Burr started to stand.

"Sit," Gillis said.

Burr sat.

"Mr. Ballantine, what did Mr. Slaughter do when he found the defendant at Thorne Swift?"

"Mr. Slaughter told me that he asked Murphy to leave."

"And what did Mr. Murphy do?"

Ballantine looked at Collin. "He refused."

Burr stood.

I actually made it to my feet without being told to sit down.

"Objection, Your Honor. This is hearsay."

Truax smiled his condescending smile at Burr. "Counsel is quite right. This is indeed hearsay, but it falls into two of the exceptions. First, Mr. Slaughter is deceased and can't testify, so hearsay is allowed.

"Second, Mr. Murphy could testify to this, but, regrettably, I am not allowed to call him as a witness." Truax looked at the jury. "Because a defendant cannot be forced to testify in a murder trial and incriminate himself. And I'm sure Mr. Murphy would incriminate himself."

"We've been through this. Overruled."

I just made it worse. If that's possible.

"You may continue, Mr. Truax."

"Thank you, Your Honor." To Ballantine, "Do you know what demeanor, what tone of voice Mr. Slaughter might have used when he asked the defendant to leave?"

"In my experience, Mr. Slaughter was kind and polite. He was always respectful."

"Would he have removed the defendant forcibly? Or laid a hand on him?"

"Absolutely not."

Collin leapt to his feet. "That's a lie. Slaughter beat me up and stole my camera."

Gillis pounded his gavel. "Bailiff, remove the defendant. Cuff him. Take him to jail and see that he's fitted with an orange jumpsuit." To Truax, "You may continue."

Swede walked up to Collin.

It was Burr's turn to leap to his feet. "Your Honor, I apologize for my client's outburst. He is upset." Burr paused. "And he *is* being tried for murder."

"Take him out," Gillis said. "Continue, Mr. Truax."

"Your Honor," Burr said, "if you remove my client, you must adjourn the proceeding."

"I don't 'must' do anything."

The same old mail-order law degree.

"Your Honor, a fundamental principle of criminal procedure is that the accused has the right to hear his accusers. You may remove Mr. Murphy, but you must adjourn the proceedings while he is absent."

Gillis put his hands on his desk and clenched his fists. "Very well. Mr.

Murphy, sit down." Collin sat. "If I hear one more word from you, you will be removed from my courtroom. Criminal procedure be damned. Is that clear?"

Collin put his hands on the defense table and made them into fists. "Yes."

"Do not make your hands into fists in my courtroom," Gillis said. To the prosecutor, "Mr. Truax."

"Mr. Ballantine, you testified that Mr. Slaughter told you that he asked the defendant to leave Thorne Swift."

"That's right."

"What did the defendant do?"

"He refused to leave."

"What did Mr. Slaughter do next?"

"He asked him again."

"And?"

"Murphy attacked Mr. Slaughter."

"The defendant attacked Mr. Slaughter?" Truax took a step back. "What happened?"

"Murphy beat him. Mr. Slaughter did his best to hold him off."

"What happened then?"

"Mr. Slaughter fled."

Collin jumped up again. "He's lying. I was the one who was beaten. Slaughter beat me and stole my camera. And my knife."

Gillis crashed his gavel. "Bailiff, remove the defendant."

Swede grabbed Collin by the arm and took him out of the courtroom. Gillis looked at his watch. "We are adjourned for lunch."

* * *

When Gillis called them back to order, they were all in their places. Except Collin. They waited. And waited. And waited. At last, the door opened. Two of Petoskey's finest brought Collin in an orange jumpsuit and handcuffs.

Now he looks guilty.

The policemen sat Collin down and belted him to his chair.

"Your Honor," Burr said.

"Mr. Murphy has no one to blame but himself." To Ballantine, who was back on the witness stand, "I remind you that you are still under oath."

Truax walked up to the not-so-dapper Dewey. "Mr. Ballantine, before we were adjourned, you testified that the defendant attacked Mr. Slaughter, who did not fight back, but retreated. Is that right?"

Collin did his best to stand but couldn't. "That's not—"

"Mr. Murphy, don't say a word. Not a single peep. If you so much as clear your throat, I will have you gagged. Is that clear?"

Collin didn't say anything.

"I asked you a question."

Collin nodded.

"Say 'Yes, Your Honor.'"

Collin mumbled something.

This is getting worse.

"I'll take that as a 'yes.' Continue, Mr. Truax."

"Did Mr. Slaughter say anything about Mr. Murphy's camera?"

"He said that he told Mr. Murphy to stop taking pictures."

"Did Mr. Slaughter say he took Mr. Murphy's camera or his knife?"

"Mr. Slaughter told me that Mr. Murphy attacked him. He said he left when he was attacked. He said he didn't have anything to do with the camera or the knife."

It's still not the right time.

"Mr. Ballantine, just to be clear, Mr. Slaughter told you he did not take the defendant's camera or his knife. Is that correct?"

"That's a lie," Collin said.

Gillis ignored Collin. "Do you have anything further, Mr. Truax?"

"No, Your Honor." Burr started to stand but knocked Zeke over. The decoy's head fell off, and some of his ashes spilled on the floor.

"Damn it all."

He cleaned up the ashes and put them back in the decoy.

"Mr. Lafayette?" Judge Gillis said.

Burr, still under the table, sat up and bumped his head.

"Damn it all," he said again.

"Mr. Lafayette," Judge Gillis said again.

Burr sat up in his chair. "Yes, Your Honor?"

"Please come up here."

Burr walked up to the judge.

"Over here," Judge Gillis said, pointing at Miss Longfinger's side of his desk. He looked at Burr, then quietly, "Mr. Lafayette, what may I ask, is that under your table?"

Burr turned around. "That's my briefcase, Your Honor."

"What's that next to your briefcase?"

"Next to my briefcase?"

Gillis tapped his fingers on his desk. "It looks quite like a duck decoy."

Nuts.

Burr ran his hands through his hair, front to back. "It is a duck decoy, Your Honor."

"What spilled out of it?" More finger tapping.

"Spilled?"

"Are you deaf? It looked like dirt."

"I didn't see anything spill, Your Honor."

"Come a little closer," the judge said.

Burr edged closer.

"Mr. Lafayette, I am not a learned man. I'm not particularly shrewd, but I'm not a fool."

Burr didn't say anything.

"I am quite sure that what is left of your close family member is in that decoy."

"Your Honor …"

"I don't want to know, but don't ever bring it back in my courtroom again."

"Him."

"Him," Gillis said, pointing under Burr's table. "Never mind." Then mostly to himself, "Why I ever let you back into my courtroom is beyond me." He looked down his nose at Burr. "If Truax finds out, there will be hell to pay. And if you have any questions for Mr. Ballantine, ask them now, or sit down."

"Yes, Your Honor." Burr took a step to the witness box. "Mr. Ballantine, did you employ Frank Slaughter at Thorne Swift?"

"He was the caretaker. In the summer."

"As part of his job as caretaker, did Mr. Slaughter watch over Thorne Swift to make sure it was not being mistreated and allow access only when the preserve was open?"

"Yes."

"As part of his duties, did Mr. Slaughter ever ask Mr. Murphy to leave Thorne Swift?"

"Yes."

"And why did he do that?"

"Because I terminated the lease and closed it."

"Did Mr. Murphy have permission to be at Thorne Swift?"

"He most certainly did not."

Burr walked back to his table and picked up a file, then reached under the table and patted Zeke.

Here we go, old friend.

Burr walked back up to Ballantine. He tapped the file on the railing. "Mr. Ballantine, this is a court order from Judge Elizabeth Abbott, judge of the Federal District Court for the Western District of Michigan. Do you know what it says?"

"No." Ballantine sat up straight in his chair, but he was still rumpled.

"Of course you don't." Burr tapped the file again. "This order gave Mr. Murphy the right to enter Thorne Swift for the express purpose of doing research on the lady's slipper. Were you aware of that?"

"No."

"Of course you weren't."

Burr went back to his table and picked up another file. He tapped it on the railing. "Mr. Ballantine, this is a transcript of a hearing in Judge Abbott's courtroom. Mr. Murphy testified that he had been at Thorne Swift doing research, as authorized by the court, when Mr. Slaughter attacked him. In the transcript, Mr. Murphy also states that Mr. Slaughter beat him and stole his camera and his Swiss Army knife. Were you aware of that?"

Ballantine looked at Johnson Smart in the gallery. Smart shook his head.

Burr took a step to Gillis. "Your Honor, the transcript shows that Mr. Ballantine was present at the hearing. Moreover, there is a court order served on Mr. Ballantine authorizing Mr. Murphy to do his research at Thorne Swift." Burr looked at the jury, then at Gillis. "Your Honor, Mr. Ballantine is lying. I move that his entire testimony be stricken from the record."

Truax jumped up. "I object, Your Honor. Mr. Ballantine is testifying as to what he believes is the truth."

"Mr. Ballantine was present at the hearing in Judge Abbott's courtroom, and he was served with the order. He is lying."

Truax cleared his throat. "It is possible that Mr. Ballantine is mistaken. That doesn't mean he's lying."

Burr shook his head at Truax. "That's slicing the salami pretty thin."

Truax rushed up to the bench. "Your Honor, these purported files have not been introduced into evidence."

Burr smiled at Truax. "Your Honor, the defense introduces the transcript and the order as Defense Exhibit One and Defense Exhibit Two, respectively."

"I object," Truax said.

Gillis arched his eyebrows. "On what grounds?"

"We are here trying Mr. Murphy for murder. The proceedings in another courtroom are irrelevant to this trial."

Burr looked up at Gillis. "On the contrary, Your Honor. They are extremely relevant. They prove that Mr. Murphy was at the Conservancy lawfully and that Mr. Slaughter beat him and stole his camera and his knife. They also prove that Mr. Murphy couldn't have murdered Mr. Slaughter because he didn't have his knife."

Truax cleared his throat. "Your Honor, these files don't shed any light at what happened at Thorne Swift. And there is no proof whatsoever that Mr. Slaughter took the defendant's camera or his knife."

Gillis sighed. "I am going to admit these files into evidence. I am not going to disqualify Mr. Ballantine." Gillis looked at the jury. "Ladies and gentlemen, you may consider Mr. Ballantine's testimony as well as these files. As the triers-of-fact, you must decide what to believe." To Burr, "You may continue."

Burr looked at the jury. "Ladies and gentlemen, this witness is lying."

Truax exploded out of his chair. "I object. This is outrageous."

"Ladies and gentlemen, you will disregard Mr. Lafayette's last comment. Strike Mr. Lafayette's comment from the record."

"I have no further questions." Burr walked back to his table and sat.

That worked.

"Mr. Truax, you may call your next witness," Gillis said.

Truax stood and faced the gallery. "The state calls Paige Turner."

Swede swore in the fiftyish, perky blonde with the pageboy.

"Ms. Turner," Truax said, "were you at Bar Harbor on the night of July twenty-first?"

"I was."

"And did you see the defendant at Bar Harbor that night?" Truax pointed at Collin.

"Yes."

"And who was the defendant with?"

"He was with Mr. Slaughter."

"Frank Slaughter? The deceased?" Truax said.

"Yes."

Truax took a step back.

As if you didn't know.

"Ms. Turner, did you hear what they were talking about?"

"I did."

Truax nodded. "And did—"

Gillis cut him off. "Mr. Truax, I do understand that you have a certain style and a way in which you'd like the testimony presented, but we're going to be here all day if you keep up with this twenty questions."

"Your Honor?"

"For mercy's sake, let Ms. Turner tell her story."

The prosecutor turned the faintest shade of red, then turned to his witness. "Ms. Turner, please tell us what you heard that evening and the tenor of the conversation."

Tenor?

"Tenor?" she said.

"The mood." One more shade of red.

She pulled her skirt down and sat back in the chair. "Mr. Murphy was angry. He was raising his voice. He wasn't shouting, but he was loud. I couldn't help but hear." She looked at Burr and smiled.

"What were they talking about?" Truax.

Gillis scowled at Truax, who pretended not to notice.

"I heard Mr. Murphy say, 'I know you've got my camera, and I want it back.' Mr. Slaughter said he didn't have it. Mr. Murphy said, 'You stole it from me, and I want it back. Now.' Mr. Slaughter shook his head. Then Mr. Murphy reached across the table and grabbed Mr. Slaughter by the arm. Mr. Slaughter pulled his arm away and sat back in the booth. Then, Mr. Murphy said 'give me my camera or I'll kill you.'"

"He said 'I'll kill you?'" Truax looked at Collin.

"Yes."

Collin started to stand. Burr held him down. "Don't say a word."

"I never said that."

"I'll take care of it, Just be quiet."

The lady's slipper really is deadly.

Paige Turner put her hands on the rail of the witness stand. "Then Mr. Slaughter smiled at Mr. Murphy and said, 'I don't have it, but I can get it.' Then Mr. Murphy said, 'Get it now.' That's what Mr. Murphy said. Then Mr. Slaughter said 'I can get it for you. For twenty-five thousand dollars.'" She sat back in her chair.

"Then what happened?"

The witness leaned toward Truax. "Mr. Murphy said, 'It's my camera. I want it back. Give it to me now, or I'll kill you.'"

Truax took a step back, horrified. "The defendant said, 'I'll kill you?'" Truax pointed at Collin again.

This is worse than the preliminary exam.

"Yes, he said, 'I'll kill you,' then he got up and grabbed Mr. Slaughter around the neck. Mr. Slaughter broke free and said, 'Get your hands off me. If you want the camera, it's twenty-five grand in cash.' Mr. Slaughter got up and left."

"What did the defendant do?"

"He followed Mr. Slaughter out."

"Did you see them after that?"

"No."

"Thank you, Ms. Turner." Truax walked to the jury. "Ladies and gentlemen, you just heard Ms. Turner testify that she heard the defendant tell Mr. Slaughter he would kill him unless he got his camera back. She also testified that the defendant physically assaulted Mr. Slaughter, then followed him out of the bar." Truax stopped, looked at Collin again, then back at the jury. "The defendant, Collin Murphy, then followed Mr. Slaughter out of Bar Harbor to the nature preserve at the end of Fourth Street, where he stabbed Mr. Slaughter to death with this." Truax walked to the evidence table. He opened up the knife and waved it at the jury. They sat back in their chairs.

Burr jumped to his feet. "I object, Your Honor. The witness testified that she saw Mr. Slaughter and Mr. Murphy leave the bar. She did not testify that she saw Mr. Murphy follow Mr. Slaughter to the nature preserve."

"Your Honor, the defendant did, in fact, follow Mr. Slaughter to the nature preserve. I apologize if I made it seem that Ms. Turner saw it."

"No one saw Mr. Murphy follow Mr. Slaughter to the nature preserve," Burr said.

"Wait and see," Truax said.

The judge rapped his gavel. "Ladies and gentlemen, the witness testified that she saw Mr. Murphy follow Mr. Slaughter out of Bar Harbor. She did not testify that she saw Mr. Murphy follow Mr. Slaughter to the nature preserve."

"Thank you, Your Honor," Burr said.

It's not much but it's something.

"Your witness," Truax said.

Burr walked up to the witness.

How could anyone name their daughter Paige Turner?

"Ms. Turner, are you married?"

She looked at him like he was crazy.

"Ms. Turner, are you married?" he said, again.

"Objection, Your Honor," Truax said. "Irrelevant."

Gillis looked at Burr like he was crazy.

"Yes. Yes, I am." She held up her ring finger with a gold band and diamond almost as big as a cocktail olive.

At least her parents didn't name her Paige Turner.

"I withdraw the question, Your Honor." To the witness, "Mrs. Turner, you testified that you were in the booth next to Mr. Murphy and Mr. Slaughter. Is that right?"

"Yes."

"And you overheard their conversation?"

"Yes."

"So, you were listening in?"

She squirmed in her chair. "I couldn't help but hear."

Burr put his hands in his pockets. "So, you were eavesdropping." Not a question.

"I most certainly was not."

Burr looked at the jury, then back at the witness. "What would you call it?"

"They were so loud, I couldn't help but hear."

Burr rocked back and forth, heel to toe. "Mrs. Turner, were you drinking that night?"

"Drinking?"

"Alcohol. It is a bar."

She looked down at her hands but didn't say anything.

"What were you drinking?"

"Drinking? I don't remember."

"How many drinks that you don't remember having did you have?"

"I may have had a drink or two."

"Or three? Or four?" Burr looked at the jury and frowned.

Truax stood. "I object, Your Honor. Mrs. Turner is not the one on trial."

"Your Honor," Burr said. "If Mrs. Turner had been drinking, which she said she had been, she may have well been under the influence of alcohol or even drunk, which makes her testimony unreliable."

She sat up straight and threw her shoulders back. "I was not drunk."

"Mrs. Turner, have you ever been arrested for drunk driving?"

"Your Honor, this is irrelevant," Truax said.

"You need not answer that question, Mrs. Turner." To Burr, "Mr. Lafayette, you are out of order. If you are going to continue with Mrs. Turner, you will change your line of questioning." Gillis slammed his gavel. "Do I make myself clear?"

"Yes, Your Honor, but if Mrs. Turner had been drinking, she may not have heard what she thinks she heard."

"I know what I heard. The whole bar heard him screaming."

"I have no further questions." Burr walked back to his table.

Gillis shuffled through his papers again. He found what he was looking for. His lips moved as he read it.

I wish I could read lips.

The judge cleared his throat. "Mr. Truax, I see that Mrs. Turner was your last witness." To Burr, "Counsel, you may present your defense." He paused, then mumbling, "Whatever it might be."

I don't have to be a lip reader to hear that.

Burr started to stand, but Truax popped up. "Your Honor, the state has one more witness."

Burr, halfway to his feet, ripped through his files. "Your Honor, Mr. Truax called all of the witnesses on his list."

Truax smiled at Gillis. "Your Honor, this witness has just now come to our attention."

"I object, Your Honor," Burr said. "You had six months to dig up anybody with a pulse."

"Your Honor, I know this is somewhat irregular, but in the interest of justice, I ask that you permit me to call this witness. It will make the state's case clear and convincing. Even more so than it already is."

"I object," Burr said, again.

"In the interest of justice, Your Honor."

"Justice stopped mattering a long time ago," Burr said.

Gillis ignored him. "Call your witness, Mr. Truax."

"Your Honor, if you permit this Ichabod Crane of a prosecutor to call his witness, I will move for a mistrial."

"Ichabod Crane?" Gillis said.

Truax turned red.

Burr nodded at Truax.

"Call your witness."

"I move for a mistrial."

"So noted." To Truax, "You may proceed."

The prosecutor, still red in the face, faced the gallery. "The state calls Walter Hughes."

A man in his late fifties walked to the witness stand. He had bushy brown hair and eyebrows to match. He turned and faced Swede.

The bailiff swore him in. Truax walked up to the witness stand. "Mr. Hughes, please tell us your address."

"530 West Fourth Street. Harbor Springs."

"And where is that?"

"It's below the bluff. The last house on Fourth Street. Right next to the nature preserve."

Truax nodded. "Mr. Hughes, please tell the court what you were doing the night of July twenty-first. At about eleven."

"I was walking my dog. I always walk him about that time. At least in the summer. Helps us both get to sleep."

Truax nodded again. "Mr. Hughes, where did you walk that night?"

"Same way as always. Down to the end of Fourth Street, around the turnaround, and back."

"Did you see anything on your walk that night?"

"There was a car parked down there. I only saw one car, but I'm pretty sure there were two. I heard a door shut, then another one a ways off."

"Then what?"

"Then hollering. One of 'em was yelling at the other."

"Did you hear what they were saying?"

"One of them said, 'Put that knife away. Give me my camera or I'll kill you.'"

"Then what happened?"

"I heard a scuffle. The other guy said, 'Get away from me.' I heard them start off down the path into the preserve."

Truax took two steps toward Burr's table, then, sotto voce, "I told you that someone saw Murphy follow Slaughter. All you had to do was wait." He walked back to Hughes before Burr could say anything. "Mr. Hughes, did you see or hear anything else?"

"No."

"What did you do?"

"I went home."

"I have no further questions." Truax started back to his table, then looked back at the witness. "Mr. Hughes, what kind of dog do you have?"

"Dog?"

"Yes, what kind of dog do you have?"

Walter Hughes smiled. "I have a Lab. A yellow Lab."

"Do you hunt him?"

"Yes. Mostly ducks."

"How old is he?"

"He's getting up there. Eleven. He's eleven."

Burr started to stand but sat down.

"I don't know what I'll do when he's gone."

Truax smiled at Burr. "Your witness."

This isn't happening.

Burr tried to stand but fell back into his chair.

"Mr. Lafayette, do you have any questions for this witness?"

"Yes, Your Honor."

Burr stood, then sat back down.

"Is there something wrong?"

Burr reached under the table for Zeke. He rubbed the back of the urn decoy. "I have no questions," he said, still under the table.

"Very well. Mr. Hughes …"

Aunt Kitty jumped to her feet. "I have a few questions." She marched up to the witness. "Kathryn Lafayette for the defense, Your Honor." She turned toward the witness.

"Mr. Hughes—"

"Objection, Your Honor," Truax said. "She's not a lawyer."

"You know damned well I am a licensed attorney."

"Not another Lafayette," Gillis said, mostly to himself.

"She hasn't entered an appearance," Truax said.

"I just did."

"The court recognizes that Ms. Lafayette has entered an appearance." Gillis looked over his glasses at Burr's aunt. "Go ahead, Ms. Lafayette, but please don't be as difficult as your son."

"He's not my son." She turned to the witness, "Mr. Hughes, did you see the faces of the two men you heard at the end of Fourth Street?"

"It was dark."

"I know it was dark. That's what happens at night." She smiled a not very nice smile at Hughes. "I asked if you saw their faces."

"No."

"No," she said. "Did you recognize their voices?"

Hughes squirmed in his chair. "No."

"So you have no idea who they were." Aunt Kitty tapped her foot. "Do you?"

"I'd know his voice if I heard it." Hughes pointed at Collin, who squirmed in his chair.

Aunt Kitty stepped to the bench and looked at Gillis. She was tall enough that she really didn't have to look up. "Your Honor, I ask that Mr. Hughes's testimony be stricken as hearsay."

Truax sprung up like a jack-in-the-box. "I object, Your Honor. Mr. Slaughter is dead and can't testify, but you can ask the defendant to speak."

Gillis cleared his throat. "Mr. Murphy—"

"Your Honor," Aunt Kitty said, "a defendant in a criminal proceeding cannot be forced to testify."

"Judge, we only need him to say a few words."

"Your Honor, if you ask Mr. Murphy to testify, you will be violating his constitutional rights, and this proceeding will end in a mistrial."

Truax was turning red. "The defendant waived his rights when he shouted in court."

"He most certainly did not waive his rights," Aunt Kitty said.

Gillis tapped his fingers on his desk, then he looked at Hughes, then Truax, and finally, at Aunt Kitty. "I am going to allow the testimony under the hearsay exception for the deceased."

Aunt Kitty rocked back and forth. "Your Honor, there is no hearsay exception for the constitutional protection afforded to Mr. Murphy."

"There is now."

"I object."

Truax walked up to the confused witness. "Mr. Hughes, didn't you hear Mr. Murphy's voice when he so rudely interfered in these proceedings?"

"You are out of line," Aunt Kitty said. To Collin, "Don't say a word."

"Ms. Lafayette, need I remind you that I'm in charge here?"

"It doesn't seem like it," she said, not so under her breath.

"I wasn't here that day," Walter Hughes said.

Gillis looked at the jury. "Ladies and gentlemen, you may give Mr. Hughes's testimony whatever credibility you think it merits."

Aunt Kitty put her hands on the bench. "Your Honor—"

Gillis rapped her fingers with his gavel, then smashed it on his desk. "We are adjourned."

CHAPTER SEVENTEEN

Jacob knocked on the door. "Burr. Burr. Open up this instant."

Burr rolled over.

Jacob knocked again, louder this time. "I know you're in there."

Burr rolled over again.

Jacob banged on the door. Burr rolled over one more time. Then it was quiet. But not for long. A key turned in the door. Jacob burst in. "Good God, man. Get up. We're late already." Jacob shook Burr's shoulder. "Hurry up. We've got to go. Now."

Burr sat up.

How did he get in here?

Burr looked over at the door. Stewart smiled at him, key in hand.

"Burr," Jacob said, "get dressed. We've got to get to court."

"I'm not going."

"Our defense starts today."

"Aunt Kitty can do it. She did fine yesterday."

"She doesn't know what to do."

"Give her our witness list."

"Collin hired you, not Aunt Kitty."

"Collin looks like he's guilty as sin." Burr laid back down. He thought he'd gotten over, or at least gotten past Zeke, but Truax's surprise witness had put Burr over the edge. Truax had cornered him on the way out of the building. He'd patted Zeke on the head. Burr had come straight back to the Harbor Inn and put himself to bed. He was damned if he'd let Truax get the better of him, but he couldn't make himself get going.

Jacob shook him by the shoulders. "You don't have time for a shower, but there is time to shave."

Burr shook his head.

"Come on, Burr. Let's go."

Burr sat there.

"I think I may have found something on Frank Slaughter."

* * *

"Ladies and gentlemen, simply put, Collin Murphy did not murder Frank Slaughter. The prosecutor's case is built on circumstantial evidence. No one saw who killed Mr. Slaughter. Mr. Murphy lost his knife. He believes Mr. Slaughter took it from him. But any one of a number of people could have found it and used it to kill Mr. Slaughter." Burr took a step toward the jury box. "While it may be true that Mr. Murphy was angry with Mr. Slaughter, that doesn't mean that he killed him. People get mad at each other all the time, and it seldom, if ever, ends in murder."

Burr walked up to the jury box and put his hands on the railing. He looked at each juror one by one. "The prosecutor's case is based on circumstantial evidence, flimsy at best."

Burr looked at Collin, then back at the jury. "Collin Murphy did not murder Frank Slaughter. You must acquit him." Burr walked back to his table.

"Mr. Lafayette, is that the extent of your defense, or do you actually have a witness or two?"

I don't have much of a defense, and I'm barely hanging on.

Burr looked up at Gillis. "The defense calls Johnson Smart."

Swede swore in Burr's witness.

Smart, in a black suit, starched white shirt, and a black-and-red striped tie, looked every bit the well-heeled developer he was. He acted like he was at least a cut above everyone else in the world, including Burr. He looked down his nose at Burr. Smart was still tan, even in March.

He must go somewhere in the winter.

"Mr. Smart, you are trying to buy Thorne Swift from Mr. Ballantine, is that right?"

Smart looked further down his nose. "I bought Thorne Swift. We closed yesterday afternoon."

Burr stepped closer to Smart. Under his breath, "You didn't."

"I most certainly did," Smart said, not under his breath.

"Speak up, Mr. Lafayette," the judge said. "We all need to hear what you're saying."

Burr stepped back from Smart.

"You lost, dear boy," Smart said.

How could this have happened?

"I beg your pardon," Burr said.

"I closed with Mr. Ballantine yesterday. I am the new owner of Thorne Swift."

Burr was shaken. He walked back to his table, picked up a file, and pretended to look at it. To Collin and Aunt Kitty, "Do you know anything about this?"

They both shook their heads.

I lost.

"Mr. Lafayette, do you have any further questions for this witness?" Gillis said.

Burr, his back to the judge, didn't say anything.

I lost every step of the way.

"If you don't have any questions for Mr. Smart, I am going to excuse him."

Burr shook his head.

What do I do?

"I take it that you don't," Gillis said. "Mr. Smart—"

Burr walked up to Smart.

This is never going to work, but it might confuse the jury.

"Mr. Smart, Collin Murphy's study could have prevented you from buying Thorne Swift. Isn't that right?"

"Collin Murphy never finished his study, and Judge Abbott ruled in my favor, time and again."

"But the pictures on his camera could have hurt your chances. You had a reason to keep them from seeing the light of day."

"I have no idea what you're talking about."

"You wouldn't want Mr. Murphy's study to block your purchase of Thorne Swift. Frank Slaughter tried to sell the camera to you. You refused to pay. You were furious. You followed Mr. Slaughter to the preserve. When he wouldn't give you the camera, you murdered him."

Smart sat back in his chair. "I did nothing of the sort."

"Mr. Smart, you had every reason in the world to want those pictures. The lady's slipper only blooms for a few weeks. If you had Mr. Murphy's camera, you could have kept him from completing his study. Judge Abbott would give her approval for you to buy Thorne Swift."

Smart gave Burr a withering look. "The lady's slipper isn't endangered. The pictures didn't matter."

"No one knew that at the time."

Smart gave Burr another withering look.

"Mr. Smart, you have a house on Lower Shore Drive in Harbor Springs. Is that right?"

"Yes."

"And you were in Harbor Springs during the time Mr. Slaughter went missing. Is that right?"

"I don't remember."

Burr put his hands in his pockets. "Mr. Smart, you have a convenient memory."

Another smile from Smart, this one amused. "I may have been in Harbor Springs then."

"Mr. Smart, where were you the night Mr. Slaughter disappeared?"

"I was with my wife."

"I'm sure you were." Burr turned to the jury. "Ladies and gentlemen, as you can see, Mr. Smart had every reason to murder Mr. Slaughter. The pictures on Mr. Murphy's camera would have ruined his plans to purchase Thorne Swift."

I hope I confused the jury.

Burr looked out at the gallery. "We already heard from Mr. Ballantine. He had the same reason to kill Mr. Slaughter." Burr pointed at Ballantine then looked back at the jury. "Both of them had a much better reason to kill Mr. Slaughter than Mr. Murphy did."

To Gillis, "I have no further questions."

Truax walked up to the witness. "Mr. Smart, did you follow Mr. Slaughter into the nature preserve the night he was killed?"

"No."

"Did you murder Mr. Slaughter?"

"No."

"I have no further questions." Truax nodded to the jury and sat.

Burr walked back to his table and picked up the file Jacob had given him about Frank Slaughter. He looked at it again, put it down, then turned to the gallery. "The defense calls Jill Slaughter."

She took the stand. Swede swore her in. The widow Slaughter wore another black dress. No jewelry and no makeup. She folded her hands on her lap.

"Mrs. Slaughter, let me start by saying that I'm very sorry for your loss."

"Thank you."

"How long were you married to Mr. Slaughter?"

"Eighteen years."

"And you have two children?"

"Yes."

Now it's going to get dicey.

"Was it a happy marriage?"

"Yes," she said, softly.

"Did you have any troubles, troubles with your marriage?"

"No. Just the ordinary things. Raising children. Jobs. Money."

Burr walked back to the defense table and picked up the file Jacob had brought. "Mrs. Slaughter, this is a police report that you filed with the Harbor Springs Police Department. Are you familiar with it?"

She took a deep breath. "No. No, I don't think so."

Burr smiled at her. "Let me refresh your memory."

Truax stood. "Your Honor, if counsel wants to talk about whatever is in that file, he needs to introduce it into evidence."

"So moved," Burr said.

Gillis admitted the police report into evidence.

Burr took a piece of paper out of the file. "Mrs. Slaughter, this is a copy of a complaint you filed with the Harbor Springs Police Department. In it, you state that your husband, Mr. Slaughter, beat you and that you were afraid." Burr looked at the gallery, the jury, then at Jill Slaughter. "Do you remember that?"

She pulled down the hem of her dress and sat up straight. "Not really."

Burr took out more papers. "There are three more complaints. Each one states that your husband hit you. Do you remember filing them?"

"Not really."

"Shall I read them to you?"

Truax popped up. "I object, Your Honor. Counsel is harassing the witness."

"Your Honor, I am trying to show Mr. Slaughter's true character and the nature of his marriage to Mrs. Slaughter."

Gillis dismissed Truax with a wave of his hand.

"You may continue, Mr. Lafayette."

"Mrs. Slaughter, each one of these complaints you filed accuses your husband, Frank Slaughter, of pushing you, knocking you down, and hitting you. Is that what happened?"

The widow Slaughter put her hands in her lap and clenched her fists. "I don't really remember."

"Let me refresh your memory. This one is dated last May, a month before Mr. Slaughter was murdered." Burr read from the complaint. "'Last night after dinner, I was doing the dishes. Frank came into the kitchen and told me I was a terrible cook. I kept at the dishes. He said it again. I still didn't say anything. He came up behind me, grabbed me by the shoulder and jerked me around. Then he yelled at me. "Answer me when I talk to you." I said I did my best. He said it was lousy and then slapped me on the face. I told him to stop. He knocked me down and kicked me.'" Burr stopped reading.

Burr's witness looked down at her feet.

"Mrs. Slaughter, would you like to hear more?"

She shook her head.

Burr walked over to the jury box and put his hands on the rail. He looked at the jurors, one by one. "Each one of these complaints details similar, if not worse, violence. Despite what the prosecutor would have you believe, Mr. Slaughter was not a saint. He was a violent man. He beat his wife regularly."

Burr walked back to the witness stand. "Mrs. Slaughter, did you finally have enough? Did you follow your husband that night and murder him?"

"No. No. I would never do that." She started to cry.

"Very theatrical," Burr said, under his breath. "I have no further questions."

Truax walked up to the teary-eyed widow. "Mrs. Slaughter, did you love your husband?"

"Yes."

"But you had a few marital problems?"

"Yes."

"Did you kill him?"

"No."

"I have no further questions."

The Honorable Judge Benjamin Gillis made a show of looking at his watch. "I see that it's almost noon. I have an engagement this afternoon and am going to adjourn these proceedings until tomorrow morning." He looked at Burr. "At which time, I expect you to conclude your defense."

I think the jury believes Frank beat her, but they don't think she murdered him.

Gillis tapped his gavel and glided out.

* * *

Jacob, Eve, and Kitty sat in a conference room just down the hall from the courtroom. Burr walked in circles around the table.

"Will you stop that?" Aunt Kitty said.

Burr changed directions.

"Stop that pacing and tell us what you've got planned for tomorrow," she said. "Who's left on your witness list?"

Burr kept pacing.

"Stop that and answer my question."

Burr looked at his aunt while he paced. "I can't believe I lost."

"Lost?" Aunt Kitty said.

"Thorne Swift."

"You have a murder trial to finish. And win," she said. "Stop feeling sorry for yourself."

"I can't believe I lost," he said again.

"This isn't about you and your oversized ego. You have to focus on the trial."

"Judge Abbott ruled against me every step of the way."

Eve put her hand on Burr as he walked by. "This isn't about you. This is about Collin. Thorne Swift can wait."

"Thorne Swift is gone," Burr said.

"It is gone," Jacob said. "We must focus on the matter at hand, which is Collin's trial."

Burr started pacing again. Aunt Kitty joined him, walking the other way around the table. "What's next?" she said.

"I'm going to call Ian and Claire. I might call Ballantine back to the stand."

"That's it?"

"Who else is there?"

"If that's all you've got, I'd say you're in trouble," his aunt said.

"What are you going to do?" Jacob said.

What happened to 'we'?

"No one saw Collin stab Frank," Burr said, "but there's plenty of evidence that makes him look guilty."

"He hasn't helped himself much," Eve said. "With his temper."

"Thank you, Eve." Burr and Aunt Kitty passed each other. "We haven't been able to make any of the cast of characters look particularly guilty."

"We just don't have any real suspects."

"Do you think Collin killed Frank?" Eve said.

"I don't know. He might have." Burr stopped. "No. In spite of everything, I don't. I really don't."

Aunt Kitty ran into Burr.

They filed out of the conference room. Burr didn't know what to do next. He wandered around the courthouse, up the stairs, down the stairs, through the hallways, going nowhere in particular, just like his defense. He stopped and put his hands in his pockets. "As long as I'm here, I might as well give it a try."

"What is it this time?" George Maples said.

Could I have another look at Frank Slaughter's personal effects?"

"You've got five minutes." Maples disappeared, then reappeared with the wire basket.

There wasn't much to look at. Just like there hadn't been much to look at before. A wristwatch, a comb, keys, a wallet, the key to the locker at Nub's. He picked up the locker key.

"That was a big help," Burr said.

"What's that?"

"Nothing." Burr picked up the wallet. "Can I look through this?"

"As long as you don't take anything."

Burr opened up the wallet. Some small bills, nothing bigger than a twenty. Wrinkled from being in the swamp. Driver's license, credit cards, ruined pictures of his family. He opened another compartment. Receipts. A lottery ticket. A scrap of paper, folded over itself. He opened it up. There was something written on it, but the ink had run, and it was hard to make out.

"It probably doesn't matter."

"What's that?"

Burr handed Maples the slip of paper. "Can you read this?"

"Not really. Looks like '*B*' something." Maples scratched his ear. "B, A. I can't make this out. Then some numbers. I can't read the first three but the last three look like 876."

* * *

Burr drove back to Harbor Springs, Zeke-the-Decoy riding shotgun, the scrap of paper in his beak. He had no idea if there was anything to it, but he didn't really have anything else. When he got to Harbor Springs, he took State Road up the hill and turned east on the narrow road that ran along the edge of the bluff. He parked across from the million-dollar cottages with the million-dollar views of Little Traverse Bay, not a soul in sight. Below him Harbor Springs, then the bay.

"Zeke, the ice is blowing around. It won't be long now."

He took the scrap of paper from Zeke's beak. He studied it, turned it over, folded it, unfolded it. Then he wrapped it around the steering wheel, but he couldn't see all of the letters and numbers. He put it on the dashboard and studied it again.

"Does this mean anything?"

* * *

Burr sat in the dining room of the Harbor Inn with Jacob, Eve, and Aunt Kitty. If they hadn't been delighted to see him after Gillis adjourned them earlier in the day, they were even less than delighted now, but Burr had offered to buy them an early dinner. Burr had a charge at the Harbor Inn, which he never paid, but there was no reason to bring that up.

They'd all ordered the planked whitefish, Stewart's specialty. Even Jacob, who asked for his without paprika.

Burr wasn't hungry, and he had important business.

He took the scrap of paper out of his pocket and put it on the table.

"Where did you get this?" Aunt Kitty said.

"It's probably better that you don't know."

"Where did you get it?"

Burr shook his head.

"Tell me this instant."

Burr looked out at the bay. "There's still plenty of ice."

"Tell me."

"I found it in Frank's wallet."

"At the evidence cage?" Jacob said.

Burr nodded.

"Sometimes I wonder who raised you. Your father would never do such a thing. Not to mention your mother."

There's always been some larceny in my heart.

"What is it?" Eve said.

Burr unfolded the slip of paper and laid it on the table. "What does this say?" They all leaned over it.

"The number looks like 61878," Jacob said.

"The last number is 6," Eve said.

"That's right," Aunt Kitty said.

"So, it's 61876," Burr said. "What about the letters?"

"What difference could this silly scrap of paper possibly make?" Jacob said.

"Probably no difference." Burr fished out his last olive. "But it's all I've got."

"The first one is an 8," Aunt Kitty said.

"That's a *B*," Eve said.

"It's *B, A, I, N*," Aunt Kitty said. "BAIN61876."

Burr chewed his olive. "What does it mean?"

"A lottery ticket?"

"A post office box?"

"It's too many numbers for a post office box, and lottery tickets don't have numbers like that."

"Maybe it's a phone number."

"Phone numbers have seven numbers."

Burr chewed his olive, then, "Harbor Springs used to have five numbers for in-town calls."

"So maybe BAIN is a name."

"I'll check the phone book."

Burr went to the bar and came back with a phone book.

"I've seen thicker comic books," Eve said.

Burr thumbed through the phone book. "Nothing here."

The waiter brought their food—the whitefish was sprinkled with paprika, dotted with capers, and dabs of butter. Burr picked at his food.

He took the slip of paper out of his pocket and read it out loud. "B-A-I-N-6-1-8-7-6. I've seen that somewhere." He jumped up from the table and ran to his Jeep.

Burr shifted into four-wheel drive. The gears ground. The transmission clunked, and the Jeep stalled.

"Damn it all."

Burr fumed.

"Why do I have things that never work right?"

He pounded on the steering wheel, shifted back into two-wheel drive, then tried four-wheel again. More grinding and clunking, then the Jeep lurched forward.

"I love my Jeep."

The Jeep crawled up the driveway into Thorne Swift. It hadn't been plowed all winter. The snow was melting in the sun, wet and heavy, and the Jeep sank almost to the bumper.

"If it gets any deeper, we'll never get out."

There was still plenty of light in the sky. There were longer days in Harbor Springs much sooner than warmer weather.

Burr slogged down the path doing his best to stay in the tracks made by the cross-country skiers. He didn't know what he was looking for, and he didn't know if he'd recognize it when he found whatever it was. And whatever it was, it would be buried under three feet of snow, but he didn't know what else to do.

Twenty minutes later, he stood on the beach—or where the beach would be once the snow and ice melted. Lake Michigan, frozen as far as he could see. He struggled back to the path. He stopped to catch his breath where the orchid had bloomed last summer.

"Was that the last time you're going to bloom?" Burr started off again. "Not if I have anything to say about it."

Then he saw it. The massive beech tree, the beech tree with the initials. With the leaves gone, the sun reached all the way to the snow, and the beech tree, its bark silver and gray, stood out like a lighthouse.

He followed a snowed-in path to the tree. He'd sweated through his shirt by the time he made it to the Tree of Hearts, his Barbour jacket was as good at keeping moisture in as it was at keeping it out.

He walked around the tree, once, twice, three times, studying the carvings.

"Those must be dates."

He took off one of his gloves and ran his hands on the bark, then traced one of the carvings with his fingers. He ran his hands over the smooth, silver bark, rough where the carvings had scarred it. "I know I saw it." Burr backed away from the tree, stepped in a hole, and fell on his back in the snow.

He sank, and the snow fell over him, covering him like one of Aunt Kitty's Hudson Bay blankets. He tried to sit up, but he couldn't move.

"I feel like the girl in the lady's slipper legend."

He pushed the snow off his coat and sat up. Then he got on his hands and knees, pushed himself to his feet, and stepped out of the hole.

Burr backed away from the tree and looked at the names cut into the back. "Anne and Bob." "Joe and Sheila." "Connie and Sam." And the initials "JB + RC," "TM + SJ." Some of them had hearts around them. Some had dates—"JR + HW 7-22-74."

He started off, stopped, and looked back at the Tree of Hearts. Then he saw it. "BA + IN 6-18-76" was carved in the tree.

Burr pulled the slip of paper out of his pocket. It read BAIN 6-18-76. He looked back at the tree again. BA + IN 6-18-76. "There's no plus sign on the paper, but there is on the tree. He nodded to himself. "It's not a name. It's initials. And a date."

* * *

"The defense calls Ian Nash."

Swede swore in the shipwright. Ian sat back in his chair. He looked like he was right at home.

Burr, for his part, had spent another sleepless night. He was sure there was more going on than a murder—not that murder wasn't enough. There was more to it, but he didn't know what it was.

But Collin looked guilty, and maybe he was. Burr was afraid he didn't have enough time to figure out what was going on or even if he could figure it out, but he thought it had to do with the slip of paper. He didn't really have any reason to call Ian, and he didn't have much to ask him. Maybe he could cast a reasonable doubt in the jury's collective mind. Maybe not. And he risked losing one of his few allies.

"Mr. Nash, you were at Thorne Swift the day Mr. Murphy was beaten and his camera was stolen. Is that right?"

"I don't know."

"Did you see Mr. Murphy get beaten?"

"No."

"Mr. Nash, did you see Mr. Murphy at Thorne Swift on the day you were there with your field trip?"

"Yes."

"What was he doing?"

"He was taking pictures."

"Do you know what he was taking pictures of?"

"I think it was the lady's slipper."

"Did you see him take pictures of anything else?"

"I saw him taking other pictures, but I don't know what they were."

"Mr. Nash, you were opposed to the sale of Thorne Swift. Is that true?"

"Yes."

"And you were part of the Friends of Thorne Swift, a group that sued to prevent its sale to Mr. Smart. Is that right?"

"Yes."

Ian sat up a little straighter.

"In fact, you were violently opposed to the sale. Is that right?"

"I was opposed."

"So opposed that you followed Frank Slaughter into the preserve and murdered him."

"That's ridiculous."

It is, but it's all I've got.

Burr took a piece of paper out of his pocket. "Mr. Nash, does this mean anything to you? The letters BA + IN. Then the date 6-18-76?"

Ian sat back in the chair. "No." He glared at Burr.

If looks could kill.

"I have no further questions."

"Mr. Truax?" Judge Gillis said.

The prosecutor didn't bother to stand up. "Mr. Nash, did you murder Mr. Slaughter?"

"No."

"Nothing else for me," Truax said.

"Your next witness, Mr. Lafayette."

Burr called Claire Fisher. He asked her about the Friends of Thorne Swift, her passion to save it, and asked her if she had murdered Frank. It was a shabby, shallow performance on his part, but it was all he had. Maybe, just maybe, he put some doubt in the jury's mind.

"You may call your next witness."

"The defense has no further witnesses."

"Really," Gillis said. "Very well, then. Closing arguments will be tomorrow at 10 o'clock sharp."

* * *

As soon as Gillis dismissed them, Burr drove to Harbor Springs and looked out at the bay. The ice had blown out—open water as far as he could see.

"It's an east wind."

He pulled into a parking lot in front of a not particularly memorable white ranch house on Lake Street, and walked into the offices of *Harbor Light*, Harbor Springs's weekly newspaper.

A chest-high counter ran across what had once been a living room. "Can I help you?" said a not particularly helpful-looking woman in her forties.

"Could I look at your archives?"

"Archives?"

"Your old newspapers."

"Archives," she said, again. "How far back?"

"1976. No, 1977."

"That's a long time ago."

"Do you have them?"

"If we do, they're in the basement. We're putting them on microfilm, or whatever you call it, but we haven't gotten very far."

"Can I see them?"

"The whole year?"

Burr counted to nine on his fingers. "July, August, September, October, November, December, January, February, March." He looked back at the clerk. "February through April 1977."

"I don't see why not." She opened a door in the counter, then another door at the back of the room. Burr walked past four empty desks.

"They're all out looking for news," the clerk said. "Not that there's much in the way of news around here." She started down a flight of stairs. "Follow me."

The basement was full of newspapers, stacks and stacks of old newspapers. It was damp and musty and smelled just like a basement full of old newspapers.

"You don't smoke, do you?"

Burr shook his head.

"Good." She walked through the stacks. She thumbed through the old newspapers. "Here you go. 1977. You can look, but don't take anything. Let me know if you want something. I'll make you a copy. Ten cents a page." She walked back upstairs.

If this doesn't work, I'm euchred.

Burr started with February. Week by week. Nothing. Then March. Nothing.

"Maybe I was wrong."

He tried April. Nothing the first week. Or the second.

"Damn it all."

Then the April 19, 1977, edition. He ran his finger under "Births."

That's what I thought.

* * *

Burr sat at the writing table in his room at the Harbor Inn. He looked out at the bay. The wind had gone to the west. The ice had blown back in, not all of it, but enough to make it look like winter again. Zeke lay on a rug near Burr's feet. Burr had finally figured out how to work the viewfinder on Collin's camera. He flipped through the pictures again. He stopped on the picture of Ian and the kids at Thorne Swift. He studied the girl who was holding Ian's hand.

"I know who that is."

A knock at the door. "It's not locked." Ian came in.

"I saw your Jeep at the newspaper office today."

You won't like what I found

"This has gone far enough," Ian said.

"It should be over tomorrow."

"Give me the camera." Ian took a step toward Burr.

"I need it for tomorrow."

"Give me the camera," Ian said, again.

"Go home, Ian. I'm not going to give you the camera."

"You're going to hurt a lot of people with that camera."

"So, I should just give you the camera and let Collin get convicted of a murder he didn't commit?"

"That camera is going to ruin lives." Ian stepped closer.

Burr held the camera in both hands. "Without this camera, Collin will most certainly be convicted."

"Give it to me."

"You're making yourself look guiltier than these pictures do."

Ian pulled a pistol out of his pocket. "Give me the camera."

"We both know you're not going to use that."

"Don't be too sure." Ian started toward Burr. He tripped over Zeke and fell on the floor. Burr grabbed the gun. "Good boy, Zeke."

* * *

Twenty minutes later, another knock on the door.

"What fresh hell is this?"

Johnson Smart came through the door. "Dorothy Parker."

Burr looked up from the camera.

At least he's well read.

Smart sidestepped Zeke. "Mr. Lafayette, let me get right to the point."

"Please."

"It's about that." Smart pointed at the camera.

I must really have something here.

Burr looked out the window. The ice was still blowing around in the bay.

Smart took a checkbook out of his pocket. "I'm prepared to write you a check. This very moment. Shall we say twenty-five thousand?"

"I'll think it over."

"I need an answer and the camera now."

"If you need an answer now, the answer is 'no.'"

"I need the camera now."

Burr took Ian's pistol out of his pocket. "Unless you can beat this, get out."

"You have no idea what you're getting yourself into."

I'm sure I don't.

Burr waved the pistol at the door. "Out."

Smart left.

Burr looked down at Zeke-the-Decoy. "The very best way for me to lose my license would have been to take that check. Not that I couldn't use the money."

Burr opened a bottle of Smith and Hook cabernet, his favorite twenty-dollar cab. He let it decant for two minutes, then poured himself a glass. "It opens right up." Back to the camera. "Why does everybody want this?" He flipped through the pictures again. And again. The lady's slipper. Again and again. The Tree of Hearts, Ian and the kids. The frog. The turtle. A man and woman in the distance, the man pointing at the Tree of Hearts.

"Who are they?"

* * *

Burr looked out in the gallery. It was full. Murders in Emmet County always drew a crowd. The Friends of Thorne Swift had turned out plus the interested parties … Johnson Smart, Dewey Ballantine, Jill Slaughter, Ian Nash, Claire Fisher. Judge Abbott sat in the back. She'd been in the courtroom for the entire trial.

She's the one I needed to be here.

"Mr. Truax, you may present your closing argument," the Honorable Benjamin Gillis said.

Truax walked toward the jury. "Ladies and gentlemen—"

"Your Honor, the defense has one more witness," Burr said, standing.

Gillis sighed. "Mr. Lafayette, yesterday you said you had no further witnesses."

Burr walked up to the bench. "There is new information that has an important bearing in this case. It has just come to light."

"We just started, and you're causing trouble already."

Truax stood next to Burr. "I distinctly remember you saying that you had no further witnesses."

"That was yesterday."

"I object," Truax said.

"Your Honor, as long as we're distinctly remembering things, Mr. Truax must remember presenting another witness after he concluded his case."

"That was different," Truax said.

"Very well, you may call your witness."

Burr smiled at Truax, then looked out at the gallery. "The defense calls Elizabeth Abbott."

"You can't do that," Truax said. "She's a sitting judge."

"Judges can be witnesses," Burr said.

The Honorable Judge Elizabeth Abbott didn't move.

Gillis took off his glasses and looked at Judge Abbott. "I'm sorry, Judge Abbott, but I am compelled to order that you testify."

She still didn't move.

"Your Honor," Burr said, "if Judge Abbott refuses to testify, I am going to ask that you hold her in contempt of court."

"My stars and little comets." Gillis looked at Judge Abbott. "I'm sorry, judge. Unfortunately, Mr. Lafayette is right."

She sat there, looked down at her feet, then slowly made her way to the witness stand. She glanced at Smart, Ian, and Collin on her way.

Swede swore her in. She smoothed out the skirt of her black suit, two-inch heels, and her signature pink lipstick.

"Judge Abbott, you are the presiding judge in the Friends of Thorne Swift versus Dewey Ballantine case. Is that right?"

"Yes."

"And you're familiar with the defendant in that case, Dewey Ballantine."

"Yes."

"And the plaintiff, represented by Claire Fisher, Kathryn Lafayette, among others."

"I am."

"And Johnson Smart, the would-be purchaser of Thorne Swift."

Truax stood. "Your Honor, Mr. Smart testified that he did, in fact, close on the purchase of Thorne Swift."

"So noted," Gillis said.

Judge Abbott glared at Burr. "Yes."

"And, of course, the defendant, Mr. Murphy."

"Yes."

"I object, Your Honor," Truax said. "All this is irrelevant."

"I am about to connect the dots, Your Honor," Burr said.

"See that you do," the judge said. "Promptly."

"Judge Abbott, you're also familiar with me since I represent the plaintiffs."

"Yes," she said, then softly, "regrettably."

"I beg your pardon?"

She shook her head. "Yes."

"Finally, you must also be familiar with Ian Nash, another of the plaintiff's representatives."

Judge Abbott didn't say anything. Burr looked at Ian, two rows back in the gallery. She still didn't say anything.

"Judge Abbott?"

"Yes."

"Thank you. Judge Abbott, growing up, you spent your summers in Harbor Springs. Is that right?"

"No."

"Really. But you did spend some time in Harbor Springs."

"A little."

I wonder if she knows where this is going.

"So, you're familiar with Thorne Swift?"

"Yes, from the litigation."

"Have you ever been there?"

"No, not that I recall."

"Really?"

Burr took a step back. "Have you ever heard of the Tree of Hearts?"

"No."

She's lying.

Truax stood. "Your Honor, this isn't going anywhere. It's all irrelevant."

Burr looked over his shoulder. "It's about to get relevant."

"Proceed, counsel, but let's move things along." Gillis shooed Burr with his hands.

"Judge Abbott, as I believe you know, there is a very old, very large beech tree at Thorne Swift. It's called the Tree of Hearts. There are carvings on it, initials mostly, some dates, many with circles around them. Surely you recall that."

"No, I don't think so."

She's starting to lose her color.

"Judge Abbott, there is one particular carving I'd like to bring to your attention. It has the initials BA + IN and then the date 6-18-76. Do you remember that?"

"No," she said.

She's pale as a ghost.

"Judge Abbott, the initials IN could stand for Ian Nash, couldn't they?"

"I have no idea."

"And, if I may, your first name is Elizabeth, and Beth is sometimes a nickname for Elizabeth. Isn't it?"

"I don't know."

"Were you ever called Beth?"

"No."

"Did you ever date Ian Nash, say, in 1976?"

"No."

"Do you know Ian Nash?"

"Only from the litigation."

"Your Honor, this is ridiculous," Truax said.

"Mr. Lafayette, you will end this line of questioning immediately. It is irrelevant, and you are embarrassing a highly respected member of the judiciary."

"Please, Your Honor," Burr said. "Five more minutes."

"You may have two minutes." Gillis shook two fingers at him. "Two minutes. That's it."

"Yes, Your Honor." Burr stepped closer to Judge Abbott, standing so that the jury could see her.

"Judge Abbott, I submit that you and Ian Nash had a romantic relationship in the summer of 1976. It was serious enough that Mr. Nash carved your initials and his on the tree."

"That's not …"

Burr talked over her. "It was so serious that you got—"

Ian bolted to his feet. "Stop it. Stop it right now."

Gillis banged his gavel. "Quiet. I will have order."

Ian looked at Burr with pure hate. "You're going to ruin innocent lives."

Burr turned around and looked at Ian. "It's too late for that."

"Sit that man down," Gillis said. "If he says one more word, take him out."

Burr turned back around and put his hands on the rail of the witness stand. "Judge Abbott, your relationship with Mr. Nash became so amorous that you got pregnant."

"I most certainly did not."

"Your family was beside itself. They hid you away in Harbor Springs until you had the baby. No one knew who the mother was, and the official story was that the mother died in childbirth. Mr. Nash was the father. He raised your daughter by himself."

Beth Abbott lost whatever color she had left. "These are lies. All lies."

"Mr. Lafayette, you are out of order," Gillis said.

Burr grabbed a newspaper off his table. "Your Honor, Judge Abbott's family did everything they could to keep this quiet, but the Harbor Springs newspaper has a section in their paper called 'Births.'"

Truax jumped to his feet.

Burr introduced the newspaper in evidence before the prosecutor could object. He opened the newspaper and handed it to the judge. "Please read this."

She pushed the paper away. Burr walked to the jury box. "I am reading from the 'Birth' section of the April 12, 1977, edition of the *Harbor Light.* 'Births. April 12, 1977, Elizabeth Abbott.'"

Judge Abbott folded her hands together and put them in her lap. She sat there, as solemn as the judge she was.

"The paper left off the father's name, but we all knew who it was." Burr looked at Ian again.

Truax, still on his feet, said, "What in heaven's name does this have to do with the murder of Frank Slaughter?"

Burr looked at Truax. "This has everything to do with the murder of Frank Slaughter." He turned back to the reluctant witness, "Judge Abbott, you said that you hadn't been to Thorne Swift recently. Do you want to take that back?"

"No."

Burr went back to the defense table. Eve, sitting in the first aisle of the gallery, handed him Collin's camera.

"Your Honor, I'd like to introduce this camera into evidence. It belongs to Collin Murphy and was stolen by Frank Slaughter."

Gillis waved off Truax's objection.

Burr held the camera in front of the shaken, but still stoic, Judge Abbott. "There is more on Mr. Murphy's camera than just pictures of the lady's slipper. He took more pictures that day. There is a picture of the Tree of Hearts, which includes the 'BA + IN 6-18-76' carving." Burr looked back at Ian. "Mr. Nash made the carving on the tree." Back to the judge. "There's also a picture of Mr. Nash and the kids on their field trip last June." Burr found Ian in the gallery again. "Including Mr. Nash's daughter. Finally, and most importantly, there is a picture of Mr. Smart with you, Judge Abbott. Mr. Smart is pointing at the Tree of Hearts."

"That's not true," she said, not quite so stoically.

"Mr. Smart was blackmailing you. It's not enough for you to be a federal district judge. You want to run for the United States Senate. Smart threatened to expose your illegitimate daughter which would, in all likelihood, ruin your chances to be a senator. But as long as you ruled in his favor and made sure he got Thorne Swift, he would keep quiet.

"Smart knew about the field trip, and he made sure the two of you were there to see Mr. Nash with your daughter. But he didn't know Mr. Murphy would be there that day taking pictures. When you saw Mr. Murphy taking the picture of the two of you, you had to have the camera."

Judge Abbott bit her lip.

"You bite your lip when you're upset. Did you know that?"

The upset judge put her hand over her mouth.

"Frank Slaughter had no idea what was on Mr. Murphy's camera. All he wanted was money. You tried to persuade him to give it to you, but he wanted twenty-five thousand dollars for it.

"You followed him after he left Bar Harbor that night. You started fighting with him. He took out Mr. Murphy's knife. Somehow you got it from him and stabbed him to death. You lost your temper and murdered him." Burr looked at the jury. "Then you stabbed in the eye just for good measure."

She grabbed the railing, her hands shaking.

"It's not true. Not any of it."

"Oh, but it is. The newspaper and the pictures tell the tale. If that's not enough, I'm sure Mr. Smart will be happy to tell us all about it, especially how you sent him to my room last night to buy Mr. Murphy's camera."

"You can't prove it," the soon-to-be former Judge Abbott said.

Burr leaned toward her. "I don't have to prove it." He smiled at her. "All I need is a reasonable doubt."

* * *

Burr looked out at Little Traverse Bay. The ice had blown out again.

For good, this time. I hope.

To his left, Zeke in the decoy. A Labatt to his right. The merry little band, Jacob, Eve, Aunt Kitty, Claire, and Collin—the reluctant star of the show, much merrier now. They had the best table in the dining room at the Harbor Inn. Ian was, unsurprisingly, absent. Burr, absolutely spent, decided against a martini.

"There's too much vermouth in this," Aunt Kitty said.

It's comforting when she says that.

It had taken the jury the better part of the afternoon to reach a verdict. The longer it took, the more worried Burr became. They came back with "not guilty" just before five o'clock.

Truax stopped Burr on the way out of the courtroom. "I still think he did it."

"He might have."

"Then why did you defend him?"

"Everyone has the right to a defense."

"You'd rather win than see that justice be done."

He's probably right.

"There's plenty of people who could have murdered Frank Slaughter. He was no saint," Burr said.

Truax marched off.

Burr took a swallow of his beer and looked at Collin. He didn't look quite as guilty, now that he'd changed out of his orange jumpsuit.

He could have done it.

"Thank you so much," Claire said, "but you didn't have to accuse me."

"I'm sorry, Claire. I was trying to confuse the jury."

"I guess it doesn't matter now."

Maybe I do like to win too much.

"How did you figure it out?" she said.

"It was the tree," Burr said. "I fell in the snow and got stuck."

"Like the girl in the legend," Claire said.

"The carvings were staring me right in the face."

"That was it?"

"It really started with the camera. When I saw Smart and Judge Abbott in the background, I knew there was more to it than the lady's slipper."

"This was a lot of trouble for a flower," Jacob said.

Eve took a bite of the pickle in her Bloody Mary. "That wasn't endangered."

The waitress took their orders. Burr dearly wanted veal morel, but it was too early in the season, and Stewart's planked whitefish was nothing to sneeze at. He decided to start with the chili, Stewart's specialty.

"Will Judge Abbott be charged with Frank's murder?" Claire said.

"I doubt it."

"But you said she did it," Claire said.

"The jury didn't believe beyond a reasonable doubt that Collin murdered Frank. It's quite another thing to get a new jury to believe beyond a reasonable doubt that Judge Abbott murdered Frank."

"It was lucky for you that she was in the courtroom. If she'd been smart, she'd have stayed away." Aunt Kitty sipped her drink.

"I think she was worried and wanted to see what was going on firsthand," Burr said.

"If she hadn't been there, you couldn't have called her as a witness," Jacob said.

"I'd have asked Gillis to subpoena her."

"He might not have agreed," Jacob said.

"It doesn't matter now," Burr said.

"You were lucky, nephew."

I figured it out and won the case. Now I'm lucky.

"The lady's slipper is the deadliest flower," Burr said.

"But it's so beautiful," Claire said.

Burr finished his beer. "It's beautiful, but it's deadly."

"It really is," Collin said.

"Is it poisonous?" Jacob said.

"No, but it might as well be," Collin said.

"Why?" Jacob said.

"For all the trouble it caused," Burr said.

Eve took another bite of her pickle. "What's going to happen to Judge Abbott?"

"She's going to be censured. At a minimum. She may have to resign, and she's definitely not going to run for the Senate." Burr finished his beer, he waved for the waitress and ordered another Labatt.

There's hope for me.

"That explains why I kept losing in Judge Abbott's courtroom. Smart was blackmailing her, and I had to keep losing so he could buy Thorne Swift."

"Maybe it was bad lawyering," Aunt Kitty said.

"Maybe it was a losing case," Burr said.

Eve took another bite of her pickle. "It's going to be a dark day if you ever think you deserved to lose."

It will be a dark day.

Jacob smiled a small smile. "Burr did drag it out. That's his specialty."

"Just long enough," Eve said.

I'll take that as a compliment.

"The big news, though, other than Collin's acquittal, is that Judge Abbott is going to have to unwind the sale of Thorne Swift and recuse herself from the litigation with Ballantine and the Friends of the Conservancy."

"What does that mean?" Claire said.

"It means the whole thing starts over," Burr said.

The waitress delivered Burr's chili. He poured a package of oyster crackers in it.

"It means Burr will take the new case." Aunt Kitty held up her glass and waved at the waitress.

I must not have been that terrible.

"What that means is that the Friends of Thorne Swift needs to raise the money to buy it."

"You can do that," Claire said.

Burr's beer came.

"I'm not doing another thing until I get paid."

Aunt Kitty started to say something, but Maggie came in carrying what looked like a shoebox. Burr hadn't seen her since Zeke had died.

She kissed him on the cheek.

I really missed you.

She put the box down next to his chowder. The box wiggled. She kissed him.

"Open it up," she said.

The top came off before Burr could open the box. A black Lab puppy peeked out.

"Say hello to Crow."

THE END

Acknowledgments

To Ellen Jones, my longtime, part-time, long-suffering assistant for her typing, copy editing, encouragement, and endless patience.

To Leland Bassett, Kieran Fleming, Charlie McLravy, Jesse Melcher, Mike Murphy, Diane Newman, Trevor Peitz, Julie Spencer, Steve Spencer, Steve Pruett, Bruce Stickle, Bob Stocker, and Eric Thuma for reading the manuscript. They made many story suggestions and helped me correct countless factual, contextual, and typographical errors.

To John Wickham for his cover design.

To Mission Point Press for all their help in producing *The Lady's Slipper*. They have been spectacular: Hart Cauchy for his editing and insight, Misha Neidorfler for being a great project manager, Zinzi Robles and Mark Pate for producing *The Lady's Slipper*, Sarah Meiers for interior design, Darlene Short for proofing, Leslie Marshall, Julie Hazlett, Terese DiMercurio, Martha Scherf-Pompa, and Anna Faller for marketing. Heather Shaw for her steady hand. Jen Wahi for her direction and leadership.

Finally, thanks to my wife, Christi, for her unflagging support during the writing of *The Lady's Slipper*.

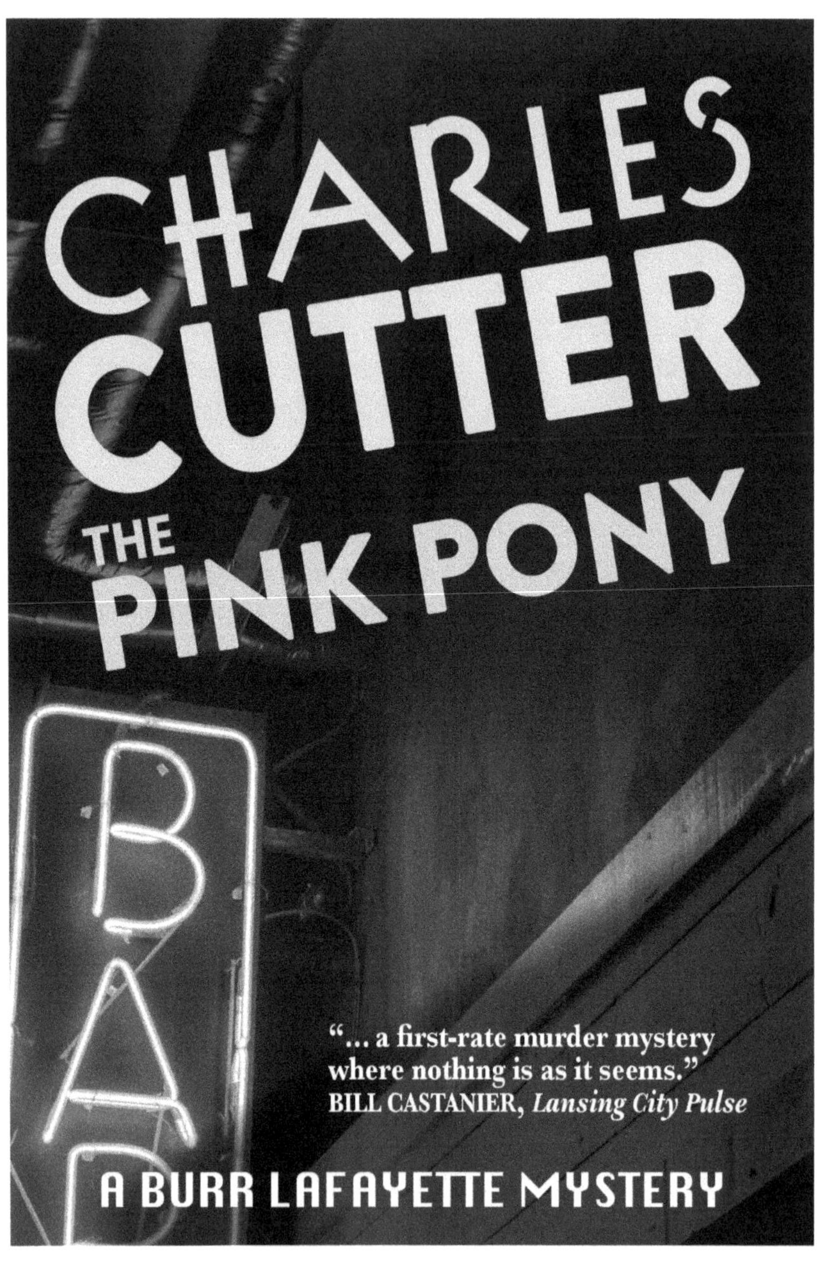

"If you can't make it to Mackinac Island this summer, it's not too late to escape through the pages of *The Pink Pony*. It's a fast-paced, highly entertaining mystery that uses Mackinac Island as the backdrop for a criminal trial."

Ray Walsh, *Lansing State Journal*

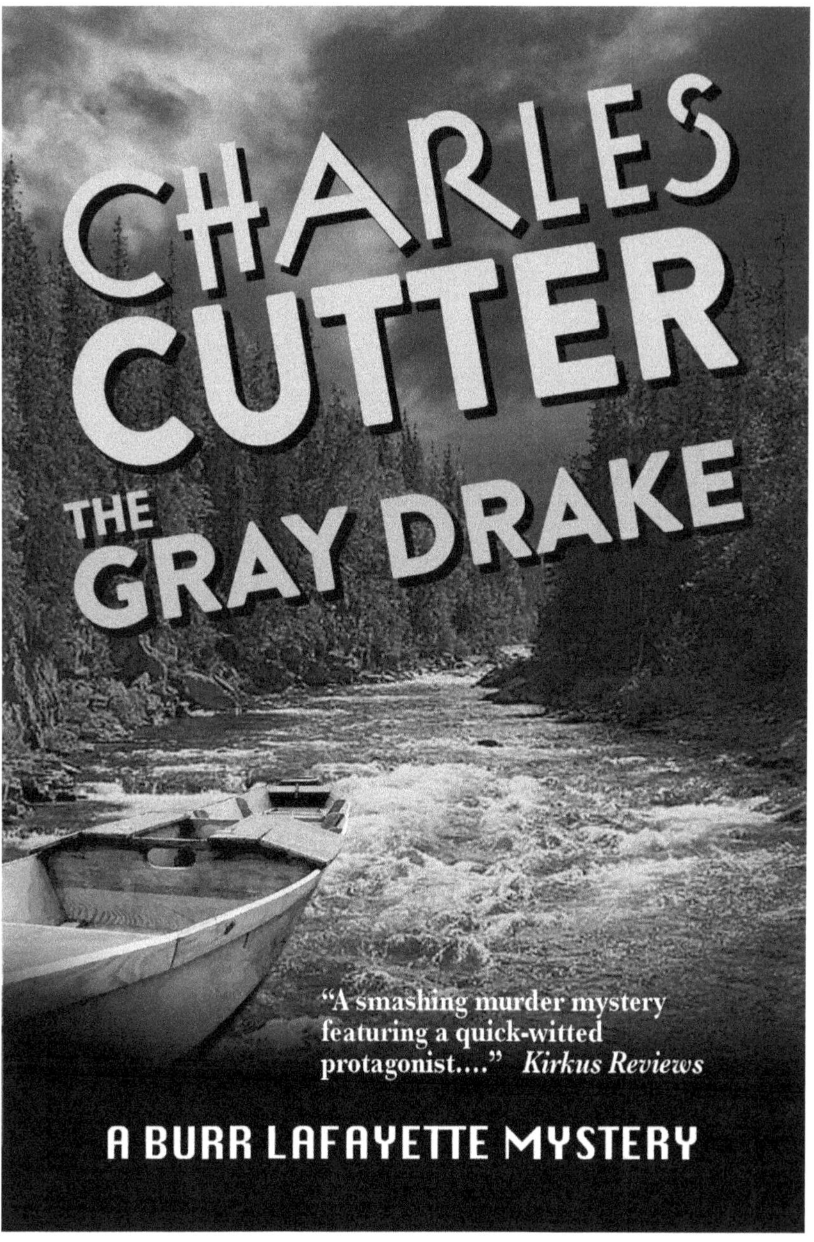

"A smashing murder mystery featuring a quick-witted protagonist... Cutter's razor-sharp dialogue in the courtroom [is] truly unforgettable."

Kirkus Reviews

"*Bear Bones* and Burr Lafayette remind us of what we have and why we love where we are. Part mystery, part ode to the last best places, Cutter's prose captures the best of what is always slipping away. A page turner of a mystery."

Glen Young, *Bear River Literary*

"Cutter's narrative maintains a relentless edge; numerous characters lie; and an unsettling ambiguity hangs over everything. Another superb, realistic installment of this Midwestern legal thriller series."
Kirkus Reviews

"*Under the Ashes* is like a good gin and tonic:
clean, crisp, and with a bite."
Steven Pruett, *Executive Chairman,*
Cox Media Group

"This is an engrossing work—the sinewy and lean prose
produces a kind of spare poetry. An absorbing story,
moving and uncompromising."

Kirkus ReviewsCox Media Group

About the Author

Charles Cutter is the author of the highly acclaimed Burr Lafayette legal thriller series. *The Pink Pony,* the first book in the series, recently won First Prize in the Global Book Awards.

Cutter is a cum laude graduate of the University of Michigan Law School and a graduate with highest honors from Michigan State University. Before his writing career, he was in the media business and was a practicing attorney.

Cutter is active in conservation, most recently serving as chairman of the board for Pheasants Forever and Quail Forever, the largest upland conservation organization in the United States. He lives with his wife, two dogs and four cats in East Lansing. He has a leaky sailboat in Harbor Springs, and a leakier duck boat on Saginaw Bay.

Books in the Burr Lafayette series include *The Gray Drake, Bear Bones, The Pink Pony, The Crooked Angel, Under the Ashes* and *The Hangman's Blind.* They are available at Amazon and your local bookstore. Cutter has also written literary fiction, short stories and screenplays. He is currently at work on the next book in the Burr Lafayette series.

For additional information, please go to www.CharlesCutter.com.

www.ingramcontent.com/pod-product-compliance
Lightning Source LLC
Chambersburg PA
CBHW040858010826

48978CB00013BA/1075